GIRL, UNHINGED

SASHA LANE

Discover other titles by Sasha Lane:
Girl, Conflicted

First published in Great Britain in 2015 by Sasha Lane
This paperback edition is the first edition

ISBN 978-0-9934562-1-3

'You deserve everything that you get.'

Chapter One

Mmm. I feel Joe's soft lips kissing the back of my neck and instantly I'm smiling. I could definitely get used to being woken up like this. It's been nearly three months since we moved in together and every day feels as special as the first. I love our home, and I love the fact that I'm sharing my life with someone who loves me as much as I love him. I'm finally in a grown-up relationship where it's not just one-sided and driven by my fantasy of what I think a relationship actually is.

'Is it really time to get up?' I mumble into my pillowcase, already knowing the answer.

'Yeah, but it's an exciting day today: your first day at college.'

Joe sounds more excited than I feel – my stomach does a little flip, no, make that a big flip. I don't know how I talked myself into this. Signing up to do a fashion design course at night school seemed like a good idea at the time. But now I feel like I'm five years old again and being thrust into Primrose Infants' along with all the other small children who've dreaded this day since their mums explained they were going to be 'big girls and boys'. I had Sophie to cling on to then, and she was brave and confident even at five. But tonight I'll be walking through those big school doors on my own, and I'll probably the oldest in the class by a decade. I must have been crazy to sign up for this.

'Come on.' Joe prods me gently on the arm. 'I'll make you breakfast before I go to the gym.'

That's one thing that hasn't rubbed off on me over the last few months. Waking up together – tick. Having breakfast together – tick. Going to the gym together – maybe not.

'Okay.' I roll over to face Joe and plant a quick kiss on his lips. 'You won me over with breakfast.' I grin. 'And there'd better be caffeine.'

That evening, following a day of complete oblivion at work trying to serve customers and do a stock check in the shop (seriously, I have no idea what I've said or done all day, and I must have miscounted shoes a hundred times – the stock check will definitely need doing again tomorrow), I drive to the college feeling a mixture of fear, anticipation and the three thousand lattes I've drunk today as a substitute for food churning around inside me. I take a deep breath and exhale slowly, hoping to keep the contents of my stomach where they belong.

The sensible part of my brain knows that I'm being ridiculous. My irrational fear is being driven by nightmares of days at school spent hiding from the cool kids to avoid putting myself in the firing line for teasing and/or downright abuse, and making up constant excuses for why I couldn't take part in the sport science class, much to my teacher's disgust. I can still see Mrs Melligan's sneer as I explained, not for the first time, that I'd tripped on my way to school and sprained my ankle. I guess nothing much has changed; I still make up every excuse possible to avoid going to the gym with Joe. For some reason, he finds this amusing rather than annoying. Unfortunately I still don't feel any cooler than I did back then, but Joe doesn't seem to care about that either.

I have to pinch myself sometimes just to make sure I'm definitely not dreaming. It all seems too good to be true. I'm actually living a grown-up life, with a guy who's not only cute but for some reason seems besotted with me. For the first time since I moved out of my mum and dad's house I've stopped living off the scant contents of the cupboard or whatever may be lurking at the bottom of my fridge (Joe can cook actual edible food, unlike me). And now I'm embarking on planning a wedding, which I've always dreamed of – but following the whole Chris debacle of being dumped over what I thought was going to be a romantic meal, which would end in a marriage proposal, never dared to believe would actually happen to me.

But here we are, six months away from the big day and it seems that wedding fever has consumed everyone around me. Sophie is the worst culprit. It's almost like she's planning her own wedding, with the intricate details she keeps trying to force on me and the constant nagging: 'Have you booked this yet? Or chosen that?' Despite my constant assurances that I have it all in hand, she's unrelenting. My mother is no better, and having thousands of miles between us seems to be doing little to dim her enthusiasm. I fear that my wedding will be judged and scored like a beauty pageant, with me spending the day hoping I get at least a 7. The whole thing is crazy, but now I'm on this rollercoaster there's no getting off and it just keeps picking up speed. Sometimes I wish I was married already, or at least that Joe and I could sneak off to a tropical island to have the ceremony, surrounded by palm trees and sand with the sea lapping at our feet, witnessed by two complete strangers who won't give me crap over the table decorations.

Oh God, I'm here already. I grasp the steering wheel with shaking hands as I pull the car to a stop, as though gripping on to the leather for dear life will somehow mean I don't really have to get out of the car and go into the building.

Come on, Emma; you can do this. You're thirty-three years old. The room will be filled with adults, not snivelling children waiting to criticise your every move.

Pushing the car door open, I gulp at the fresh air. My little speech is convincing enough, and I know I have no choice but to 'man up' and get on with this. What is it my mother always says to me? 'You're the only one who can change things if you're not happy with them.' Even in the face of my fear I have to acknowledge that my mum is right.

I hover nervously, staring as the glass sliding doors like they're a ring of fire that I must propel myself through. My new satchel hangs casually at my side, containing a pretty pink notebook and matching pen set, and I cringe inwardly. What was I thinking – trying to improve my career prospects, challenging myself to do something more? Joe's voice is loud in my head:

'*What have you always wanted to do?*'

'*Work in fashion, I guess, but not dressing grey-haired ladies in a snobby boutique.*'

'*So why don't you try to do that, work in fashion?*'

'*Come on, Joe, what do I really know about what material is best for this, and what cut suits that?*'

'*Don't you want to find out?*'

I take a small step forward, battling between facing my fear and at least making it to my first class, or running for the hills. I have about three seconds to make that choice.

'Hey, are you running late too?'

A jovial voice interrupts my wayward thoughts and I turn around to see a tall, dark-haired Italian-looking guy approaching me at a jog.

'Are you here for the business management class too?' he asks, reaching my side, and I notice his lovely golden-brown skin as he smiles inquisitively at me.

'Um, no,' I stutter, glancing around to make absolutely sure that he's addressing me. (I've made that embarrassing mistake before when replying to what I perceived to be a question directed at me only to find it was actually for the person standing behind me whom I'd failed to notice. This in itself is embarrassing enough but my humiliation was greatly enhanced by the fact the guy was smoking hot and so far out of my league I should have realised my error immediately but I have that problem of mouth never engaging brain syndrome.) 'I'm here for the course in...fashion,' I mumble, which sounds incredibly girlie compared to his sensible manly business course.

'Oh.' He smiles warmly at me. 'Well, I'm Tom anyway.' He steps throughout the now open sliding glass door.

'Um, Emma,' I state still rooted to the spot.

'Nice to meet you, Emma. Aren't you coming in?'

I take a deep breath and exhale. I guess I am. And with that, I stride into the college building, resisting every urge to flee.

'Hope to see you around.' Tom half waves at me as he walks quickly through the open door of a classroom.

'Yes, you too,' I call out after him, just to be polite.

Right, now comes the task of finding room 3C. I scuttle down the corridor and see a group of girls filing into a classroom, chatting loudly and giggling as only teenage girls do, and my heart sinks. It's classroom 3C, and it looks like I'm going to be surrounded by people who are young enough to have never appreciated Madonna's Immaculate Collection. I'm practically old enough to be their mother.

As I enter the classroom, following the last teenage girl in, I scan the room for a vacant chair. It's like maths class at secondary school all over again – the only class Sophie and I weren't in together (she's slightly better at numbers than I am, so she got pushed to the elite class). I notice another daunted figure sitting nervously on a plastic chair, and for once God appears to be smiling down on me as not only does she look at least twenty-five but there's an empty chair at the side of her. I quickly slip onto it.

'Hi, I'm Emma,' I offer as an introduction as I take my notebook and pen set from my bag and place them on the desk in front of me.

'I'm Carly.' The girl smiles, appearing relieved. 'I'm so glad to see someone who was born after nineteen ninety-five. I thought I was destined to spend the next year sticking out like a sore thumb.'

'Me too,' I confess. 'I've been hovering outside for the last ten minutes contemplating just giving this up as a bad job before I even start.'

'Ladies, can I have your attention, please?' calls a rather funkily dressed middle-aged woman with black-rimmed glasses from the front of the class. A hush falls over the room. 'Good evening to you all. I'm

Sara Davies, your tutor for the next ten months. Today's class is purely an introduction and a course overview. It's nothing to worry about. The hard work starts next week.' She smiles warmly.

As she proceeds to hand out textbooks, I glance at Carly next to me and allow myself to relax a little. I'm glad now that Joe talked me into this course; I think I might enjoy it after all.

The class whizzes by in a blur of information. My hand hurts from constantly writing – honestly I don't think I've written so much in the last ten years. I'm starting to get severe cramp in my fingers and, looking down at my notebook, I realise that my handwriting became ineligible three pages ago. My head feels like it's spinning as the clock ticks onto eight o'clock and Sara bids us all goodnight.

As the rest of the class files back out of the room, I carefully put away my notebook and pen set – clearly I underestimated the amount of notes I'll have to make and I make a mental note to buy a much larger book to write in.

'So do you live around here?' Carly asks as we make our way out into the corridor.

'Not far, a ten-minute drive. Do you need a lift home?' I ask, suddenly conscious that that may have been what she was hinting at.

'Oh, no, I'm fine, thanks.' She looks quite embarrassed. 'My sister is picking me up.'

'Hey, Emma.' Tom is standing right in front of me, smiling broadly. 'How was your class?'

'Oh, um, great, thanks.'

'Good. Hope to see you next week,' he calls as he hurries towards the glass doors.

'Do you know him?' Carly asks, wide eyed.

'Tom? No, I only met him tonight on my way in here.'

'He's gorgeous.'

'I'm engaged,' I state, waving my left hand in the air to display my ring.

Carly raises her eyebrows. 'So does that mean you don't notice good-looking Italian guys any more?'

'No, I can see that he's good-looking. I'm just not interested in anyone else. I have a lovely fiancé.'

'So does Tom have a girlfriend?'

'Carly, I met him for, like, two seconds as I came into class.'

'So you won't mind if I find out next week?'

'Go for it.' I shake my head amused at her enthusiasm and blatant lack of fear of the opposite sex. I never dared to ask boys out. 'See you next week.'

'Sure. Maybe we can grab a beer or something afterwards?'

'That sounds good.'

I wave goodbye as we reach the door and Carly heads off to a waiting car – her sister's, presumably – while I stroll back to my own car in the car park. I'm relieved the first class is over with. I'm kind of looking forward to the work. I know it's going to be hard and time consuming, but at least it will be interesting, and it looks as though I've found a companion for the time being.

Joe's waiting for me as I step through the front door, a glass of red wine in each hand.

'How was it then?' he asks.

'It was great.' I move forward and give him a lingering kiss. 'Thank you for encouraging me to do this.'

He hands me a glass. 'I knew you'd enjoy it. Now come on, tell me all about it.'

As we snuggle on the sofa I tell Joe about meeting Carly. 'The room was full of young girls; I felt so old!'

'Not old – experienced!' Joe admonishes. 'Think of all the extra knowledge you have because you've already worked in a clothes shop.'

'You're too sweet sometimes.' I shake my head at him.

'What does that mean?'

'It means I'm the luckiest girl in the world.' I gulp at my wine, a little embarrassed. It's not usually me coming out with the romantic one-liners.

Joe moves the conversation on: 'What's your tutor like?'

'She's middle-aged, quite trendy, and thankfully she seems nice. Today we just got our textbooks and she outlined the course and what we're expected to do over the ten months, building up to our final submission of work in June next year. But you get marked on stuff throughout the course, so your final grade isn't just judged on the last project, which is a relief.'

'That seems fair.' Joe squeezes my hand. 'It won't be long before you're designing your first collection.'

'My first collection?' I raise my eyebrows skywards.

'What?' Joe laughs. 'I read stuff. That's what they call it.'

'I know that's what they call it.' I can't help but laugh too. 'I'm just amazed that you know that.'

'Well, I do, and that's your ultimate aim, isn't it?'

Mmm...I guess it is. It's all a bit overwhelming. I haven't really allowed myself to dream that I'd achieve such unimaginable things as designing my own clothing line. I mean, I've just started a night school class to gain a Diploma, that's all. No pressure, or so I thought. But maybe people are now expecting me to do something amazing. I thought I was just doing this for myself; I never really thought about other people's expectations of me.

I look at Joe, unsure of what to say, but thankfully I'm saved from answering by the bleeping of my mobile phone. I reach for it in my pocket.

'Hi, Mum.'

'Hello, darling. I'm just ringing to see where you are with the wedding plans.'

'I'm fine, thanks for asking. How are you?' I state with a hint of humour, although I'm a little fed up that every time she rings me it's just to see what's going on with our wedding plans. It's not the only thing in our lives at the moment.

'Tsk. I know you're fine, darling. I could tell as soon as you answered the phone.'

'How?'

'Because I'm your mother,' she states with authority.

I guess there's no arguing with that.

'So, the wedding plans,' Mum continues regardless.

'I don't think we've made any more since we last spoke, Mum.' I shrug, forgetting she can't actually see me. Then I glance at Joe, but his expression is unreadable.

'But all you've done is book the venue, darling. What about your dress, the bridesmaids' dresses, the flowers?'

'Why does everyone keep going on about my dress?' I can feel a trickle of annoyance building. 'I've got plenty of time, Mum. You do realise that I don't get married for another six months, don't you?'

I hear her sigh at the other end of the phone, which grates on my nerves.

'I've sent you some suggestions on your email, Emma. Just take a look. They're a bit pricy, but I can help with that.'

'I'll have a look tomorrow, Mum. I'm a bit tired from my first class at college tonight.'

'Oh, of course, darling. That totally slipped my mind. How was it? Can I look forward to you debuting at New York Fashion Week?'

'Well –'

'We must go, Emma, so you can see what you're aiming for. I'll arrange tickets, okay?'

'That would be good, Mum.'

'Right, I'll leave you to it. Don't forget to look at those dresses, though.'

'Bye, Mum.' I bite the inside of my mouth.

'Bye, darling. Love to Joe.'

I toss the phone dismissively to one side and catch Joe frowning at me.

'What?' I ask, but I already know what he's going to say.

'Why do you give her such a hard time? She's excited, that's all.'

'I know, but it feels like the wedding is the first thing she wants to talk to me about.'

'You're her only child, and you're getting married, and she's thousands of miles away.'

Oh God, I can feel the guilt smothering me.

'I know, I know.' I down the last dregs of wine.

'Just cut her some slack.'

'I will.' I gulp, feeling a little emotional. I can feel tears hovering and I force them back. Becoming increasingly overemotional seems to keep happening to me and I don't really know why. Maybe I'm just a bit tired.

Chapter Two

Jenny greets me with a coffee and a smile as I walk through the back door of the shop into the small kitchen area.

'So, how was your first night at college?'

'Yeah, it was good, once I'd got over my "I'm far too old to be doing this" drama.'

'Great. I'm pleased for you. You never know, it might kick me up the arse and force me into doing something interesting and more meaningful with my life.'

'I'm not sure fashion is meaningful, but still…'

'I've always wanted to speak Italian.'

'I'm sure they do courses locally for that too, you know.'

Jenny tips her head slightly. 'So you weren't the oldest one there then?'

'Oh no, I was.' I grin. 'But I managed to find a friend who was at least nearer to my age than the other teenagers who'd turned up for the class. I don't know, I can barely remember being eighteen or nineteen; it feels so long ago.'

'Tell me about your course then. What does it entail? Am I going to have to be your live manikin for the next year?' Jenny sighs emphatically.

Just at that moment Lola walks in all twenty-three years young with long gangly limbs and I catch Jenny's eye as we both appear to silently acknowledge that perhaps Lola might make a better manikin.

'What are you two gossiping about?' Lola asks, unwrapping herself from a giant blue tartan coat that's quite fabulous and something I only wish I was cool enough to wear.

'Nothing.' Jenny smiles at her. 'Emma was just telling me about her first class last night.'

'Ooh, how did it go?'

'Really good, thanks, Lola. My tutor seems pretty nice and I made a friend…oh, and I met a nice guy called, um, Tom.'

I see Jenny's eyes widen at this revelation.

'Calm down.' I laugh. 'I just said that I met a guy. I didn't say we're eloping.'

'I know, I know, it just…oh, he must be gay.'

'What? How did you reach that conclusion?'

'What straight men are interested in fashion?' Jenny retorts.

'Well, lots of men,' I protest. Honestly Jenny can be so closed-minded and over fond of stereotyping.

'Name one.'

I hear Lola giggling at this exchange as she quietly minds her own business and busies herself making a cup of tea.

Not one male, famous or not, who likes fashion but isn't gay will spring into my mind.

'That's not the point, Jenny,' I continue regardless. 'The point is you're so quick to judge.'

She responds to this accusation by raising her eyebrows at me, which is highly annoying.

'And anyway, he wasn't even on my course. He's doing business management or something.'

'So how come you ended up talking to him?' Lola must feel it's safe to re-join the conversation.

'I was loitering outside the doors,' I say sheepishly, 'um, building myself up to actually going in, and he sort of appeared from nowhere. I guess he was running late or something. We simply exchanged a few polite words before going into our respective classrooms, okay?'

'Oh.' Lola appears to feel that this is acceptable, but Jenny is still studying me with scepticism.

'But then I saw him again as we came out.'

Why? Why did I say that? There was no need. I could have just left the conversation there. Now Jenny pounces.

'Was he waiting for you?'

'No…no!'

She looks unconvinced.

'We kind of bumped into each other as everyone was filing out.'

'And what did he say?'

'I don't know.' I wave my hand, exasperated. '"see you next week" or something.'

'And what does he look like?' Jenny now has her hands on her hips, in full judgmental mode. I can't believe she's getting so upset about this.

'He's about twenty-five, twenty-six, I guess.'

'And he's cute?'

'I wasn't looking. I'm not looking. Hello – I have a fiancé! And I really think you're overreacting.'

'That means he is cute.' Jenny looks at me with a disapproving expression.

'You're being ridiculous, Jenny,' I snap, more than a little annoyed now.

'I'm just saying, you need to be careful.'

'Be careful? I met this guy for, like, two seconds, and now I have to be careful? I think you've watched too many movies, Jenny. This is real life, and I'm sure he was just being friendly'

'That's how it starts out,' Lola cuts in.

'How what starts out? What are you saying? Men and woman can't just be friends?'

Lola shrugs. 'There's no such thing as a platonic relationship.'

'Don't be silly. Anyway, I'm not his friend.'

'Mark my words.' Jenny nods knowingly. 'He'll ask you to go for a drink, and one thing can lead to another.'

The doorbell jingles, indicating that the first customer of the day has arrived, and I'm extremely grateful for the interruption.

'Right. That's enough of this rubbish. I'm going to go and serve that customer and I want no more said on the matter.'

I don't wait for a response before I flounce out of the kitchen onto the shop floor.

I spend the rest of the day ignoring both Jenny and Lola. Childish behaviour I know, but I feel I need to make a point. The conversation this morning was crazy. I love Joe. I'm going to marry Joe. It doesn't matter how many cute guys I meet who might ask me to go for a drink at some point, I'll never be interested. Jenny and Lola should both know that by now. I went through enough relationship crap in the last year to know when I've got it good. They're being ridiculous anyway, suggesting that men and women can't be friends. This is the twenty-first century, not nineteen thirty-six or some really old time when men ruled the world and women were insignificant. We can now have a multitude of friendships and relationships with both the same and the opposite sex, and that's that!

'See you tomorrow,' I call finally as I pull on my coat.

'Hey, fancy a glass of wine after work tomorrow night?' Jenny pops her head around the door to the staff area.

'Sure,' I say flatly, not feeling ready to resume our friendship. I want to sulk a bit more about our earlier exchange.

'Okay then. See you in the morning.' Jenny half smiles at me.

I just nod and close the door quietly behind me as I leave.

As I walk through the front door I find the hallway floor decorated with rose petals. A mixture of pink and red lay the trail towards the stairs and I grin as my heart flutters. How romantic! I slip my shoes off and bend down to pick up one of the petals. Holding it close to my face I inhale deeply and the wonderful scent ignites all of my senses and I feel a tingle of excitement dance up my spine. What did I do to deserve Joe Stark? I'm so lucky to have such a wonderful fiancé who isn't afraid of showing me exactly how he feels about me.

I fold my fingers around the petal and hold it tightly in the palm of my hand as I climb the stairs following the floral path. They lead, of course, to the bedroom and as I hover in the doorway, a swirl of anticipation surrounds me as I see Joe, laid in just his boxer shorts, on the bed with a dozen red roses splayed around him.

'Hi.' He says raising his eyebrows in a slightly provocative way.

'Hi yourself.' I lean on the doorframe.

'Good day?' Joe smiles widely.

I step into the room and walk over to the bed sitting down on the edge 'Um, okay, I guess. But I have a feeling it's going to end really well.'

'It doesn't sound okay.' Joe plants a gentle kiss on my lips.

Going into the whole 'men and women can have platonic relationships' with Joe doesn't seem like a good idea. Plus I don't want to dampen his whole romantic gesture. Rose petals and a semi-naked man in your bed – what more could a girl ask for? I push all thoughts of my argument with Jenny and Lola to the back of my mind and focus on Joe who's right here in front of me, waiting to seduce me.

'I just had a disagreement with Jenny. It's nothing really.'

'Are you sure it's not something you want to talk about?'

'No, but thanks. Right now I want to concentrate on just me and you.' I shuffle further on to the bed.

'I'm sure you two will sort it out tomorrow,' Joe says reaching forward and stoking my cheek with the back of his palm and my stomach does a little flip at his touch. Even now, a year into our relationship, Joe still instantly turns me on.

He sits up kneeling on the bed and I swing my legs around so I'm facing him and I kneel in front of him. We're face to face, our body's only inches away from each other and the heat between us is undeniable. Joe reaches forward and places his hand on the top of my chest and my heart thuds against it. Our eyes lock as we're caught in the moment, erotic sensations coursing through our bodies. My earlier frustrations from the day instantly forgotten.

Joe slowly unzips the back of my dress and I feel his gentle touch as his fingers caress my spine. Slowly he peels my dress from my body and

I gasp at his fingers brush my hypersensitive skin. My body tingles and I reach forward placing my hand on each side of Joe's face and I pull him closer to me. Our lips brush gently and then he grasps the back of my head and presses his lips against mine, kissing me roughly, passionately, his tongue searching for mine and finding it wanting.

I pull away from him and slide out of the remainder of my dress. Joe's hands make their way down my lower back removing my knickers with expertise. I unclip my bra and discard it over the side of the bed lying back on to the soft quilt.

Joe takes off his boxer shorts and lays down on top of me, his warm body pressing against mine and my own body immediately responds. I close my eyes and allow myself to sink into the bed as Joe's hand slides under my bottom pulling my hips towards him. I feel the familiar surge of adrenaline as my body touches his. Without fail, I'm instantly aroused by Joe; his gentle, yet confident touch. It's slow and sensual and like nothing I've experienced before, and as he pushes himself inside me I wrap my legs tightly around his body we slowly make love.

Chapter Three

The following morning I arrive at work feeling a little apprehensive.

As I turn the key at the back door of the shop I'm greeted by a cup of steaming tea on the worktop along with a heart-shaped cookie with 'We're sorry' swirled in white icing. I can't help but smile. Just then two faces appear, hovering around the door that leads through to the shop.

'Hey,' Jenny says softly, 'we both felt really bad about yesterday.'

'Really bad,' adds Lola.

'It's okay, you're both forgiven.' I take off my coat and hang it on a hook on the wall, feeling relieved that the tension has been broken and we can just get back to normal. 'But don't think for one moment I'm going to share that cookie,' I laugh, hoping to show that there are no hard feelings. I guess on this occasion we're going to have to agree to disagree.

As I screech to a halt in the college car park later that day and jump out of the car, almost strangling myself on the seatbelt as I do, I catch a familiar figure jogging towards the glass doors.

'Hi, Emma.' The figure stops and turns to face me and instantly I find myself smiling as Tom grins at me. 'We meet again.'

'Yeah, running in at the last minute seems to be becoming a habit for us both.'

'I know. Must try harder!'

I giggle as we march towards the doors. 'Must try harder' seems to be my life's mantra!

'Have a good class.'

'Yeah, you too…Hey, Emma?'

'Yes?' I glance over my shoulder as I walk towards my classroom.

'Fancy grabbing a beer after class?'

'Um.' I hesitate, conflicted. I'm sure Tom's just being friendly, but Jenny and Lola's words from yesterday are ringing in my ears.

'See whether Carly wants to come too – that is her name, isn't it?'

See? You should trust your instincts, Emma.

'Yes, it's Carly, and I'll ask her.'

'See you both at seven thirty then.'

'Okay.'

I hurry down to the classroom and sneak into the chair next to Carly just as our tutor, Sara, takes her position at the front of the room and clears her throat, signalling for us all to quieten down and pay attention.

'Hi. You're late.' Carly glances over at me.

'Yeah, I usually am. I'll work on that.'

Carly just nods, grinning.

'Good evening, everyone,' Ms Davies begins. 'Can you all turn to Chapter Three of your textbooks.'

I lean towards Carly and whisper, 'So, do you want to go for a drink with Tom tonight?'

'Are you kidding?'

'Shush.' I see Ms Davies throw a glance in our direction. 'I'm not kidding. He just asked me in the corridor if we both want to go for a beer.'

'He is cute.'

'So that's a yes?'

'He's very cute.'

'Just open your textbook.' I shake my head to suppress a giggle. Carly seems completely smitten. Watch out, Tom!

As the clock ticks over to seven thirty, Carly's already sliding her pen and notebook into her bag.

'Thanks, everybody. Don't forget the deadline for your essay is next Tuesday. Contact me in my office hours by phone if you need any assistance. See you all next Thursday.' Sara dismisses us for the evening.

Carly's already on her feet. 'Come on, hurry up.' She nudges me none too gently. 'Tom will be waiting.'

'Okay. A couple of things. Firstly, he asked us to go for a drink, so he's not going to leave without us, and secondly, you need to tone down the crazy a bit.'

'What do you mean?'

'I mean that you act like an excitable puppy around him, and you'll scare him off behaving that way. You need to act a little more calm and relaxed in his company.'

'I know. I just like him, and, well, it's been a while since I've had a boyfriend. My last relationship didn't exactly end well.'

Mmm. I've been there and done that. And in reality, who am I to be doling out relationship advice? I've got it wrong more times than I've got it right.

'You know what, Carly?' I stand up, collecting my things. 'If you really like him then you should just be yourself.'

With that, we head out into the corridor and find Tom slouched against his classroom wall. He looks up as we approach and smiles brightly, and I think Carly might actually explode. As we head outside I send a quick text to Joe so he doesn't worry where I am:

Just going for a quick drink with my new friends. Won't be home too late. xx

A few moments later we're sitting in a booth of the pub across the road from the college. Soft indie beats fill the room, reminding me of my younger days spent listening to Oasis on repeat on my CD player. It's weird, I never thought I'd feel old at thirty-three. I glance over at Tom, and before I can engage my brain, my mouth moves into action.

'How old are you, Tom?'

'Emma!' Carly admonishes me.

'Sorry. Was that rude?'

'It's all right, I don't mind.' Tom chuckles softly. 'I'm twenty-eight.'

'And why are you doing a...' Rather embarrassingly, I forget exactly what course Tom's taking.

'Why am I back at college?' He raises his eyebrows at me.

'Well, yes.'

'I could ask the same of you, Emma.'

'Well, that's easy.' I shrug dismissively. 'I long for a career where I'm not answerable to an uptight dragon and I don't spend my days unpacking stock and pandering to the unreasonable needs of overly rich women.'

'I'm almost scared to ask what job you do now.' Tom looks at me inquisitively. 'But me? I've been working in sales for a while in the finance industry and I wouldn't mind setting up my own business one day.'

'That sounds like a good plan.' I kind of like the idea of being my own boss, making my own decisions, not being answerable to some snappy old dragon. Sounds pretty good to me.

'So what do you do in your spare time?' Carly leans forward and I swear she flutters her eyelashes.

'What spare time?' Tom laughs lightly. 'I barely make it to class on time.'

I can definitely appreciate that.

'And although it seemed like a good idea at the time, I just hope that I can commit enough time and energy to this course to do it justice. If not, I'm just tiring myself out for nothing and achieving very little.'

Huh...can Tom read my thoughts? It's like a mirror image of what swirls around my head on a daily basis.

'Do you have a girlfriend?' Carly asks, blushing far too crimson to make the question sound breezy.

'Oh, um, no,' Tom fumbles.

Carly smiles, appearing content with that response for now, and I signal for the barman to brink me another Diet Coke.

As I drive home later I find myself chuckling at Carly and her attempts to woo Tom. I admire her optimism and wonder when I became so jaded about relationships. Although I'm very happy with Joe, I've had to kiss a lot of frogs before finding my prince. But Carly could do a lot worse, as it turns out Tom is pretty good company. However, despite her very obvious flirting and giggling like a schoolgirl, Tom seems pretty oblivious to Carly's charms.

'Hi,' I call down the hallway into the darkness as I close the front door softly behind me. 'Joe?'

I throw my coat over the bannister and climb the stairs towards the sliver of light coming from under the bedroom door.

'Hey.' I push the door open to find Joe in bed, half asleep, with his tablet balanced on his lap.

'You're a bit late, aren't you?'

'Sorry. I lost track of time.'

'So you're making new friends. That's nice.'

'Yeah, hopefully it will make doing this course a little more enjoyable.' I start to undress, pulling my dress up over my head. 'And Carly's certainly going to be one to watch.'

'How so?' Joe switches off his tablet and places it on the bedside table.

'Well, she obviously fancies Tom –'

'There's a guy called Tom on your fashion course? He must be gay.'

'No, Tom's not on our course.' I remove my tights with some difficulty while trying to remain upright. 'And I'm pretty sure he's not gay.'

'Oh, so if Tom's not on your course then how come you and this Carly girl ended up going for a drink with him?' Joe looks at me with a completely blank expression and I feel the hairs on the back of my neck start to prickle.

'There's nothing to be jealous of,' I state.

'I didn't say that there was.'

'Well, it was implied.'

'I just asked how you ended up going for a drink with him, that's all.'

I pause for a moment and consider my answer. I decide very quickly that I've done nothing wrong, so the truth is the way to go on this.

'I met him last week when I first got to the college, and Carly spoke to him on our way out. He's a nice guy and he's just being friendly.'

'Men don't do "just being friendly", Emma.' I swear Joe scowls for a second before changing his expression back to neutral.

'So what are you saying? That all men have an agenda?'

'Pretty much.' He shrugs. 'Are you going to turn the light out? It's late.'

And with that he pulls the covers up around him and rolls onto his side, facing away from me. I'm left standing in my bra and knickers feeling a mixture of shock at this conversation, complete surprise at Joe's obvious jealousy and outrage at what appears to be his total lack of trust of me – like I'm going to jump into bed with some random guy I've just met at college when I'm already in a committed and loving relationship.

Right, well…how annoying that Joe appears to have dismissed our conversation and signalled his lack of desire to continue it by abruptly pretending to go to sleep.

I march over to the door and flick the light switch off before flouncing into bed, making a big deal of getting comfy by swishing the quilt around me. Sleep evades me long into the night. This is the first time that Joe has ever reacted like this, and it feels totally out of character. I can't quite believe that he's behaving this way after me having drinks with Tom and Carly. It's not like I went out with Tom on his own. Joe has no right to be jealous, and no right to treat me like I've done something wrong.

I toss and turn for what seems like years, trying desperately to ignore the prodding thought: What if Joe went for a drink with another girl – alone or not? I'm sure if that were the case then I would be completely reasonable about the situation.

Who am I kidding? I would kill him in his sleep.

Hmm…

Chapter Four

'Hey, what do you fancy for dinner tonight?' I call through to the kitchen where I can hear Joe making coffee. I really should make more of an effort to be a good girlfriend around the house. I don't think I've made dinner all week. Joe seems to have taken on that role, even putting food in Tupperware pots I didn't know we owned and leaving them in the fridge for me to heat up when I'm late home.

'Why don't we go out? It'd be nice to spend the evening together.'

'You're right,' I concede.

The wedding and my newfound need for knowledge are taking their toll on my social life, our social life. I'm starting to behave like a boring girlfriend, old before my time and falling asleep on the sofa the minute I sit down and waking up to find I didn't even finish my glass of wine before snoring into the sofa cushion.

'So, shall we say Ernie's at eight?' Joe suggests.

'Yeah, and I'll meet you there.'

'You'll meet me there?'

'Yes. It'll be like we're on a date or something.' I grin.

'Okay.' Joe appears in the living room doorway. 'A date it is. See you tonight.'

He walks over to me and I smile. 'See you tonight. Don't be late.'

'I love you.' He leans in and kisses me and I revel in the warmth of his touch. I realise I've missed this. We need to make more time for intimacy so we're not just physically close when I've fallen asleep on him!

'I love you too.'

I'm relieved that things seem back to normal between me and Joe, with the nothing more said following our exchange of words about me going for drinks with Tom and Carly. Either Joe has realised that he overreacted and wants to just forget about the whole thing, or he's keeping his feelings about it hidden and I can expect an explosion of words at some point in the near future if I dare to mention Tom's name again, which right now I have no desire to do. Call me an ostrich if you want, and maybe I am burying my head in the sand, but I don't see the point in provoking an argument when we've both said our piece and we still disagree. It would just be arguing for arguing's sake, and that's not productive.

In the meantime I've made a mental note not to discuss college unless I'm talking about actual coursework, in which case Joe is always very supportive. Sometimes it's better to avoid confrontation, although I still don't think I have anything to feel guilty about. Having said that, a sliver of hesitation forms in my mind whenever I bump into Tom in the corridor, which, quite honestly, happens nearly every week.

As I arrive at work, I'm greeted by an unexpected scene. Jenny is embracing Lola in a bear hug and tears are flowing. I bump into them as I step through the back door of the shop.

'Hey, what's going on? Is everything okay?' An emotional Lola pulls away from Jenny as they make room for me in the small space.

'Yeah, everything's fine.' Lola wipes at her cheek with the back of her hand.

'So why are you crying?'

'She's leaving us,' Jenny states. 'Lola's going to travel the world while we stay here and play dress up with the manikins.'

'You're leaving!' I take hold of Lola's hand. 'But why? When did you decide this?'

'I'm going to Australia with my friend Kate.' Lola smiles clearly trying to contain her excitement, but who could blame her 'We're both twenty-five and single, so we just decided to do it while we've got nothing stopping us.'

'Australia. Wow, that's amazing. Why haven't you said anything to us before?'

Lola shrugs. 'Kate and I have been talking about it for some time – we got our visas sorted a while ago. I've been putting some money to one side and honestly, I didn't think we'd ever get to the point of actually doing it but last night we decided to take the plunge and book the flights.'

'Wow,' is all I manage to say as I struggle to process this bombshell. 'When are you going?'

'We leave in three weeks.'

'I can't believe you haven't said anything until now. How long are you going for?'

'A year.'

'A year?' I repeat, still a little shocked by this announcement.

'A whole twelve months of sun, sea and sand. It sounds too good to be true.' Jenny sighs.

'We must have a leaving do. Just the three of us out on the town again,' I suggest.

'We can have a tequila night!' Lola squeals.

'I don't think so – not after the last time!' I cringe inwardly, remembering that night in the bar when Connor (a.k.a Johnny) sent over a drink for me. I was inebriated and vulnerable which was a toxic concoction as I was easily charmed back to his flat, drunk and disorientated, where I then proceeded to sleep with him, which was the catalyst for a whole heap of crazy stuff that followed. He turned out not to be "Johnny" but to be Connor, Sophie's new boyfriend, and it all went wrong from there. He knew who I was and played me against Sophie, forcing her to choose between him and me, making me out to be the bad guy when it was him all along. It was only through my sheer determination to show him for the liar and disturbed individual that he was that Sophie finally saw through him. We're lucky that our friendship survived.

'Maybe you're right,' Lola concedes with an apologetic smile.

'I'm really happy for you, Lola, but I'm going to miss you. It just won't be the same here without you.' And I mean it. The three of us get on so well it will be weird without her.

'That's a really good point.' Jenny starts filling the kettle and I grab three cups from the cupboard for our morning coffee. 'Who's going to take your place as chief manikin dresser? You're the only one who can get clothes on those damned things.'

'Erm, an even more pressing question is: Who's going to deliver the news to Marissa Bamford?' The owner of the business, and a harsh evil dragon. My heart sinks at the thought.

'Rock, paper, scissors?' Jenny holds out her hand.

Honestly?...Okay.

Chapter Five

The day seems to fly by and I take the opportunity to fit in a bit of studying at the library once I've finished work. Seemed like a good idea, but I was so immersed in reading my new textbook that I lost track of time, and now the car journey home seems to have been sent to test my patience as it appears that every living soul within a ten-mile radius has chosen this moment to come out in their car and clog up the roads.

Once I finally make it home and rush through the front door, I catch a glimpse of the clock. Seven fifteen. I have twenty minutes to get ready before I need to be in a taxi, heading to the restaurant to meet Joe for our date night. Climbing the stairs two at a time, I discard clothing as I go. I jump in the shower and pull on the shower cap, careful not to let any water or steam interact with my hair – there's no way I'll make it out of here in the next eighteen minutes if my hair morphs into Marge Simpson's style. As the hot water hits my shoulders I feel the tension seeping from them slightly. I'm so mad at myself. I should never have gone to the library to study after work. I seem to be putting myself before "us", as in Joe and me. He seems to be last in the queue for my time at the moment and I know that needs to change. He's not specifically said anything but I can sense that he's getting a bit fed up just from the odd comment here and there.

Jenny warned me to just come home and chill out a bit and get ready to enjoy my evening out, but no, I thought I knew best and that I had time to do everything. What is it with time recently? It feels like it's passing twice as quickly and I have no time at all to do anything, even sleep. Speaking of running out of time – I rinse the last of the bubbles from my skin, grab a towel from the rail and fling it around me as I stride with wet feet to the bedroom.

Switching on the bedroom light, I peer at my reflection in the mirror. It's not great: dark circles appear to be forming rapidly under my eyes, more rapidly than I expected at the age of thirty-three, but a quick touch-up of makeup tonight will have to do. I swirl on face powder followed by blusher, and finish with a black steak of eyeliner around my eyes and two coats of mascara. That should just about do it. I look slightly more human than I did five minutes ago.

I can hear my mobile phone ringing in my handbag at the bottom of the stairs. I hurry down them, grabbing my dressing gown on the way and pulling it around me tightly. I grab the phone from my bag and see Sophie's name flashing on the screen.

'Hey, Soph. How's things?'

'Yeah, I'm good, thanks. I just thought I'd call as it feels like forever since we had our usual coffee and muffins for breakfast and had a good catch-up. What are you doing tomorrow?'

'I'm not working this Saturday and don't have any particular plans. We could do coffee in the morning. I can meet you in our usual place at, say ten?'

'Great. So how are things?'

'A bit manic if I'm honest. I'm really sorry but I don't have time to talk now. I'm meeting Joe for dinner and I need to leave in about three minutes and I'm not even dressed yet.'

'Oh, that sounds nice. Where are you going to eat?'

'Ernie's.'

'Oh, I love it there. Although I haven't been for ages. In fact I haven't been out on a date for ages.'

I feel a stab on guilt. I know Sophie hasn't even contemplated going out with a guy since the whole thing with Connor. It really shook her confidence after she realised he had played her and convinced her to believe all his lies. It's been nearly seven months and I know she's starting to feel lonely. I must make more time for her.

'We're having a date night.'

'What's that? You're already going out with him, and you live together, so how can you be going on a date?'

'Well, it's simple: we're just making that bit more effort to spend some time together doing what we used to do before we became buried under workloads, housework, studying et cetera.'

'Oh, I see.'

'I suggested it. I thought it'd be fun,' I say. I don't want to admit to Sophie that I actually suggested it to offset my guilt, which may be from an imaginary issue rather than a reality but I feel like I've been too busy with work and college to be a good girlfriend over the last few weeks. I've fallen asleep in my text book more times than I care to recall and domestic chores have become almost non-existent to me.

'That sounds sweet. A date night. It's romantic.'

My gaze catches the clock on the kitchen wall. 'Soph, I'm really sorry but I need to get off the phone I'm going to be late and Joe will kill me.

I made this big deal about it being a "date" and now I'm going to ruin it by arriving late.'

'How can you ruin it? You're already in the relationship. You're getting married for God's sake!'

'I know, I know. But I don't feel like we've been spending much time together recently. It might just be in my head but...' I leave the sentence hanging. I never could hide the truth from Sophie. 'And Joe's been really patient with me, even though I've hardly had any time to spare. I just want us to have a nice romantic evening together without me having to worry about textbooks, essays, stock takes or what colour wedding napkins are going to be on the tables.'

'Okay, I get it. But...don't shoot me down for saying this...'

'What?' I sigh, already anticipating what Sophie is going to say.

'Do you think that you've taken on too much? It's a lot to do a part-time course at college alongside your job, but to do all of that while trying to plan a wedding, well...'

Hmm. It's a bit late for that now. I feel like I'm hurtling down a hill and there are no brakes to apply.

'Emma?'

'Yes.'

'I'm just worried about you.'

'I know, and maybe you're right, but I can't change things now. I need to keep working to pay the bills. I want to do this course to try to improve my career prospects, as I don't want to spend the next thirty years of my working life hanging up clothes. And I want to be married to Joe.'

'You said, "I want to be married to Joe."'

'Yeah, I do. What are you getting at, Sophie?'

'You didn't say, "I want a wedding."'

'What? I did. That's the same thing.'

'No, it isn't. You do actually want to plan your wedding, don't you?'

'Of course I do.' I can hear the snappy tone of my voice. 'Why would you even ask that?'

'Because of this. Every time anyone mentions your wedding, you snap at them.'

'That's not true, Sophie. It's all in your head. I want to marry Joe and I want to have a wedding. Now I really have to go or I might not have a groom at the end of this night to marry anyway.'

'Emma –'

'Bye, Soph.' I press the 'end call' button, squishing my thumb into the keypad.

I don't know why but I feel a wave of irrational anger towards Sophie when she starts ranting on about my wedding. I mean, it's my wedding, and yet everyone seems to think they're entitled to an opinion on it.

Damn it, that's the taxi beeping outside. I head back upstairs and pull on my purple dress, which I know Joe loves, and then grab my handbag and a pair of simple black high heels. Slamming the front door behind me, I clamber not so elegantly into them and stumble hurriedly to the waiting car.

'Hi, sorry, Ernie's restaurant, please', I say breathily as I climb into the back of the taxi and pull on my seatbelt ignoring the disgruntled stare from the taxi driver. Honestly I only kept him waiting for two minutes, not two hours.

The car pulls away and I exhale, trying to calm myself. I always seem to be charging from one place to another recently, and Sophie nagging me on the phone doesn't help. No, that's not fair. She's right: we haven't had coffee together for a few weeks, and it used to be our regular Saturday morning pastime. I know she's found it hard to deal with trying to get back to normal following everything that happened with Connor. He was her new boyfriend but he targeted me in a bar one night, took advantage of my drunken state and enticed me to sleep with him all the while knowing that I was Sophie's best friend. He then played us off against each other until Sophie was so convinced by his lies that she ended our friendship.

It took me a while, and I had a few failed attempts, but I finally got Connor to admit to me that he had planned it all, it was just a game to him, simply because he could and I was sneaky enough to record that conversation on my mobile phone to prove to Sophie that he was the bad guy in all of this not me. But Connor caught me in the act and as we tried to escape him a speedy pursuit in our cars ensued resulting in a terrible accident.

I know Sophie blamed herself, and still does, that I ended up in hospital, apparently near death's door, although I don't really remember that part of it. But it was all Connor's fault. He was sick in the mind and we just happened to be his victims. But Connor paid the ultimate price as he didn't survive the car accident. No matter what he'd done, neither of us would have wished that to be the outcome.

All I wanted was for him to leave me and Sophie alone. I still think about him sometimes, and the horrible upbringing that he had - a mother that abandoned him and a violent drunk of a father. He never really stood a chance of being a normal, decent human being, and I can't help feel a strange mix of guilt and relief when I go over the events of those few months in my head. But I try not to think about it too much. Sometimes you just have to say, 'That happened, and I couldn't have done anything to change it,' and you put it to one side and carry on with your life.

'Miss, we're here.'

'Oh, sorry.' I snap out of my trance and look up to see the bright lights of Ernie's restaurant reflected in the car window. I hand a five-pound note through the gap in the Perspex window and climb out of the car.

As I pull open the door to Ernie's, I can already see Joe standing at the bar.

'I'm so sorry, I'm running late.' I rush over to him and plant a kiss on his lips. 'It's Sophie's fault,' I lie. 'She kept me talking on the phone.'

'It's okay, calm down. You're here now. I took the liberty of ordering you a drink.' He hands me a glass of white wine and I'm reminded of what a great guy Joe is. I really am lucky to have met him, and it feels good to be out in a restaurant on a Friday night, just the two of us, like we used to do.

A waitress appears from behind me. 'Are you ready to be seated?'

'Yes, please.' Joe smiles at her.

She escorts us to a booth and hands us a menu each while listing the specials of the day, before stating she'll return in a couple of minutes to take our order.

I take a sip of my wine. It tastes expensive. I must try not to gulp it like pop, which is a habit I fall into when drinking with Sophie; I must savour it instead.

'So, how was the shop today? Was it busy?' Joe reaches across the table and takes my hand in his, gently stroking the back of my hand with his thumb.

'You know what? I don't want to talk about the shop tonight, or my studies. I just want to…talk.'

'That sounds ominous. Do you want to talk about anything in particular?'

'No, just nice, easy conversation. I love the atmosphere in this place. Let's just enjoy the evening.'

'Okay. I just need to mention one slight wedding thing.'

I purse my lips.

'My mum called today and invited us to dinner with the whole family next Sunday.'

'Why is that a wedding thing?'

Joe shrugs. 'I don't know. She just said it would be nice for us all to have dinner together.'

'Who's "all"?'

'Um, Mum, Dad, my two brothers, Matt and Paul, and Paul's wife Melanie.'

'That doesn't sound too bad.'

'And Paul and Melanie's two kids.'

I want to scream 'No!' and that it sounds like the last thing I'd want to do on a Sunday and that I'd rather be lying on the sofa in my pyjamas drinking wine and stuffing crisps and dip simultaneously into my mouth while attempting to read a textbook. But instead I force a smile onto my face and nod.

'So I can tell her yes?'

I just nod, unable to trust myself to speak.

'Good, because I kind of already agreed that we would go.' Joe laughs a little nervously.

'Hmm. Why do I feel like I've just been manipulated?' I raise my eyebrows but Joe just grins at me, and then the waitress appears, saving him from answering.

'Are you ready to order?' she asks.

I glance down at the menu. 'Can I have the tortellini, please?' I smile courteously at the waitress as I hand my menu back.

'The sirloin steak, please.' Joe adds. 'Cooked medium.'

'Of course.' The waitress scribbles something indecipherable on her minuscule notepad. 'And to drink?'

'A beer, please?' I think a night off the wine is required (if you exclude the initial glass of wine that Joe got for me). I feel like I'm a test dummy for a theory on pickled humans at the moment, but I'm not off alcohol altogether. It is Friday night, after all.

'Make that two, please.' Joe hands his menu back to the waitress and she heads off to the bar.

'Lola announced today that she's leaving the shop.' I fiddle with the napkin on the table in front of me going against my own rule of not talking about work.

'How come?'

'It's nothing bad. She's decided to go travelling for a year with her friend. She's so excited, but honestly I'm dreading having to start from scratch with someone else. She and Jenny have become more than just work colleagues; they're friends.'

'That's a shame. I know how much you three like to drink wine and gossip at the end of the working day.' Joe raises his eyebrows at me.

That's true. We've always been there for each other, ready with wine, to address whatever calamity had befallen one of us. It feels like the end of an era.

'I know. I'm really going to miss her.'

'When does she leave?'

'In three weeks.'

'Wow, that's quick. What are you going to do about replacing her?'

'Jenny's going to have to have that conversation with the old dragon.'

'How'd she end up with the short straw?'

'We played rock, papers, scissors.'

'Seriously?'

'That's how we make all the major decisions.' I can't help but laugh at the astonishment in Joe's voice. 'We have to entertain ourselves some-how, you know.'

The waitress reappears and places two bottles of beer on the table.

'To us.' I pick up my bottle and tip it toward Joe.

'To us.' He clinks his bottle against mine and I take a sip, enjoying the refreshing taste of the ice-cold beer.

'Can you promise me now that rock, paper, scissors isn't how we're going to make important decisions in our future, please?'

'Of course.' I grin. 'It'll be much simpler. I'll make the decision and you'll just go along with it.'

'Oh, really? Is that your idea of a mature relationship involving give and take?'

Joe's looking at me now with eyebrows raised even higher, as if chal-lenging me to continue down this path, but I'm having fun. I'm enjoy-ing the banter and I feel more relaxed than I have done in ages. No wed-ding talk, no textbooks, and it's past eight o'clock and I'm still awake, which is a bonus given my recent existence.

'So let me get this straight.' Joe takes a swig of beer. 'Once we're mar-ried, you get to make all the rules and I just get to play along nicely.'

'If you know what's good for you.' I bite my lip to stop myself laugh-ing out loud.

'Carry on like that and I'll show you who's in charge in this relation-ship.' Joe shoots me a daring look.

We barely make it through the front door before Joe's pulling my dress up and grabbing my bum as his lips smother mine. It's as if all of the tension from the last month or so has bubbled to the surface and is escaping through sexual desire. I run my hands through Joe's thick, dark hair and tug at it roughly. He murmurs in my ear before pulling my dress up to my thighs and scooping me up. I wrap my legs around his body and hold on as he carries me upstairs towards the bedroom.

As he lays me down on the bed, I feel his lips demanding mine and instantly adrenaline starts coursing through my body. His tongue gently pushes my lips apart, in search of mine, and I can feel my body starting to tingle all over. I've just been so tired and so preoccupied with everything that I haven't made time for Joe, for this, and I had no idea how much I've missed his enjoying his company.

I reach around Joe's back, sliding my hand underneath his jeans and down his pants, grabbing his bottom and pressing his body closer to mine. I can already feel him hard against me as he peels off my dress, and I lean up slightly while he pulls it gently over my head and discards it on the bedroom floor. He rolls over to the edge of the bed and stands up while taking off his own shirt and jeans, and I feel incredibly aroused and, weirdly, a little emotional. As Joe climbs back onto the bed I reach out and touch his lips with my thumb.

'I love you,' I whisper.

'I love you too,' Joe says softly.

And then the love-making is slow and sensuous, like we're both in need of the other's touch and we want to savour every moment, every emotion. Joe's hand strokes my thigh as an electric current surges through my body forcing every nerve in my body to stand to attention and it's like the first time Joe touched me all over again. His mouth is on mine and I can feel his heartbeat as his chest presses against me. It's as though we're exploring each other for the first time and every touch, every kiss, is intense. The energy in the whole room has gone up a notch and the tension of the last few months is beginning to dissolve as we find comfort in each other's arms. I reach up and pull my fingers through his hair as he traces down my neck to my breastbone with kisses, and I lay back, a tingling sensation washes over my entire body as his kisses head south.

'Your life as you know it is over.'

Chapter Six

I make my way across the crowded coffee shop amid a variety of whizzing and hissing noises, and finally reach Sophie in the far corner, lounging on a squishy brown sofa in what used to be our usual Saturday morning spot.

'Morning. Sorry I'm late,' I gabble, hugging her as I flop down next to her on the sofa.

'No problem. I guess your date night went well last night. Couldn't tear yourself away from Joe this morning?'

'Well, yes, something like that.' I don't really want to divulge that after last night's love-making I had the best night's sleep I've had in weeks and I simply overslept.

'I got you a latte.' She pushes an oversized mug in my direction. 'And a blueberry muffin.'

'Thanks, Soph. I'm in desperate need of caffeine.'

'So how was last night really?'

I take a swig of coffee and relax back into the sofa cushions. 'It was lovely, the whole evening. We had nice food, easy conversation…it was exactly what we needed, to concentrate on the two of us for once, to get that moment back of when you're just in your own little bubble. No talk of textbooks or essays, no discussions over flower arrangements –'

'You haven't chosen your flowers for the wedding yet?'

I shoot Sophie an annoyed glance.

'Sorry.' She bites her lip.

'It was a perfect evening.' I pull off a chunk of muffin and chew it gratefully deciding that I must have burned off plenty of calories last night and I can hear my stomach grumbling its annoyance at my late breakfast. As I watch Sophie as she mindlessly drinks her coffee I wonder whether I'm about to speak out of turn. But we're best friends, and if you can't have an honest conversation with your best friend then who can you talk to?

'Sophie.'

She glances up from her coffee mug. 'Yes?'

'Don't you miss it?'

'Miss what?'

'Dating.' I press my lips together, hoping that she won't be offended. We used to talk about our relationships all the time; but for a while now I've been the only one raising that subject.

Sophie looks a little uncomfortable with this line of questioning and I hesitate for a second before continuing.

'Why are you focusing on my love life?' Sophie asks.

'Why are you being so defensive?'

'I'm not. It's just...'

'Look, Soph, I know you were pretty shaken by everything that happened with Connor –'

'It's not that.'

'But you need to let go and move on and...What do you mean it's not that?' I stare at Sophie, but she won't quite meet my eye and instead picks at the crumbs of blueberry muffin on her plate.

'Soph. Have you met someone?'

'What? No, no, I'm...' She pauses, her whole body looking uneasy. 'You're right,' she says after a moment. 'I'm just not ready to have a new relationship yet. Now can we change the subject, please?'

Reluctantly I nod and we move on to the more pressing topic of my other best friend, Simon, and his blossoming relationship with James – his latest love fad who seems to have turned into something serious which has surprised us all given Simon's reluctance to commit to anyone previously always claiming he was too much of a free spirit to be tied down to one person. Every time I meet James, I blush crimson at the memory of walking in on him and Simon having sex on the sofa in Simon's flat. I think that image will remain etched on my memory for eternity – though believe me, I've tried everything I can to forget!

'How was Sophie?' Joe calls from the lounge as I arrive home an hour later.

'I'm not sure.' I hover in the doorway.

'In what respect?' Joe switches off the television and turns his full attention to me.

'I can't put my finger on it but something's going on with her. I know her too well and she has a crap poker face.'

'Going on with what? A guy?'

'I think so.'

'Didn't you ask?'

'Yes, but she got all defensive and forced us to change the subject.' I flop down on the sofa next to Joe and he gives me a quick kiss. 'I just didn't want to push it with her.'

'She's your best friend. She'll tell you whatever it is when she's ready. You'll be the first to know what's going on, I'm sure.'

'I know. You're right.'

'So what are you going to do with yourself for the rest of the day?'

'Why? Where are you going?'

'Football practice, remember?'

'Of course.' Actually it had totally slipped my mind and I'm a little disappointed. Having spent the morning with Sophie, I was looking forward to enjoying time with Joe this afternoon. 'What time will you be back?'

'I might go for a beer with the guys after practice, so around six o'clock.'

'Great. I'll get a few beers in and we can have a takeaway.'

'Sounds good to me.' He glances at his watch. 'I'd better get going. I said I'd pick Ben up on the way.'

'Have fun.' I force a smile and kiss him on the lips. 'See you later.'

I hear the swish of the front door opening and closing and then silence descends on the house. I sit there for a moment, relishing the sound of, well, nothing. After the craziness of the last few weeks it's nice to have time to reflect. I stare around the room aimlessly, trying desperately to focus on the meditation mantra from that yoga class that Sophie dragged me to the other month – something about envisaging yourself as an old oak tree. I close my eyes and take in a deep breath…

Maybe I'll just pop to the off licence now to get the beers, then they'll be chilled for tonight.

I open my eyes and stand up, grab my handbag and coat and go out in search of alcohol.

'Hello, miss.' The cashier smiles at me before giving a sideways glance at the six-pack of beers and the bottle of white wine in my hand basket as I place it none too ceremoniously in front of him.

'Um, hi.' I smile back out of courtesy before adding, 'They're for tonight.'

Like I need to be judged by the off-licence man. He relies on customers to buy alcohol – that's the point of his business. And anyway, it's not like I'm in here all the time. Although I did call in twice last week on the way home from work and then college, but that was an exceptional week, not the norm. Not usually anyway. Am I trying too hard to convince myself here?

As I reach home again, I glance absentmindedly at my watch. It's only three thirty. In the kitchen I open the fridge and place the beers and wine on the shelf, then take the bar of chocolate and the fashion magazine from the bag and make my way through to the lounge. I flop heavily down on the sofa and switch on the television, in need of some sign of life. After flicking through the music channels I settle on 'Back to the 80s' and, tapping my foot to Michael Jackson's 'Beat It', I open my magazine and start scanning the pages of designer shoes and clothes that I'm no way cool enough to pull off.

Is it too early for a beer? It is the weekend. I mean, lots of people must already be enjoying alcohol in pubs, catching up with friends, watching football on television screens. And Joe will be having a few drinks with his friends after football practice, so I might as well just have one.

I find myself in front of the fridge door, opening it and reaching in for the bottle of wine. One glass will be absolutely fine.

It's nice not having to stress about work, although Lola's leaving and that's not good; I don't like change. And it's nice not to have an essay to work on this weekend, although I'm really enjoying learning more about fashion, and Carly is lovely. I don't know what I was so scared about that first evening at college. I wish I'd done this course ages ago. I should have done more when I was younger. I certainly had the grades too but I was in too much of a hurry to earn some of my own money, learn to drive, buy a car; have some independence. Maybe it was being an only child that drilled that in to me, or perhaps mum and dad separating when I was sixteen was my catalyst to support myself. Although they have remained amicable, and their love for me was never in doubt, I do sometimes wonder if I would be a different person had they stayed together. Maybe I wouldn't have had so many failed relationships having fallen for the wrong guy. Who am I kidding? I've always made bad choices, I'm too easily led. I need Sophie to keep me in line.

Belinda Carlisle is now playing on the television and I'm tempted to get up and dance around the living room like Sophie and I have on too many drunken occasions but after only one glass of wine I remain seated on the sofa and my thoughts drift back to Sophie.

It's six o'clock. Where's Joe? What time did he say he'd be home?
Maybe I'll just have another glass of wine.

It's eight o'clock. Where is he?

I'm starving.

Why is there no wine left?

Ah, I bought beers.

I'm wearing the carpet out in a circular pattern as I pace the living room floor. Admittedly it's a slightly wobbly circle due to the wine and beer that I've consumed on an empty stomach, but that's not my fault. I was here, ready for dinner, two and a half hours ago.

The front door opens and closes, interrupting my silent rant.

'Hi.' Joe appears in the doorway not looking nearly sheepish or sorry enough to douse my anger.

'Hi.' I glare across the room.

'Sorry I'm late.' Joe remains glued to the spot, clearly sensing my prickly demeanour.

'Late would have been six thirty. This?' I look at my watch purposefully. 'This is just plain rude.'

'You're drunk.'

'No, I'm not.' I'm careful not to slur any of my words, although defiance is fuelling me as I know full well that I left sober behind about an hour ago.

'How much have you drunk?'

'That's neither here nor there. I've been sitting here on my own for the last however many hours waiting for you. It's not my fault you weren't here to share the alcohol with me.'

'So now I can't have a few beers on a Saturday with my mates?' It's Joe's turn to have an attitude now.

'I'm not saying that.' I find myself folding my arms defensively.

'Well, that's what it sounds like, Emma.'

'I was just looking forward to spending some time together today, but you chose to stay out with your friends instead of coming home.'

'But it's different when you go for wine with Jenny and Lola, or Sophie, or Carly and Tim from college.'

'Tom.'

'What?'

Is that what this is about? He's jealous because I went for a drink with another guy, not alone or anything, but with another friend too.

'Never mind.'

'And now you want me to drop my friends and come home early just because it suits you.'

'No, I wanted you to come home when you said you would and have dinner with me and a few beers, as we agreed at only lunchtime earlier today."

'Well, I'm sorry to ruin your schedule. You'll have to see when you can next fit me in.'

'That's not fair.'

'No?'

'No. You encouraged me to do this course and you know that things have been crazy busy at work too. Now you're punishing me for going for a quick beer with two new friends from college just because one happens to be male.'

'That's not what this is.'

'That's exactly what this is, Joe, and I can't quite believe it of you. Don't you trust me?'

'It's just...' He shoves his hands into his jeans pockets and looks down at the floor.

'It's just what, Joe? Come on, let's hear it.'

'It just feels like I never see you, and when I do you're falling asleep on the sofa, but you seem to make time for other people.'

I swallow down the mixture of hurt at the accusation and guilt at the realisation that there may be some truth in that statement, but I don't feel quite ready to face that yet.

'You know what, I was looking forward to this evening and now I'm just...' I exhale slowly. 'I'm going to go to bed and put an end to this day.'

'Emma, wait.'

Joe grabs hold of my arm as I walk past him to leave the room. I try to force back the tears that are building but I fail miserably and a big, fat tear slides down my cheek and plops onto my jumper. We just look at each other in silence and I feel my heart being squeezed so tightly that for a second I don't think I can breathe.

'I'm sorry,' Joe says earnestly and I bite my lip to stop the surge of emotion overflowing into a complete breakdown.

'I'm sorry too.'

He kisses me softly on the lips. 'Please stay down here and spend the rest of the evening with me.'

'Okay.'

I can't help but feel that the bubble of closeness between us last night has burst, emphatically leaving a deflated shape that now resembles our relationship tonight.

Chapter Seven

'I can't believe that today's been your last day.' I hug Lola as we stand in the staff area of the shop as Jenny locks up for the day. Our last day together. It just seems so sad.

'I'll miss you two.' Lola looks a little tearful.

Jenny appears in the doorway. 'Come on, don't get all misty-eyed. We've got plenty of drinking to do. Get your coats on; there's a shot of tequila each waiting for us.'

'No way.' I shake my head vigorously. 'There's no way I'm drinking that stuff again.'

My protest falls on deaf ears and not ten minutes later I find myself huddled around a tall circular table with a shot of tequila in my right hand and salty crystals on the back of my left hand. I know this isn't a good idea – I've experienced the aftereffects of tequila with Jenny and Lola before – but there's no convincing them.

Jenny downs her shot and glares at me until I follow suit.

Urgh! The mixture of salt and liquid poison sloshes down my throat and my stomach protests at the intrusion, making it swirl around before finally settling, much to my relief.

'Another round?' Lola waves her empty shot glass around.

'I'll go,' I quickly offer so I can get myself a vodka and Coke instead of more tequila without getting grief from Jenny and Lola beforehand.

I squeeze through the large crowd of Friday night revellers. It's busier than I expected so early in the evening. I collect the drinks from the bar and I can already see the look of disapproval from Jenny as I make my way back to the table.

'What is that?' She points at my glass.

'Vodka and Coke,' I say dismissively.

'Oh no you don't.' She shakes her head at me. 'You can't wimp out on us on Lola's last night.'

I glance at Lola and she's giggling at the exchange between Jenny and me as she reaches for her replenished shot glass.

'All right, all right. I'll join back in the drinking of disgusting petroleum on the next round, okay?'

Jenny nods and then downs her second shot as I sip slowly from my glass, determined to make this drink last as long as I can.

I'm sweating and gasping for breath. I have no idea how long we've been dancing but it feels great just to let go with no cares tonight. There's a lot to be said for escapism. Jenny is jigging at the side of me to some lively dance tune and Lola is being flung around the dance floor by some surfer-type guy to whom she's clinging for dear life, although I expect that's more to do with how cute he is rather than her drunken state.

'I need a break,' I mouth to Jenny, but she has no chance of understanding me so I tug on her arm and point towards the bar.

'Drink?' she shouts.

'Yes.'

'I'll come with you.'

'When did we become old and unfit?' I slouch on the bar for support to stay upright. 'I remember the days of dancing long into the night, and early morning for that matter, and it doesn't feel that long ago in my head, but my body's telling me it was.'

'We hit thirty and that's the tipping point,' Jenny says, a little breathless too.

'So that's it? We're on the scrap heap at thirty?'

'In regards to clubbing – yes.'

'Why? How does this happen?'

'It's simple really.'

'It is?'

'Yes. The answer to the following question defines whether you've reached the point when you can no longer pass as an appropriate age for nightclubbing.'

'Okay...'

'Did you bring a coat out with you tonight?'

'Um, yes, my red winter coat. It's cold.'

'I rest my case.'

'But –'

'Three double vodka and Cokes, please,' Jenny shouts to the barman over the music.

I just stand there, reflecting on my apparently lost youth.

Ouch. My head hurts. It's suddenly become too heavy to even lift off the pillow. I am never drinking tequila again...ever! I am no longer friends with Jenny.

Mmm...is that coffee I can smell?

Chapter Eight

It's Monday morning already and as I drive to work I feel a weird sense of uneasiness. All Jenny and I have been told is that we have a new employee starting today to replace Lola and that whoever it is has been appointed by Marissa Bamford. None of that bodes well.

'Morning, Jenny,' I call as I walk through the door to the back room of the shop. The lights are already on, so Jenny must be somewhere. 'Do you want coffee?' I turn to hang my coat on the hook on the wall.

'What time do you call this?' a clipped tone echoes behind me, and I turn back around, startled.

The woman addressing me is impossibly thin, looks no older than twenty-five and is presented immaculately in a fitted red dress that looks like it was made to measure for her bony frame. Her makeup is applied with perfection: black eyeliner is streaked across both upper eyelids with what can only be fake eyelashes protruding from each eye, and bright red lips, the exact colour of the dress, are pursed, clearly awaiting my response.

'Um –'

'As I understand it the shop opens at nine a.m.; is that correct?'

'Um.' I glance down at my watch. It's only eight forty-five.

At this moment Jenny appears, creeping in the doorway behind this ridiculous woman who has descended upon us.

'From now on I expect you to arrive at work promptly, and no less than thirty minutes before the shop is due to open, giving you plenty of time to prepare for the day.'

Prepare for the day? What on earth do we need thirty minutes for? It takes a whole three minutes to arrive, take off my coat, make a coffee and then open the shop doors. Now we're expected to start work a whole thirty minutes before we start getting paid? She's got to be kidding.

'I'll be out in the shop checking the displays,' the random woman announces before marching purposefully out of the staff area in her black patent three-inch heels.

I just stare, dumbfounded at Jenny, who looks completely shell-shocked herself.

'Who the hell is that?' I hold my hands out in a gesture of despair.

'That?' Jenny whispers, making sure the door to the shop is closed properly behind her, 'is Julia Bamford.'

'Julia Bamford? Bamford? Oh no!'

'Oh yes. Say hello to Marissa Bamford's niece, i.e. Lola's replacement.'

'Seriously?'

'You want to start looking for a new career?'

'Based on first impressions, I'm going to say yes.' I sigh heavily. This is all I need at the moment. As if life weren't already stressful enough, God thought that he'd have some fun with me and send the devil's niece to control my work day. Usually this is my time to escape the other madness and chaos that swirls around my existence, and now I have to deal with some uppity woman's agenda too.

'I have a very bad feeling about this, Jenny.'

'Me too.'

Julia Bamford swings the door open. 'Come on, ladies. There's work to be done. You aren't paid to chitchat.'

Oh my God. We haven't just been sent the devil's niece; we've actually been transported to hell.

Chapter Nine

'Hey.'

I feel Joe nudging me awake, and as I start to stretch out my body twinges in pain and I realise that I'm scrunched on the sofa with what feels like a textbook lodged somewhere that it shouldn't be.

'You didn't make it to bed again.' His voice is soft but with a hint of disappointment.

Guilt washes over me and I feel a sharp stabbing pain in my heart. It's been three weeks since that awful Saturday night when we had the fight, after which we both promised to spend more time with each other. It looks like I'm already failing.

'I'm sorry.' I roll up to a seated position and rub my eyes, hoping to dislodge the sleep that still feels like it's descending on me. The guilty realisation that this is becoming an all-too-common occurrence nestles unpleasantly in my stomach. 'Let me make you some breakfast,' I offer, a small consolation.

'Thanks, but I need to get going.' Joe stands up and I notice he's already showered and dressed in his gym gear.

'At least a coffee.'

'Sorry, Emma. You do breakfast tomorrow.' He leans down and kisses me on the lips. 'See you tonight.'

'What time will you be home?'

'Around six.'

'Have a good day.' I force a smile, but as I hear the front door close behind Joe I can't help but feel a hint of sadness.

When we moved in together I didn't foresee that we would quickly become two ships that pass in the night, or in the early morning as it would seem to be. But the fashion course is taking up more of my time than I imagined. I didn't expect it to be easy – well, okay, maybe I did, but I'd forgotten how much time it takes to read textbooks and write essays. It feels like a lifetime since I was whizzing through stuff like this at school, getting consistently good grades. And then there's planning the wedding. Between Mum constantly ringing for an update on where we are with things and repeating, 'But, darling, you've only booked the venue – what about your dress?' like some demented parrot, and Sophie morphing into bridezilla on amphetamine, I'm starting to wonder why we didn't just elope to a small tropical island and steal two waiters to be witnesses. Then we could just share the pictures by social media and be done with it – the twenty-first century wedding. A virtual one with no fuss!

I guess I need to make more of an effort at home, and at least try to not fall asleep on the sofa tonight. I think I'll get a bottle of red wine, Joe's favourite, on the way home from work at the shop today, and maybe order a Chinese takeaway. For now I need to get a move on or I'll be late for work and will be in Jenny's bad books too.

I force my weary body up from the sofa (yet another night of falling asleep in my text book. This is becoming a far too frequent event given Joe has stopped even trying to wake me up and get me into bed) and I head into the kitchen, where I make myself an extra-strong coffee from the new machine with its little foil pods.

It's nearly seven thirty and I've been nursing the same glass of wine for the last hour. Joe said this morning that he would be home for six. I pick up my mobile from the kitchen worktop and hit redial, but for the fourth time tonight I'm greeted by Joe's voicemail. Where is he? I place the phone back down none too gently on the worktop. My hand hovers over the phone for a second and I press redial.

'Hey, you're through to Joe. Leave a message after the beep.'

I take a deep breath.

'Hi, it's only me. Just wondering where you are. I bought wine and I thought we could have a takeaway…Anyway, give me a ring to let me know you're okay.'

I feel like a fraud, leaving a happy-go-lucky message in my singsong voice when I really just want to shout, 'Where the hell are you, and why aren't you answering your phone?' Picking up the glass I down the lot in two gulps before refilling it and heading through to the lounge grabbing the remote control and flicking angrily through the channels before deciding on some rom-com film that I've seen a hundred times. I scowl at the loving couple on the screen as they kiss and cuddle, whispering and giggling together. Why don't people in the movies have real lives where they get on each other's nerves and have to balance a career and family commitments with friends and relationships, instead of this 'Isn't everything romantic!' bullshit? I ponder this for a moment before concluding that if entertainment was as frustrating and annoying as real life then we'd probably all want to commit suicide as we left the cinema. I guess we need an escape from reality.

I gulp at my second glass of wine. I don't know why I'm so mad at Joe. It's only – I glance at my watch – quarter to eight and he doesn't have to report back to me. But it's common courtesy, isn't it, to let your girlfriend know that you're going to be late home? Especially when she's bought wine and planned takeaway food (although he doesn't know that bit). It's rude not to call. Maybe I'm just angry because Joe's spoiled my attempt at easing my own guilt at being such a crap girlfriend recently. But why isn't he answering his phone?

'Emma…Emma.'

I swallow but my mouth is so dry.

'Emma.'

Oh no, I immediately panic. I fell asleep again.

I sit up quickly and realise that I'm still on the sofa but the romantic comedy from earlier is long gone from the television screen. Joe is hovering above me with his coat still on.

'What time is it?' I squint at my watch.

'Just after ten.'

'Where were you?'

'You fell asleep again.'

'Well, I was awake at six o'clock when you said you were going to be home,' I snap quickly.

Joe has the decency to look contrite.

I stand up, a little groggily, so we're face to face. 'Didn't you get my messages?'

'My phone battery died and I left the charger here.'

'Right. But you still haven't told me where you were.'

'I just went for a drink with some guys from work, that's all. It's no big deal, Emma.'

'Of course it's no big deal to go for drinks with your work friends, but you could have called me to let me know. I was worried.'

He shrugs. 'I just thought you'd be studying again or something.'

'Well, I wasn't. I was waiting for you to come home so we could spend some time together.'

'Come on, Emma, give me a break. You've had your head in a textbook for the last month, and when you finally give it a rest you fall asleep on the sofa. I've lost count of how many times I've woken up in bed alone, and now you're giving me grief for having a few beers with my work mates.'

A big part of me wants to yell at him that he's not being fair. I'm just trying to get ahead on this course so I don't fall behind. It's so long since I last studied anything that I'm scared I might just be a gigantic failure at it. But I'm struggling to keep the textbook info plus the day job plus a load of wedding stuff inside my head. It feels like there's too much swimming around in there and something is going to have to give. But I don't tell him all that. Instead I bite my lip and take a moment to compose myself.

'I don't want to fight.' I look up into his soft brown eyes.

'I should have called.'

I lean up and kiss him gently on the lips. 'Let's just go to bed. It's getting late.'

It's only when I'm snuggled up against the warn comfort of Joe's naked body that I realise he never actually said sorry.

Chapter Ten

Today is wedding dress shopping day. Sophie has reached apoplectic heights. I'm going to have to try really hard to calm her down a notch or two!

'Let's go grab a coffee first,' I suggest as I drive us into town. 'It's still early.' I count nine thirty in the morning as far too early to be on a wedding dress quest, but this was as late as Sophie would allow me to pick her up.

'Okay,' she agrees reluctantly, 'but just a quick one.'

'A quick one.' I smile, already looking forward to my latte. This used to be mine and Sophie's regular date, coffee and pastries that we shouldn't be eating, but it's been weeks since we've done this.

'So do you have an idea in your head of what you want your dress to look like?' Sophie asks once we're seated in the coffee shop armed with lattes and croissants.

'Something...elegant.' I ponder. 'Nothing frilly or lacy or with a skirt so big that you have to pick it up and carry it around with you for the whole day.'

'You do realise that this is a wedding dress you're choosing, don't you?' Sophie looks at me sceptically. 'They are, by the very nature of a wedding dress, supposed to be big and extravagant and maybe have some lace or...ooh, I don't know, diamantes.'

Sophie's eyes light up and I stuff some croissant into my mouth to prevent the disparaging comment in my head from escaping. I take a swig of coffee and try to think something encouraging to say.

'I guess I'll just know the right dress when I see it. That's what everyone says, isn't it?'

'Yeah, absolutely,' Sophie agrees somewhat half-heartedly.

About an hour later I find myself standing in front of a large full-length mirror in which a huge, white, frilly meringue stares back at me. The minute we arrived in the bridal shop Sophie gets all over emotional, gushing at everything from a diamante tiara to a little tiny purse which, apparently, is essential for carrying a lip gloss on the day for 'touch-ups'. I, on the other hand, have felt a weird sense of detachment since being faced with everything white and lacey, like this whole episode is happening to someone else.

'Oh! You look gorgeous.' Sophie sniffs, wiping a tear from her eye.

'Sophie,' I chastise slightly, 'we talked about this. No crying, and tell that shop assistant no bloody meringues.' I realise that, ironically, I'm starting to sound like one of those overly demanding women that I'm usually serving and complaining about to Jenny in the store room.

'I know, but...' Sophie acknowledges my stern stare and just nods. 'I'll ask whether we can look at some alternatives.'

'Thank you...Wait – what are you doing?' A flash and click simultaneously occur.

'Your mum rang me and asked me to take photos of you in each dress for her to see.' She shrugs innocently. 'It's hard for her being so far away while you're planning all of this.'

Here comes the guilt trip again.

'It's not my fault that she lives in New York,' I protest. 'It's not like she can just fly over every time I try a wedding dress on.' And I'm convinced, without any wavering, that my mother would pick the most hideously frilly and extravagant dress of them all for me to wear.

'She knows that,' Sophie reasons softly. 'She just wants to feel...involved.'

'I get that.' I take a deep breath and slowly release it. 'Now, how about I try that one over there.' I point to a simple off-white, floor-length dress with a very small train and only the simplest of pleats across the front of the bodice.

'What do you think?' Sophie asks a few moments later when I emerge from behind the changing room curtain. She looks me up and down repeatedly, trying without success to hide the frown on her face that tells me she really doesn't like the dress and is hoping I don't declare it as my wedding dress of choice.

The truth is, I don't know. I thought I'd feel different when I actually tried some wedding dresses on, that I'd suddenly feel magical and 'princess like' and I'd know instantly once I'd found the perfect dress, gushing deliriously, 'This is the one!' I had a vision of myself swishing down the aisle towards a waiting Joe, looking extremely handsome in his morning suit, but so far I've felt nothing even close to that. In fact, every dress I've tried on (and there have been many today) has felt heavier than the last one, until I feel like I'm being crushed under the vast weight of them. Surely that's not right, metaphorically or in reality.

'So...' Sophie prompts.

'Maybe the last one.' I smile to appease her.

Not twenty seconds pass between me arriving home and my mobile phone ringing shrilly in my handbag. It's no surprise at all to see Mum's number flashing on the screen.

I answer the phone while heading straight to the kitchen to pour myself a large glass of wine. 'Hi, Mum.'

'Oh, darling, you look lovely in all of the dresses. It's brought a tear to my eye.'

Oh God.

'I take it Sophie's just sent the pictures to you.'

'Have you decided on one?'

'Um, not yet.'

'Why ever not, Emma? The wedding day is drawing near, you know.'

I do know that, thanks, I want to scream. Instead I take a gulp of wine and answer calmly.

'There were a few I liked,' I lie. 'But I want to be sure that I make the right decision. I don't want to rush it.'

'Rush it? But Emma –'

'I've made another appointment to try on the three I liked most next Saturday, so I can decide then.' Another lie.

'Oh, that's wonderful, Emma.'

Good. That seems to have satisfied her.

'Which three did you like?'

Oh, dear God...

'You've ruined my life; now it's my turn to ruin yours.'

Chapter Eleven

'Emma, can I ask you something?'

Sophie sits across the table from me in Henry's bar which used to be our regular haunt. It's Thursday night and we decided to celebrate the fact that it's nearly the weekend with a glass of wine – just the one. My wine consumption seems to be getting more frequent these days so much so that I'm counting the grapes as one of my five a day of fruit and veg.

'Of course, Sophie, you can ask me anything.' But the instant the words are out of my mouth I regret them, as I know exactly what question is coming.

'You don't seem very…um…excited about the wedding stuff.'

She coughs awkwardly and I take a large gulp from my glass of wine to buy myself some time before I say out loud the thoughts that have been ricocheting around my head for a while now. I've been desperately trying to bury them in a deep, dark corner, because if I acknowledge them, then that might mean that they're real and it will be like letting off grenades.

'I love Joe,' I state, even though I know that's not an answer to the question I was asked.

'I know that.' Sophie looks at me with a worried expression on her face.

I take a deep breath and exhale. 'I just feel like I'm suffocating a bit.'

'Suffocating? I don't understand. I thought you wanted to get married.'

'I do, or at least I think I do. No, I do want to get married. It's just that I have so much going on at the moment, trying to fit in reading textbooks, making sense of essay questions, balancing work now that the devil's sidekick is ruling the roost and spending what feels like every spare minute being asked and deferring questions about my wedding. It's too much.'

I reach for the bottle of wine and refill our glasses (okay, maybe two glasses tonight not one) in an attempt to mask the uncomfortable silence that hovers as Sophie tries to digest what I've said. Hopefully she doesn't think I'm the world's biggest bitch. She reaches for her replenished glass and takes a sip.

'Have you spoken to Joe about any of this?'

'And how would that conversation go, Sophie? "Hi, Joe, you know you asked me to marry you and I was really excited? Well, now it's causing me to become stressed out because there are too many pressures in my life. So although you've given me everything I wanted, I'm now not so sure I want to go ahead with the wedding."'

'You don't want to go ahead with it?!'

I really need to engage my brain before speaking.

'I didn't say that…'

'You don't want to marry Joe?'

Sophie looks at me, all wide-eyed, and I feel sick. My stomach is doing somersaults and the thudding in my chest that I've been managing to just about keep under control is now thundering in my ribcage, and it feels like someone has reached into my chest and is squeezing my heart with an ice-cold hand.

'I want to be married to Joe, I really do, more than anything. But I don't understand why it has to turn into a circus. Why can't we just get married, just the two of us on a beach somewhere hot and exotic, and that just be it? We get married, we live happily ever after, that's it. Without the need for me to be dressed in a meringue that weighs half of my body weight; without having to decide between roses and lilies; without devising a seating plan that won't offend anyone; without choosing random place-cards that no one will care about but apparently are an important part of my wedding day; and without having to pay three hundred pounds for a cake!'

I hear the hysteria in my voice. It feels like the top has just blown off my emotional volcano and scary lava is going to pour out and start disappointing people, smothering them with my over-honesty. This might be the tipping point of the last few months where I start to crack.

'Because you should want to share your special day with family and friends who love you, and who want to take part in your wedding, and who want to celebrate your big day with you. I mean, you do really want to do that, right? You wouldn't just sneak off and get married without telling anyone?'

I think about this for a moment and relish how appealing that scenario is to me.

'No, of course not. For one, my mother would kill me.'

'So would I.'

Chapter Twelve

There are many times in our lives when we wish we could go back in time and change things: not say something, or not do something. Today was definitely one of those days. Halfway through the following conversation with Joe I realise what a catastrophic mistake I've made.

'So, just you and him went for a drink?'

'Um, well, Carly was supposed to be coming too, but then she had to…' I see Joe's mouth twitch and then set in a straight line. 'There's nothing going on with Tom,' I snap feeling a little indignant. I haven't done anything wrong, for Christ's sake. I went for a quick drink with a fellow student.

Tom had asked us both out for a drink after class on the way in. I'd initially agreed, but then Carly, looking completely crestfallen, said she couldn't as she had to go straight home after class for her sister's birthday meal. Given that I'd already said I would go, I felt it would be incredibly rude, and a bit weird, if I then said I wouldn't. This was clearly mistake number one.

'Look, just because everyone is so hung up on the fact that people of the opposite sex can't just be friends that doesn't mean that they can't, okay?'

'I never said that.' Joe's tone is clipped. 'But who says that they can't?'

'Well, it was Jenny and Lola. They were…um…'

This was my second mistake.

'They were what?'

'They were saying that there's no such thing as a platonic friendship,' I mumble, looking down at the floor.

'I see, and why were they saying this? Were you talking about him? Were you talking about Tom?'

'Not in that respect, honestly. I was just telling them about people at college, that's all. Don't you trust me, Joe?'

'Of course I trust you. If you say there's nothing going on then there's nothing going on.' He shrugs, which just infuriates me.

'Are you sure? Because you don't sound that convinced.' My tone is harsher than I perhaps intended.

'Look.' Joe steps towards me and takes hold of my hand and I resist the urge to pull away. His expression is unreadable but the usual softness in his eyes is no longer there. It feels like I'm being accused of something here and I'm starting to get angry. 'It just feels like I hardly see you any more. I miss you, Emma.'

'So this has nothing to do with Tom?'

'No. Why would it have something to do with Tom? You're being ridiculous.'

'Am I? Because you say it's got nothing to do with him, but you flip out whenever I mention his name, and although you're saying the right things Joe, you're eyes are giving you away.'

He blinks and glances to the side before looking back at me 'Well, it seems like since he's come on the scene you're pushing back on everything to do with the wedding. It's almost like you don't want to get married at all!'

'I can't do this.'

'Can't do what?'

'It's just too much. Everything. I'm trying to keep everything going, but something's got to give.' I can hear hysteria creeping into my voice but I can't do anything to keep it from exploding. The blue touch paper has been lit and now I have no choice but to stand back and watch the fireworks. 'I'm trying to balance writing essays while refraining from punching that stupid Julia women in the face at work, and then I come home and try to be the best girlfriend I can be, but it's too much pressure. I can't do it all. I put up with all Julia's attitude at work and then come home to this.'

'I feel like I don't even know you any more, Emma.' Joe shakes his head and he lets go of my hand and stuffs his hands into his pockets.

'I'm sorry.' I feel sick, instantly sick. My whole world seems to be falling apart right in front of my eyes and I can't seem to do anything to stop it. It's as though everything I say just makes it worse.

'I want things to go back to the way they were.' Joe sounds defeated.

'Me too.'

A tear slips silently down my cheek and as Joe reaches forward and wipes it away softly with his thumb the floodgates open and I sob. As Joe pulls me into a hug I feel overwhelmed emotionally by everything. The walls have come crashing down and I'm exhausted from trying to keep everything together.

As I lay in bed late that evening, snuggled into the crook of Joe's arm, it feels like the divide between us has closed slightly and this whole thing might just blow over. Perhaps we needed to reach explosive heights to release the pressure that has been building for both of us. We've cleared the air and can now move on. I might even go and try on some more wedding dresses this week.

But things get much worse, and a week later we find ourselves back in the same argument:

'What are you saying, Emma?'

I can see hurt and confusion etched across Joe's face.

'I...I don't know. It all just feels too much.'

'All?'

'Working at the shop, trying to do this degree, trying to plan a wedding. People just keep pushing and pushing and I feel like I'm suffocating.' I throw my hands up in the air. 'I just....I need a break.'

'A break from what, Emma?' Joe's voice is quiet but accusing. 'A break from me?'

No, no, not from you! I want to scream. I want things back to the way they were, that's all. But then I hear words come out of my mouth, words I never, ever thought I'd say:

'Maybe we should just...postpone the wedding.'

Silence hangs heavily in the room and for a second I wonder whether I actually said that out loud, but then I look Joe and I know full well that he heard every word. He looks crushed. I can hear my heart hammering in my chest and I open my mouth to say something, anything, but no sound will come out.

'I need some air,' Joe grunts. He grabs his car keys from the table and strides past me and out of the kitchen, towards the front door.

'Joe!' I call after him. He turns back at the door for a second before he opens it and then it's too late: the door slams heavily behind him, shattering the atmosphere.

Breathe Emma....breathe...

I open my mouth and gulp at the air. That is so not how I wanted that conversation to go. I hold my head in my hands, trying to dispel the urge to sob, but it's no use. Tears slip, one by one, down my cheeks and I sniff loudly.

It's okay. We just had a fight, that's all. He'll come back. We can sort this out.

I walk back into the kitchen and reach for a wine glass from the cupboard. I'm grateful to find an unopened bottle of white wine chilled and waiting. I pour a generous measure and down it practically in one before refilling the glass with a still-trembling hand.

What feels like an eternity passes, filled with a constant replay of our fight swirling round and round my head, before I finally hear the front door open and the soft thud of Joe's footsteps in the hallway.

'Hey,' I croak as Joe appears in the doorway. I want to run over and wrap my arms around him but I can't move a muscle. He looks different somehow.

'Hey.' He puts his keys down on the kitchen worktop and I swear I see him exhale deeply before he turns to face me.

'I'm so glad you're home,' I stutter, placing the empty wine glass I've been twirling around in my hand down on the kitchen table. I gingerly step forward. 'I've just been sitting here, going over and over in my head what I said –'

'And did you mean it?' Joe's voice sounds flat. 'Did you mean it that you want to postpone the wedding? That you don't want to marry me?'

'Joe, I didn't say that I don't want to marry you!' I creep towards Joe, but he stays standing still, stoic.

'Just not right now?' The tone of his voice is accusing and cold. I've never heard him like this.

'It just feels...a lot right now. A lot of pressure.' I can feel the tears from earlier swarming and I blink them back.

'If it feels like too much pressure to be marrying me then maybe we shouldn't be doing this?'

'This?' I swallow nervously.

'This.' Joe shrugs awkwardly, his body language jarred.

'What does that even mean, Joe?' Although the somersaulting of the wine around my stomach tells me that I already know where this is heading.

'If you don't want to marry me, Emma, then what are we doing here?'

It feels like a knife has been thrust between my ribs and twisted in every direction until it hurts too much to even speak.

'I thought we wanted the same things...'

We do. I do.

'Maybe we only thought we did.' He wipes at a stray tear before it can escape.

I swallow down the urge to throw up. 'So what...is this it? Are you saying it's over?' I can hear the shock and sadness in my voice. It's all right. We just had a fight. He'll come back...

'I'm sorry, Emma. I don't want to be with someone who isn't where I am right now.' He does nothing to hide the tears now and they flow freely, mirroring my own.

'This can't be it,' I whisper. 'It can't be over.'

But with those words out loud, in the open, I know that it is. It's over. My happily ever after is over. And the only sound that fills my ears is the shattering of glass as it hits the floor and smashes into a thousand pieces mirroring the breaking of my heart.

Chapter Thirteen

Please be in, please be in, please be in, I beg silently as I knock repeatedly on Sophie's front door.

'I'm coming, I'm coming,' I hear her call as a light illuminates the glass panel above the door.

'Hey, Emma, where's the fire?' Sophie smiles as she opens the door, but her face soon drops as she takes in my overnight bag. 'What's going on?'

I shake my head, pressing my lips together before tipping my head upwards, trying to force the tears I know are imminent back into their hiding place.

'Emma...?'

'It's over.' I gulp. 'Joe and I are done.'

Sophie steps forward just in time and envelops me in a bear hug. My knees give way and I collapse, sobbing, in her arms.

'I just don't understand how this has happened.' Sophie looks at me in bewilderment once she's managed to half carry, half push me inside the house and into the kitchen. She hands me a large vodka with a splash of tonic. 'Here, drink this.'

'I don't know either.' I sniff back the last of my tears, for the moment anyway. I take a sip of the vodka, then down it in one gulp. 'That's a lie,' I state, holding out the glass for a refill. Sophie hesitates for a second before pouring more vodka into the glass.

'What's a lie?'

'Me, I'm a lie. I've felt the pressure building over the last month or so and I didn't say a word to him. I just kept pretending everything was all right.'

'Oh, Emma. Why didn't you say something – to me, at least, even if you couldn't to Joe?'

'Because I'm stubborn. Because I have a built-in mechanism that won't let me admit that I'm not brilliant at everything. I have a burning desire to exceed at everything and to please everyone.'

Sophie nods gently in acknowledgement. I've always been the same and she knows that.

'I don't know what to do, Sophie.'

She sighs. 'For once, Emma, I don't have the answer either.'

'Why do I always do this? Why do I mess up every relationship I ever have?'

'Not every relationship, Emma. You've been friends with me and Simon nearly all of our lives and we've made it.'

'If you don't count the three months last year with Connor...' I hate myself for even saying those words, but they're true. I slept with Connor and nearly destroyed my friendship with Sophie – my fault or not, it still happened. I almost nearly ruined everything.

'That was neither of our faults. Connor was sick and twisted and he played us both – not just you.'

'What if I'm so emotionally inept that I can't make a relationship last? Is this all my fault? I do want to be married.'

I pause, exhaling slowly 'I want to marry Joe.'

Sophie looks down at the floor, for once seeming unsure of what to say to me.

'So why, having been proposed to and actually planning that wedding, am I now here, back in the depths of despair, having carpet-bombed everything?' I ask the unanswerable question.

'Look, I'm sure when you've both calmed down and slept on this you'll wake up tomorrow with a clear head and you'll be able to sort everything out.'

I don't share Sophie's optimism. Right now it feels like I'm buried up to my neck in quicksand and I'm sinking rapidly.

'You didn't see how hurt he looked, Soph. He's given up on us. He's sick of me. I'm sick of me. I don't know why I've flipped out recently. My head's just been all over the place and I've taken it out on Joe, when he's really the one I want to hold me and tell me that it's all okay.'

'So you need to tell him that.'

'He's angry and jealous, and I'm not sure I blame him. I've been spending so much time doing everything except being with him over the last few months, and I didn't really realise how much I was doing that. I guess I pushed his patience too far, and this whole friendship thing with Tom has been blown everything out of proportion.'

'So there's definitely no underlying feelings there for Tom?'

'No, he's just a friend who happens to be cute. That's it. It's Joe I love.' A big, fat tear runs down my cheek and plops onto the collar of my coat. 'What if I've lost him forever?' I swallow down the lump of regret threatening to choke the life out of me. 'What if I've just ruined the one good relationship I've ever had?'

Sophie's silence speaks volumes.

'Please tell me you have more vodka.'

I open one eye a crack and feel the sunshine warm on my face. I roll over and reach out for Joe, his warm, soft skin, and then the sledge-hammer hits, smashing my already broken heart into a million pieces, obliterating it completely. I'm not next to Joe. I'm not snuggled up in my own bed. It's over.

I sit up abruptly, forcing both eyes open fully now. I'm on Sophie's sofa with a quilt tucked around me, resembling a sausage roll. I remem-ber drinking vodka – that explains the dull headache – and wailing long into the night until I finally cried myself to sleep. I resist the strong urge to crawl under the quilt and die a slow and painful death, and opt instead for caffeine, dragging my body unsteadily off the sofa. I catch a glimpse of myself in the wall mirror on my way to the kitchen and I don't even recognise my reflection. Red, swollen eyes are protruding from my face like I'm a boxer at the end of a twelve-round fight that was very one sided, and my skin has taken on a grey tinge.

I fill the kettle and scowl at it. I want my posh coffee machine that makes fresh coffee from a tiny little pod. Mine and Joe's coffee machine.

'Hi.' Sophie's soft voice interrupts my wallowing. 'How are you feel-ing this morning?' she asks. I turn around. 'Jesus Christ, Emma!' She puts her hand to her mouth.

'I know, I look like someone ran over me then reversed back over my head just for good measure.'

'Oh, Emma. What are you going to do?'

'For now? Drink my coffee, have a shower, then I need to drag myself to work. Is it okay if I crash here today?'

'You're welcome to stay here as long as you need, you know that. But you might want to move your stuff into the spare room; the sofa can't be that comfortable.'

'Thanks for covering me up last night.'

'I didn't want to wake you once you'd finally gone to sleep. But what about you and Joe? Surely you can work this out?'

'I don't know, Sophie. Maybe the damage is done. I don't feel up to facing Joe today. I'm not sure I could cope with the reality of his rejec-tion all over again, and even if I could, I don't know where to begin. I so desperately want to talk to him, but I don't want to hear what he's going to say. I can't bear to hear him say it's over for good.'

Sophie reaches for my hand and gives it a squeeze. 'Don't leave it too long, that's all. Don't let the distance between you become too wide to close.'

I nod, unable to speak. I know in my heart that, as good as Sophie's advice is, I've allowed that gap between me and Joe that started off as a tiny crack to morph into a crater. The reason I'm not ready to try to talk to him is that I already know what he's going to say.

It hurts. It physically hurts. Far more than I ever imagined it could. I'm heartbroken, there's no other word to describe it; my heart has been torn in two and even breathing aches. And beneath the pain I'm angry that I allowed myself to fall so hard. I allowed myself to trust in Joe, to let my guard down and show him who I really am, to feel safe in his arms. And now there's nothing but an empty space, a big empty space that seems to be squeezing the life out of me. It's weighing down on my chest, crushing every feeling I've ever had for Joe and then bludgeoning them into a pulp until there's nothing left to feel. The pain is so acute that I can't even cry for my loss.

Was I stupid to think we could make it? That for once all my emotional baggage wouldn't ultimately poison our feelings for each other; that my own stupid behaviour wouldn't somehow destroy the one good relationship that I've ever had? More fool me. I should have known better. I'm bad news. I don't know how to have an adult relationship – a simple glance at my dating record proves that.

I don't know how Joe and I even got here. To go from being so in love to…this. We're broken, and no amount of superglue can stick the pieces of our relationship, or my broken heart, back together.

I fell too deep.

I let myself believe in true love.

I won't make that mistake again.

Chapter Fourteen

Once I've prised my heavy body off Sophie's settee, I drag myself wearily up the stairs and into the shower. The hot water does nothing to release the crick in my neck which has formed from sleeping in a foetal position squished into sofa cushions, but at least I've removed yesterday's smeared makeup. I grab some slightly crumpled clothes from my overnight bag (I was far too distressed at the breakdown of my relationship to apply moderate common sense and actually hang up my clothes), and I pull straighteners through tangles – in vain: my hair refuses to comply and remains slightly crimped on one side where I lay on it all night.

Never mind. That will have to do. I no longer care if I look like a hideous replica of my former self. That's how I feel.

'There's coffee and toast in the kitchen,' Sophie says softly as I clunk down the stairs, 'to fuel you up for work.'

Every bone in my body rebels at the thought of going into work today, but I know there's no chance in hell that the new Ice Queen will let me have a "personal day" to deal with my emotional disaster and pull myself together. No, I'll just have to paint a smile on my face and get through the next eight hours.

'Thanks, Soph.'

'What time will you be home tonight?'

Home? I don't have a home any more. I have a house where my fiancé lives.

'Um, around six, I think.'

'I'll cook something nice.'

'Thanks. And Sophie?'

'Yeah?'

'Thanks for letting me crash here.' Tears pool in the corners of my eyes.

She stops at the door with her coat on and turns back to face me. 'You're welcome here as long as you need. But…can I be honest?'

'You're my best friend. If you can't be honest with me after all these years then we have a problem.'

'Okay.' She exhales deeply. 'I think you should go and see Joe today. Don't leave it too long. You still love each other, I'm sure of that, and I don't want to see you throw it all away.' She coughs nervously.

'You're probably right,' I say to appease her.

'So you'll go and see him?'

'Maybe.' I nod, and she heads out the door.

I go into the kitchen and drink a mouthful of coffee, then grab the toast and head out to my car to begin the journey to work.

When I arrive at work Jenny immediately sees that something's wrong. I don't know what gave it away, the dark circles under my puffy eyes or the fact that my hair would give Medusa a run for her money.

'What's happened? Is everything alright?' She thrusts a mug of steaming coffee at me as I slide off my coat.

'It's over. Joe and I broke up.' I catch my voice before it cracks and gulp in air. It still shocks me to say the words out loud. It's like a slap around the face, reminding me this is real.

Jenny's mouth flaps like a goldfish for a second before she composes herself.

'How did this happen? I thought you guys were so happy?'

'I don't really know. One minute we were arguing about me not organising the wedding, and the next thing I knew Joe was saying that he didn't want to be with me if we didn't want the same things.'

'Oh...' Jenny looks at me apprehensively and takes a sip of her own coffee.

'I said I wanted to postpone the wedding,' I blurt out, nearly causing Jenny to spit coffee across the room.

'Why the hell did you say that? Do you want to postpone the wedding?'

'Yes. No. I don't know.' I wave my arms around, sloshing coffee from my mug onto the carpet. 'I wanted...I don't know what I wanted. All I know is that I've ruined everything, and this is definitely not how I envisaged things at all.'

'Oh, Emma. What are you going to do? Where's Joe now? How did you leave it with him?'

'I spent the night at Sophie's. We haven't spoken since...since...'

My shoulders start heaving and Jenny takes the mug from my hand and pulls me into a hug.

'It'll be alright, Emma. You'll figure this out. You and Joe are too good together not to make it.'

I sniff into her shoulder, unable to speak. It feels like my whole body is failing and losing control, as well as my mind.

The door to the shop is flung open, causing us to jump apart.

Julia's harsh voice booms into the small room: 'Oh good, Emma, you're here. I need you to redo the window display with the new stock that arrived on Friday.'

I nod and sniff in acknowledgment, then head towards the door to the shop.

'Hold it right there.' Julie holds up a manicured hand, halting me with sharply pointed bright-red nails. 'You can't go out there looking like that. How dare you come to work in this boutique looking like you've been dragged through a hedge backwards?'

Jenny opens her mouth to speak, but Julia pushes her hand in Jenny's direction. I grit my teeth, holding back the retort that's threatening to escape.

'Here…' Julia thrusts her handbag in my direction. 'Use whatever you need in there to make yourself look presentable, and make it quick.' And with that she disappears back onto the shop floor.

'Are you kidding me? We shouldn't have to put up with being spoken to like that. Surely there are rules about insulting your employees.'

Jenny cringes. 'She is the boss's niece. I don't think we have much choice.'

'There must be employment laws or something that mean you can't be treated like a piece of crap at work…urgh.' I discard Julia's handbag on the table and fold my arms defensively. 'I should tell her to shove her job up her –'

'Emma!' Jenny admonishes.

I huff. 'I know, I know.' I reach for Julia's handbag. 'I'll make myself presentable and get out there.'

'Are you going to be alright?'

'Honestly? No. I feel like my world has fallen apart overnight and I have no idea how to deal with that, let alone the devil with an attitude out there jabbing me with her pitchfork.'

'Emma?' Julia bellows my name from the other side of the door. 'I meant at some point today, you know.'

I suck in my cheeks and glare at Jenny. I'm in no mood for this today.

'I'll go and make a start.' Jenny hurries towards the door. 'Take a minute to compose yourself before you join me. The last thing I want is you getting sacked today and leaving me alone in this torture chamber.'

I nod, pressing my lips tightly together, not trusting the words that might come out of my mouth.

As the day of punishment comes to an end and Julia finally leaves me and Jenny to lock up, I contemplate whether to go straight to Sophie's house or go home and face Joe. Sophie's words from this morning ring loud and clear in my mind: 'Don't leave it too long.' Maybe I can salvage our relationship after all. Maybe it's not too late. I don't want to lose Joe forever; it's got to be worth a try. I need to make him understand my point of view.

I drive to our house with a thousand butterflies flapping wildly inside my stomach, but as I pull up outside the house I see it's in total darkness. Joe's not home. Hovering on the doorstep, I feel a weird sense of apprehension, like I'm trespassing or something, as I put my key in the lock and open the door. It's only been twenty-four hours since I left but it feels a lifetime ago.

I flick the lights on as I step inside and walk through to the kitchen. Somehow it seems rude to just help myself to a drink, which is crazy as this is still my home. I gaze, with a lump in my throat, at my beloved coffee machine and reach for a latte pod from the cupboard. A few seconds later my latte is ready and I stand staring into the quiet darkness as I take a sip.

The front door opens and closes, disturbing the silence around me, and my heart leaps into my mouth as I hear Joe's familiar footsteps approaching the kitchen.

'Hey.' Joe's voice is soft.

I turn around to face him. He looks pale and tired. I could find some peace in that fact, as it means he isn't dealing with this well either. But I actually find myself wanting to rush over and comfort him, to wrap my arms around his warm, familiar body and tell him that I love him, and if getting married in some big ceremony is what it takes to make him happy, to keep us together, then that's what I'll do.

But I don't rush over to him; I stay frozen to the spot. Because I know in my heart that as much as I love him, I can't do the whole big wedding thing. Not right now. I know that's what he needs to hear from me, but I'd be lying to myself as well as him if I said I wanted to get back on that roller-coaster. So I take another sip of coffee and simply say 'Hey' back to him.

'How are you?' Joe looks at me, frowning a little.

'Okay, I guess,' I lie. I'm not okay; in fact, I'm at the opposite end of the spectrum from okay. 'You look tired.'

'I didn't sleep much.' Joe clears his throat and I swallow nervously. It's hard to believe that we used to tell each other everything and now we're having to force a conversation.

'Are you back?' Joe shoves his hands into his trouser pockets. 'Are you staying?'

'That depends.'

'Have you changed your mind?'

'About what? Us, or getting married?'

'Aren't they the same thing?'

'No. No, they're not. I love you, Joe, I really do –'

'But not enough to marry me.'

'Why isn't it enough that I love you? Why do we have to get married right now? Can't we just be happy knowing that we both want to be together?'

'I thought you wanted to marry me.'

I stare down at the floor, willing myself not to cry as tears prick the corners of my eyes.

'I want to get married,' Joe continues. 'I want to marry the person I love, the person I want to spend the rest of my life with. I want that bond, that declaration of love, that commitment. It's who I am.'

Tears defy me, one by one, trickling silently down my cheeks and sloshing into my latte.

'But it's not what you want, is it, Emma?'

'I thought I did.'

'But now you don't, and that's not going to change, is it?'

I shake my head slowly.

'Then there's nothing left to say,' Joe states flatly.

I walk over to the sink and place the cup down with a shaking hand. It takes all my strength not to throw myself on the kitchen floor and sob. How can it have come to this? How is love simply not enough?

I walk toward the kitchen door and stop in front of Joe. He looks at me with sad blue eyes.

'I do love you, Joe.' I wipe tears from my cheeks. 'I wish that was all you needed.'

Joe looks like he's going to say something but he stops himself and his mouth forms a stern line.

'Goodbye, Joe,' I say quietly and I walk silently from the room and out of the house, not trusting myself to look back, not even once, as I close the door on my relationship with Joe for good.

With wobbly legs I hobble to the car. It takes three attempts for me to get the key in the ignition. My whole body's shaking violently and I feel sick.

I make it to Sophie's – I've no idea how – and thankfully she's there as I fall through her front door. She grabs me and half-carries me to the sofa.

'What happened?'

'I…I…saw…him,' I manage between sobs. 'But it's…it's no use.'

'It's really over?' I hear the sadness in her voice.

I nod, biting my lip.

'I'm so sorry, Emma.'

'So am I..I really am. I cccan't believe this is it, but I know in my heart that…that it is. He looked at me with such sadness, like…like I've bbbroken him, and maybe I have. But I'm broken too,' I sob.

The rest of the evening is a blur as I lie snuggled in Sophie's spare bed in a fitful sleep, drifting from blissful dreams of Joe to heart-wrenching nightmares from which I wake confused and then devastated. I vaguely recognise Sophie's voice intermittently, calming and soothing me, but it does little to dispel my torturous demons.

Chapter Fifteen

'Are you sure you don't want me to come with you?' Sophie asks as I pull on my coat the following evening.

'No, I'll be okay, anyway I have to go to college first. But thanks for offering.'

'Simon won't take this well, you know.'

'I know.'

'If you're sure.'

'I'll be fine, Sophie,' I say with more confidence than I feel.

It's been twenty four hours days since I left my house after going back to see Joe and I realised that our relationship was over. The distance between us, emotionally, seemed vast. We've drifted too far. Other than Jenny and Sophie, no one knows that Joe and I have separated, and I'm dreading having to tell family and friends who love me, sure, but also love Joe.

My mum is the person I'm trying to avoid the most. I can't bear the disappointment I'll hear in her voice when she's faced with yet another relationship failure of mine. She'll be gutted that the wedding she's already planned a thousand times in her head won't actually be happening. That's harsh, I know. My real fear is having to explain to her that I've royally messed up the one solid chance I've had to get it right. She saw from the start that Joe was one of the good ones.

So Simon is first on my list, followed by Dad and Margaret, whom I'm seeing tomorrow for Sunday lunch. I'll have to break the news over roast beef and Yorkshire puddings, but hopefully Margaret's jam roly-poly for dessert will cushion the blow.

'I'll see you later,' I call to Sophie and I grab my keys and handbag and head despondently out of the door.

As I arrive at college, for the first time since I started this course I find myself with little enthusiasm. My focus has completely gone, overcome by despairing thoughts of my failed relationship instead. I haven't even looked at a text book for days.

I breathe in deeply and exhale as I climb heavily out of the car and trudge towards the college building. I'm cutting it fine for the start of my lesson, not for the first time, but I make no attempt to hurry.

As I walk through the glass doors I pray that I don't bump into Tom.

I don't feel up to making cheerful conversation tonight, but thankfully the corridor is practically bare signalling how late I actually am. As I make it to my classroom the door is already closed and I sneak in just as Ms Davis is addressing the class. She glances at me as I slide into my usual seat beside Carly but thankfully doesn't reprimand me in front of everyone. Carly looks sideways at me, frowning slightly. I smile as brightly as I can force myself to and retrieve my text book from my bag and open it staring intently at the words.

Somehow the class passes quickly this evening, although I've no idea what was said throughout. As Ms Davis dismisses us for the night I shove my books back into my bag and head straight for the door waving goodbye to Carly. I can vaguely hear her calling after me but I just need to get out of here tonight.

As I walk into the coffee shop a short time later, I spot Simon slouched on a sofa in the corner, engrossed in a conversation on his mobile phone. He waves me over, raising his eyebrows skywards, and I giggle for the first time in days.

'I've got to go, Dan. Someone far more interesting has joined me so I'll call you later.'

'What do you want to drink?' I ask, trying hard to keep a blank expression on my face.

Simon stares at me hard. 'You look like hell.'

'Thanks, Si.'

'I'll get the coffees.' He jumps up and heads over to the counter.

I take off my coat and breathe in deeply and then exhale slowly, trying to calm the hammering of my heart.

'I thought you could do with this.' Simon slides a huge slice of chocolate cake across the table to me. 'It won't mend your broken heart but it might make you feel a little better for five minutes.'

I gulp. 'You know about Joe?'

'Sophie called me.'

I press my lips together tightly and nod. Typical Sophie, trying to make things easier for me by preparing Simon for my news.

'I'm so sorry, babe. I thought you two would go the distance.'

'Me too.' Ignoring the fork placed neatly on the side of my plate, I pull off a chunk of chocolate cake with my fingers and stuff it into my mouth.

'What happened, Em?'

'I made a huge mess of everything again, Si, like I do in every relationship.'

'That's not true. Chris was a total idiot who cheated on you with someone half his age.'

'I guess so.'

'What are we going to do with you, Emma?' He pulls me into a hug and kisses the top of my head. 'Want to hear something that'll cheer you up?'

'Yes, please.' Although I doubt that anything could lighten my mood right now.

'I got caught speeding in my car the other day.'

'That's not funny.'

'I was having phone sex with James at the time and wasn't exactly paying full attention to the speed limit.'

'What? Simon!' My voice is high and alarmed, causing people look up from their coffees and newspapers and glance over at us – with curiosity or annoyance, I'm not sure.

'Not full phone sex,' Simon whispers, glancing over his shoulder to make sure we're definitely out of earshot. 'He was just describing what he wanted to do to me when we were both naked, that's all.' Simon takes a slurp of his coffee.

'That's all? You say it like that's a normal, everyday event, Simon.'

'Well, it might be, for all you know. Anyway, I got flashed by a camera doing forty in a thirty-miles-per-hour zone.'

'You're unbelievable.' I shake my head in sheer wonderment at the situations Simon gets himself involved in; usually sex is involved somehow.

'At least it was a roadside camera that caught me, not a policeman. I don't know quite how I'd have explained my way out of that one.'

'Oh, Simon!'

I'm laughing now and Simon's laughing too. Then I'm drawn back to that shocking moment I walked in on him and James naked and I laugh even harder. What is it with Simon being caught in the act? For some reason, no matter how hard I try, that memory is never far from the front of my mind.

'Thank you.' I grab Simon's hand and give it a squeeze. 'It feels good to laugh again.'

'Glad to be of service.' He squeezes my hand back. 'You'll be alright, Emma, I promise.'

'I know, Si. I really liked Joe, though…loved Joe.'

'We all did, honey.'

The laughter has suddenly evaporated and I reach forward and grab another chunk of cake.

When I get back to Sophie's later that day, I find the house empty. The silence is welcome. I pad around the lounge, slowly breathing in and out, trying to regain some equilibrium. I'm half-glad and half-annoyed that Sophie had pre-warned Simon about the break-up. At least I didn't have to get the actual words out myself. I think that would have been a struggle. Which brings me to the phone call I've been dreading, and therefore putting off, to my mum.

I realise my padding has increased to pacing, and I'm marching up and down the living room wearing a track into the carpet. I need to get this over with, or I'm only going to feel worse. Maybe it'll be one of those moments where the fear of the act is worse than the reality... maybe not.

Okay, here goes. Taking my mobile phone from my jeans pocket, I dial Mum's number and bite my lip nervously as the phone rings shrilly in my ear.

'Hi, darling. How lovely to hear from you!'

'Hi, Mum.' I try to sound normal.

'What's wrong, Emma?'

'Why would you immediately think that something's wrong?'

'Emma?'

I exhale a breath I didn't even realise I was holding in. 'Joe and I broke up,' I blurt out quickly and rather bluntly.

There's a pause and I brace myself for her disappointment.

'Are you alright?' Mum's voice is calm and concerned.

'Not really.' I bite my lip harder.

'Do you want to tell me what happened?'

'I don't really know exactly,' I mumble – excluding the minor detail that I said I wanted to postpone the wedding.

'Emma, in all honesty I've been expecting this call.'

What?

'You have? But why?'

'Because I felt your emotions building up the last few times we spoke. You didn't sound like your usual self.'

'What do you mean "building up"?'

'You've been trying to do too much, Emma. You've been putting yourself under too much pressure.'

When did my mum become so smart?

'Something was bound to give,' she says.

'I guess so,' I concede.

I remember the stress mounting inside me to the point of eruption:

my outburst as I blurted out to Joe that it was all "too much". I hang my head. Why couldn't I have seen this coming and handled it better? Maybe I could have defused the emotional bomb before it exploded.

'Emma?' Mum's voice penetrates my thoughts.

'Yes?'

'Do you want to come over here for a few days?'

'Thanks for the offer, Mum, but I can't get on a plane and hide in New York every time I cock things up.' As tempting as that is, I'd be constantly flying back and forth.

'Shall I come to you then?'

'No, Mum. I'm fine, honestly. And I don't want to interrupt your life just because I've made a mess of mine.'

'I don't mind.'

'I know that, and I appreciate it. But I need to get my head sorted right now, and find somewhere else to live.'

'Joe's staying at the house?'

'Yeah, it seemed easier for me to leave at the time, but right now I don't really know why.'

'Where are you staying?'

'With Sophie.'

'That's good. At least you're not on your own. Do you think that you and Joe can work through this?'

'No. I've tried, but when I said I wanted to postpone the wedding –'

'Oh, Emma.'

'I know, but when I said it, I meant it. It felt like the whole planning of the wedding day was turning into a pantomime.'

'And I guess I didn't help with that.' I hear Mum sigh heavily.

'It all got a bit too crazy,' I say, avoiding answering her point directly to save her feelings. In all honesty, Mum phoning me weekly to talk bridesmaid dress colours and cake flavours really didn't help with the overall calmness of the situation.

'None of that matters now, Mum,' I say flatly.

'What can I do, darling?'

'Nothing. I'm okay, or at least I'm going to be at some point.'

'I'm only on the end of the phone any time you need me.'

'I know that, Mum, thanks.'

'I'll call you in a couple of days then – to check how you are.'

'Okay, thanks. Bye, Mum.'

I hang up the phone, relieved that the conversation is over and surprised at Mum's response. I was expecting a whole heap of guilt at my utter failure, but actually I feel better having spoken to her. I have Dad and Margaret to contend with tomorrow, then I'll have declared the failure of yet another relationship to all those of importance in my life.

I head through to the kitchen and open Sophie's fridge, confident that I know my friend well and she won't let me down. She doesn't: I see three bottles of white wine lining the fridge door. Smiling, I reach in and grab a chilled bottle of Pinot Grigio and pour a generous measure into a wine glass.

Back in the living room, I open my laptop, suddenly feeling positive for the first time in days. After loading the search engine, I type in "houses to rent" and filter the results to a five-mile radius. A couple of pages of properties load up and I scroll through them. Three fit my budget and aren't so small that I'd be able to touch all four perimeter walls from the centre of the house without having to stretch my arms.

I um and ah, wondering whether this is the right move. It feels incredibly final to be finding a new place to live, like the final nail in the coffin for me and Joe. I take a sip of wine and reach for my mobile phone. The harsh truth is that it's over for us whether I continue to crash here as Sophie's sidekick or I find my own place to rent. And as much as I love Soph, I think we get on much better with a little space between us, rather than me waking up either squished into her sofa with yesterday's makeup smeared on my face or star-fished in her spare bed, neither of which is a long-term solution.

So I dial the first of the three estate agents and prepare to arrange viewings for what may become my new home. I confirm appointments to look at two properties on Monday evening after work, and the final one on Tuesday. As I hang up on the last call I feel strangely empowered, like I'm taking control of my life again (I realise it's been less than a week since Joe and I separated, but emotionally it feels like so much longer).

I hear the front door open and Sophie calling, 'Emma? Are you home?'

I decide then and there not to say anything to Sophie about viewing houses. She'll only panic unnecessarily that I don't like living with her, or that I'm going to jump in the bath with my hairdryer plugged in the moment I'm left alone to my own devices. Once I've viewed the properties and decided one way or another, then I can tell her if needed. I quickly click off the estate agent's website.

'Hey, through here,' I call and she appears in the doorway seconds later.

'How was Simon?' she asks, looking a little sheepish.

'It's alright, Sophie. I'm not mad that you told him about Joe.'

'Honestly?'

'Honestly. I doubt I'd have got the words out in any functioning order anyway, so you saved me from that humiliation at least.'

'Okay.' She visibly relaxes.

'I helped myself to some wine.' I pick up my now-empty wine glass.

'That's fine. I told you, while you're here what's mine is yours.'

'Thanks, Soph…for being here, you know, and letting me stay even when you haven't really got room.'

'You're welcome here as long as you want.' She smiles. 'And let's face it, I'm not entertaining any male company at the moment so you're not cramping my style.' She looks away and I could swear that the "oh so liberal" Sophie actually looks a little embarrassed. That's strange.

'I'll get a refill then and grab you a glass.'

'Perfect.'

I hand Sophie a rather full glass of white wine when I return to the lounge a few minutes later. 'I phoned my mum this afternoon and told her the wedding's off.'

'How did she take it?' I hear the cringe in Sophie's voice.

'Better than I thought.' I take a gulp of wine. 'And a lot better than I did.'

'Fancy Chinese food for tea?' Sophie asks in what I perceive to be an attempt to distract us both from that statement.

'I'd love some.' I clink my glass against hers.

'When the person you love leaves you. It hurts.'

Chapter Sixteen

I try to make the journey to Dad and Margaret's last as long as possible to delay the inevitable conversation about the cancelled wedding plans and my disastrous relationship status. When I drive past the spot where less than a year ago Joe shot out of nowhere on his bike, dressed from head to toe in yellow Lycra, and bounced across the bonnet of my car, my eyes fill with tears and I have to pull the car over. I remain stationary for a good five minutes trying to compose myself as I wipe at my eyes so my vision isn't impaired by big, fat tears.

Finally I pull onto the driveway at Dad and Margaret's house, having reapplied face powder and mascara to disguise my now slightly blotchy face, and I climb out of my car with a heavy heart and head slowly towards the house.

'Hey, Dad,' I call, pushing the back door open. As I step into the kitchen aromas of roast pork and stuffing fill my nostrils and make my stomach grumble loudly.

'Emmie.' Dad shuffles into the kitchen and I realise that the arthritis that was barely noticeable seems to have got worse overnight. He wraps his arms around me. 'It seems like ages since we last saw you.'

'Sorry, Dad. I know I haven't been over in a few weeks.' The reality is that it's more like a month since I last visited. I've been so busy with work and college that our regular dinners together have kind of slipped.

'That's okay, Emmie. I'm sure you're busy, what with college and planning a wedding.'

'Um, yes, well, about that.'

'About what?'

'The wedding.'

'Oh, what about the wedding?'

I brace myself for his look of disappointment as I announce that Joe and I aren't even together any more, let alone getting married, but before I can answer Margaret breezes into the kitchen in her usual bold manner.

'Hello, Emma. Nice to see you. It's been so long.'

'Sorry about –'

'Anyway, I've been meaning to call you because I saw a lovely outfit in the department store last week that I'd like to wear for your wedding.'

'I was just trying to explain to –'

'It's lilac, you see, and I wanted to check what colour your mother's wearing as the last thing we want to do is clash for the photographs.'

'But you see, there's not actually –'

'Even worse if we were to turn up wearing the same colour.' Margaret guffaws.

Oh my God, will this woman not shut up for one minute!

'Well, as it turns out, Margaret, you don't need to worry about any of that,' I snap.

Margaret and Dad looked shocked, but the momentum is taking me now and I don't care about treading softly any more, trying to spare people's feelings. I need to get this out of me before this ridiculous conversation about wedding outfits continues.

'Apart from the fact that I don't think my mother has ever worn anything remotely lilac in her life, so you could be one hundred per cent sure that you and she wouldn't turn up in the same colour, it really is irrelevant. There actually isn't going to be a wedding, not now, not ever.'

My voice has reached an unrecognisable pitch and I clamp a hand across my mouth to silence any further outburst.

'Emma?' Dad's voice is cautious. 'You're not making any sense.'

Margaret's staring at me with what looks like a mixture of hurt and surprise. She opens and closes her mouth repeatedly but no sound comes out.

'I'm sorry.' I take a deep breath and exhale. 'That's so not how I wanted to have this conversation. I was hoping to get through it a bit more articulately and with a little less shouting.'

I glance at Margaret; she still resembles a goldfish out of water gasping for air. I dismiss her, perhaps unfairly, and return my attention to my dad. 'It's over, Dad,' I tell him. 'I broke us. I ruined everything.'

Dad swallows noisily, then steps towards me and hugs me. 'Let's get you a cup of tea, Emmie, and you can tell us everything from the start.'

Dad makes the drinks as I hover nervously before he silently hands me a steaming mug and ushers into the lounge and into a seated position on the sofa. Dad sits calmly next to me and waits for me to speak.

I start to explain in the best way I can about the mountain of pressure I found myself under, and the fact that Joe's adamant that he wants to get married now and I'm not able to do that for a number of reasons.

The conversation continues way into dinner, but any appetite I had when I arrived at the house has long since evaporated.

Chapter Seventeen

I used to feel okay on Monday mornings. Work wasn't so bad with Jenny and Lola to pass the time with. Now work feels like I'm being slowly tortured until I submit and give Julia Bamford the satisfaction of telling her where to stick her job. But I can't do that. Not yet. I need to keep work ticking over until I finish my college course and get my life back on track. Leaving a home and job in quick succession may lead to a complete nervous breakdown; I can only sustain so much change before my brain goes into "drink wine and stick head in sand" mode.

I drag myself to a seated position from under the quilt on Sophie's sofa, ignoring the crunching of my shoulder blades as they protest at my makeshift bed, and I realise I fell asleep last night reading a textbook for about the hundredth time.

I know I'm doing the right thing by going to look at some properties this evening, even if I'm not looking forward to telling Sophie I'm moving out.

As I make my way through to the kitchen for my necessary caffeine fix, I can hear Sophie already in the shower. I busy myself preparing coffee mugs as the kettle boils and I pick idly at grapes in the fruit bowl on the counter, in awe that Sophie has a fruit bowl with real edible fruit in it. She's such a grown-up.

Sipping the hot coffee, I make my way to Sophie's bedroom. I place her cup on her dressing table, next to her huge makeup bag. It contains a multitude of expensive products, and I make a mental note to upgrade my shabby collection and treat myself to some new makeup – a new me deserves a new look. I guess I'm going to have to get used to being a new me as I slide back onto the road of singledom again…alone…again.

'Morning.' Sophie appears in the doorway in her dressing gown with a large fluffy towel wrapped turban-style around her head.

'I made you coffee.' I gesture towards the cup. 'I'd better get in the shower.'

'Thanks for the drink.' Sophie picks up the mug and takes a slurp. 'What do you fancy doing tonight?'

I pause as I'm leaving the room. I'm viewing properties tonight.

'I'm going for a quick drink with Jenny,' I lie, having decided that's the best course of action at the moment. No point in saying anything until I'm sure. 'I might be home a bit late.'

'No worries. Call me on your way home and I'll put some food in the oven for us.'

'That sounds great.'

By the time I get out of the shower Sophie's already left the house. I grab some of my clothes out of her wardrobe – she very kindly hung them up for me after I left them folded not so neatly in the bag I packed in haste when leaving home. They could do with an iron, but I really don't have the time. I'm sure the creases will drop out. I wish I could be one of those women who plans her outfits ahead and gets up with ample time to carefully apply makeup, instead of pulling on the first clean thing and swiping face powder and blusher across my face while simultaneously pulling hair straighteners through my defiant locks. It's difficult, however, to be an organised, immaculate person when you're faced with sleeping in a scrunched-up ball on a sofa and storing your toiletries in an overnight bag.

I leave the house already behind schedule and spend the journey to work shouting abuse at other drivers (honestly some of them don't appear to know where their accelerator pedal is) and trying to refrain from using my horn (I fail when a huge double-decker bus pulls directly into my path and it's only by miracle that it misses me by an inch instead of side-swiping me into oblivion).

I arrive at work with three minutes to spare before the revised deadline of eight thirty, when I must be present and accounted for. As I creep into the staff area and hang up my coat and handbag, I can already hear the shrill tones of Julia Bamford snapping instructions at Jenny.

'Emma, is that you?' Julia booms. Before I can answer she appears, hawk like, hovering in the doorway to the shop. Her hands are clamped firmly on her hips, displaying perfectly painted cerise nails.

Argh!

'Morning, Julia,' I say over-brightly. I've decided to kill her with kindness instead of reacting to her hideous behaviour, but it's far more challenging than I thought to remain civil, let alone keep a huge smile on my face and use a sing-song tone.

She glances at the clock on the wall above my head and I bite my tongue to silence my retort. I'm not late. I'm exactly on time.

'Help Jenny unload the stock that's arrived this morning and price it up. You need to change the window displays too, but make a coffee first. Mine's black, remember? Don't give it me with milk again like last week.'

Grrr!

I want to yell in her face: 'I think the words you're missing are "could you", "please" and possibly "thank you".' But instead I press my lips together.

Julia glares at me in a way that says, 'You're nothing,' and then twirls around and the door to the shop closes behind her.

I hate her. I hate her. I hate her.

It's childish, I know, but ranting silently in my head does appear to help, at least until I can create a voodoo doll that resembles her so I can stick pins in it all day long.

Giggling at this vision, I get on with making the coffees. I allow my thoughts to drift to this evening and I feel a mixture of fear and excitement. Regaining my independence in my own home is a step in the right direction from a "moving on from the hideous collapse of my relationship" position. But I'm alarmed to find myself imagining the tortured life of a spinster. I'm back on the shelf at thirty-three, and my previous relationship errors fill me with little hope of ever finding long-lasting love.

I realise that these are irrational thoughts. I am, after all, only in my thirties and until a few weeks ago I was in a relationship with a good man who loved me back. It's just that finding myself alone again and camping out in Sophie's living room has allowed depressing scenarios to creep into my mind and extinguished positive flickers of hope.

'Emma!'

Julia screeching my name nearly causes me to throw burning-hot coffee all over myself, and I slam the mugs down on the draining board, causing brown liquid to slosh everywhere.

Crap!

I grab a cloth and mop up the spillage. Then, after taking a deep breath and exhaling slowly, I pick up the three coffee cups and head through to the shop floor.

Jenny is surrounded by heaps of clothing still wrapped in plastic covers, an expression of bewilderment on her face as Julia hands her items while rambling instructions. Jenny raises her eyebrows skywards and I supress a smile.

Julia takes the cup of black coffee from my hand. 'I've got some paperwork to do in the back office. I presume I can leave you both to unpack this stock?'

'Of course,' I mutter, and take a slurp of my coffee. Honestly, she doesn't always have to treat us like idiots.

Once the door to the back office is closed and Jenny and I are definitely alone, I turn and stick my tongue out at the door that's now thankfully shielding us from Julia.

'I don't know about you,' I whisper, 'but I feel constantly on edge with her hovering about and watching over our every move. I wish she'd…I don't know…leave in the puff of smoke in which she appeared!'

'I know.' Jenny unloads numerous plastic-wrapped garments from her arms onto the floor. 'But I get the distinct feeling that she's not going anywhere. Some days it's hard not to –'

'…stab her with the scissors.'

Jenny laughs and I wag a finger. 'Humour isn't allowed, Jenny. If you're laughing then you're not working.'

'Come on.' Jenny hands me a batch of new dresses. 'Let's get these hung up and then you can change the manikins.'

'Why is that my job?'

'Because it was Lola's job and she left, and as we speak she's probably lying on a beach in Australia having forgotten all about us in her enjoyment of sun, sea and cocktails.'

Hmm…what I would do to be lying on a beach right now with a cocktail in my hand.

'You're going to have to do it, Jenny. Those manikins are evil. They know I hate them, so they resist every manoeuvre I try to make to get them into clothing.'

'You're being ridiculous. They're made of plastic. They have no ability to understand your hate towards them.'

'You don't know that.'

'Emma.'

'Okay. Okay! I'll dress the stupid manikins.' I roll my eyes elaborately at Jenny.

'See, was that so hard?'

'Ask me in an hour, which is probably how long it's going to take me.'

'Never mind all that. How are things with you?'

'I'm going to look at some properties to rent tonight.'

'Really? That's good.'

'Is it?'

'What does Sophie think?'

'I haven't told her.'

'Oh. Why not?'

'I don't know if I'm going to like any of them, so I thought it was better to say nothing until I know for sure.'

'That makes sense, I suppose. Do you want some company?'

'Thanks, that's kind of you to offer. But I feel like I need to do this on my own.'

'Maybe a glass of wine after work tomorrow instead? You can tell me about the properties then.'

'Sounds good.'

I pull up to the first of the three properties that I'm viewing and already I can't see myself living here. It looks…I don't know, it just looks wrong.

Come on, Emma. Keep an open mind. Everywhere will look wrong given that you don't want to be living anywhere right now other than back in the house you shared with Joe, back in your own bed.

Okay. Here goes. Open minded…

I climb out of the car and plant a smile on my face as I walk towards the two bedroom semi-detached house. It looks like it's lacking any personality, just plain and boring, although I don't know what exactly I was expecting. Maybe that's the problem; I'm expecting too much.

'Hi, I'm Nancy.' A petite blond woman – the estate agent, I assume – strides towards me with a hand outstretched.

'Hi, Nancy. Very nice to meet you.' For some reason, maybe to offset my initial dislike of the property, I feel the need to be over-polite.

We shake hands and then she unlocks the door and I edge cautiously inside.

Nancy goes into her spiel. 'The house is occupied at the moment, a lovely young couple who got married only two months ago. They're starting a family.'

'How lovely.' I maintain my fake smile.

'Yes, it is, isn't it? They need somewhere bigger now there's a little one on the way. Other than that, they've been happy here for years.' Nancy smiles broadly.

'Um, right.' Maybe some of their happiness will rub off on me if I do move in here. But no, I think as I look around the cramped hallway, I really can't see myself here.

'Let's go through to the kitchen.'

Nancy ushers me forwards and I play along with her clearly practised routine. It's is my first mistake of the evening, as she then proceeds to take me around the whole house and won't let me out of her sight, so I have to keep up my pretence of enthusiasm, which is a waste of everybody's time.

Oh my God! I finally make it back to my car, having insisted to Nancy that I'll let her know in the next day or so. That's an hour of my time that I won't ever get back. I didn't think she was ever going to let me out of there. The "kitchen" was barely big enough to house my coffee machine, let alone function as somewhere to prepare food. I think her tale of the happy couple may have incorporated some poetic licence.

I'm now late for my second property viewing, and I hurtle the three miles to the flat next to the park which leads to the river. As I drag myself out of the car the second it comes to a halt, I see a very tall man tapping his long fingers on a black leather folder and looking at his watch.

'I'm sorry I'm late. You must be Mr Woods.' I rush over to him, pulling on my coat and flinging my bag over my shoulder, nearly garrotting myself in the process.

'Miss Story?'

'Yes, sorry again. My last viewing, um, overran.'

'Not a problem. Follow me.'

He marches through the external building door and takes the stairs two at a time. I struggle to keep up with his incredibly long legs. By the time we reach Flat 24 on the second floor, I can barely breathe, let alone speak.

'It's a nicely spaced flat, Miss Story, with two bedrooms, one with an en-suite, and a main bathroom, along with a kitchen and lounge area,' he states as we walk into the small entrance area and through to the living room.

This feels completely different. Straight away it feels like home. The décor is neutral and clean, with lovely mirrors and abstract canvases on the walls. It looks like a show home, and I struggle to believe that anyone lives here. But then I remember that not everyone lives in a whirlwind state of madness like I do, and the current resident probably has time to clean the apartment and browse homeware shops at the weekend for gorgeous items.

'I'll let you look around at your own leisure, Miss Story.'

Much better, thank you.

Mr Woods stands guarding the front door as I wander through to the kitchen, which is, pleasingly, big enough to prepare food in – or at least open takeaway cartons and wine.

As I take in the master bedroom and en-suite bathroom, I'm already visualising where my belongings will go and I need no convincing that this is my new home.

I catch Mr Woods staring out of the lounge window at the view of the park below. 'Okay, I'll take it. Where do I sign?'

'You want to take it?' He sounds surprised, which perhaps should make me cautious, but I choose to ignore that vibe and persist.

'Yes, please. I'd like to sign the agreement now if I can.'

'Of course.' He flaps some papers around before presenting me with a contract. 'It's month's rent as a deposit, so I'd need two months upfront to secure the agreement.'

'Right.'

I can hear Sophie's disapproving voice in my head, chastising me for not trying to negotiate. She refuses to accept things at face value, always believing that there's a bargain to be had, whereas I prefer the path of least resistance. I sign the document and promise to make the payment required over the telephone tomorrow morning.

With that done, Mr Woods swiftly shakes my hand, locks the flat behind us, escorts me back out of the building and then disappears in his car.

I stand there on the street outside of the block of flats and watch the steady flow of traffic, finding the hum of engines weirdly calming. Then I realise that not only have I signed a six-month contract to rent a flat I've only just seen, but I've completely dismissed the third property I've arranged to view tomorrow.

Maybe it's fate. Sometimes you simply have to go with your gut feeling. Or perhaps I'm actually crazy after all...

Never mind.

It will all be perfectly fine.

I'm ready for this.

Hmm...

'I've been to see a flat to rent, next to the park beside the river,' I tell Sophie the following evening, 'and I think I'm going to take it.'

I glance sideways at her as I put the kettle on to boil, and then take out fresh strawberry and cream cupcakes from the box that I picked up earlier in the day. (They very nearly didn't make it home as I almost sat on them in the bar across the road from the shop earlier tonight, when Jenny and I went for a drink.)

'Are you sure you're ready?' Sophie's voice is tinged with hesitation.

'I need to get some normality back in my home life,' I explain. 'I can't spend the rest of my life sleeping in your spare room.'

'I know that.' Sophie sighs. 'But I've enjoyed you being here.'

'Me too.' I smile.

'Despite the circumstances in which you arrived,' she adds hastily, swiping buttercream from a cupcake with her finger.

'Of course,' I say as I continue to make cups of tea. I've enjoyed spending more time with Sophie, and without her to lean on I think I'd have curled up in a ball under a quilt and have given up on life temporarily.

'Can I at least look at the flat with you before you agree to sign the lease?'

I feel a swell of emotion (it keeps happening at the moment) and I tip my head back slightly to roll back the impending tears. Sophie's always worrying unnecessarily about me. We'll okay, maybe not always unnecessarily, but she does sometimes forget that I'm an actual grown-up.

'Sure,' I say, though I know full well I've already signed the lease. 'We can look at it tomorrow night if you're free. I'll ring the estate agent in the morning.'

'That would be good.'

'Right then. Now that's sorted, eat your cupcake.'

I hand Sophie a mug of tea and the large, pink, sugar-infused creation that bears her fingerprint.

'It's a bit small, isn't it?' Sophie glances around the flat the following evening as she takes a few steps down the hallway.

'Small? It's not small. There are two bedrooms, a lounge, a kitchen, a bathroom, and an en-suite.'

'Oh.'

I get the feeling that she doesn't really think it's small; she's just feeling conflicted about me leaving – as am I.

'Sophie, there's only going to be me living here and I don't take up that much room, honestly.'

'Mmm, what about the four bin liners' worth of stuff squeezed into my bedroom?'

'Point taken.' I hesitate briefly. 'But look…' I stride into the bedroom. 'There's plenty of storage in these built-in cupboards.'

'Are you sure you're ready for this? It's only been a couple of weeks since you and Joe…' She shrugs, not needing to end that sentence.

'I'm sure,' I say confidently. 'I'm absolutely ready for this.'

Chapter Eighteen

I'm so not ready for this, I realise the minute I close the door behind Sophie and Simon after they've spent the day helping me move in. I felt quite optimistic when I collected the keys from the estate agent. It may only be a six-month lease, but it felt like a new start, helping me to move on, to push Joe and the future I thought we would have together into my past. But now, as I stare around the blank cream walls of the flat, I feel nothing but panic and despair.

I trudge over to the large window in the lounge and stare out at the park below. I thought the view would be relaxing – looking at the greenery, watching children kicking footballs around, people sunbathing and sitting under the large, sweeping trees, dog walkers following the same route day after day. But as I look down at the vast green open space, it's empty, like my heart.

I glance around the room. Everything's neatly in its place, all of my things in a foreign environment which, despite my initial rush of love for the flat, I now doubt will ever feel like home. I take one more look out of the window and then head out of the door and to the nearest off licence for a bottle of wine.

I only intended to get a bottle of wine and have one glass, but as I pour another double vodka and tonic I realise that this was a much better idea. I note guiltily that the vodka is already a third gone, but then it occurs to me – why am I feeling guilty? Who actually cares if I drink myself to death in my new flat with nothing but vodka as my friend? Well, alright. There's Mum, and Dad and Margaret, and Sophie, and Simon and...okay, so I have family and friends who care, but it's not the same. It's not the same as being woken up every morning by a warm kiss and the feeling of Joe's toned body snuggled against mine. It's just not. I take a gulp of the vodka and tonic, feeling slightly wobbly in surroundings that have taken on a fuzzy edge.

He hasn't even so much as sent me a text. Nothing. No communication at all.

It's like our relationship never existed, for him anyway.

Is that how he really feels? Have I simply become someone he used to know? Did I mean nothing to him? After all the time we spent together. After everything we planned.

Right!

The vodka is fuelling my anger and indignation. I reach for my laptop. As I load up my email account, I push back the sensible part of my conscience that's frantically waving and yelling at me that this isn't a good idea. That I'll regret this once the effects of the vodka have worn off, and most probably it will come back to haunt me. My judgement is clouded and ruled by my emotions, which are frayed and in desperate need of validation.

Dear Joe, I type into a new email message, feeling full of bravado (or maybe alcohol).

But in an instant the bravado is gone, replaced by raw, overwhelming sadness. I don't want to be angry at Joe. I just want him to hurt, like I do. To feel like his heart's been ripped out and put through a blender like mine. So I type:

Dear Joe,

I miss you. I miss us; so much it physically hurts. I know the reasons why we aren't together. But I'm angry at you. I'm even angrier at myself for letting my feelings for you deepen to the point where I could only see my future with you. Where lying in your arms felt exactly where I was supposed to be. I allowed myself to fall in love with you, to crave your touch.

I really wish that we could have made things work. I wish relationships weren't so complicated.

I know at some point I will have to move on. I will have to find the lips of another man to kiss like we used to do. But there's one problem with that, and this is where I'm really struggling. You see, the fundamental issue here, Joe, is that you own my heart. There are no other words to describe it.

You own my heart.

And I'm really scared that you always will do.

I may meet others who'll charm me and I may pretend to be happy for a while, but you'll always be there at the back of my mind. You'll always be the one that I was meant to be with, the one I was supposed to find happiness and live happily ever after with.

You might be the one who owns my heart forever. In fact, I think you are.

I stare at the screen with blurry eyes. My heart is hammering in my chest. I hover the curser over the "Send" button but then press "Delete" and the screen goes blank. After wiping the tears from my cheeks, I down the remains of my glass of vodka and tonic in one and pour another large measure. Drowning my sorrows in alcohol is becoming a habit and I ignore my conscience as it gives me a sharp jab.

I pick up my mobile phone and my finger hovers over Joe's number. I know that I'm drunk and this is probably a bad idea but I doubt very much whether I would have the guts to call him when sober. But what am I even going to say? We haven't spoken since I collected my belongings and moved out of our home.

I press the button to instigate the call deciding not to overthink things. I'll know exactly what to say when I hear his –

'Hello.' a female voice purrs down the phone.

Holy shit.

I just stare at the mobile phone in my hand like it's a grenade waiting to explode.

He's seeing someone. Already…he's over me.

I hang up the call and descend into a very dark emotional place.

What's that noise? What is that noise?

I pull the quilt over my head to try to block out the annoying buzzing sound, but it persists. Then the realisation dawns that it's the intercom for the flat.

'Go away!' I shout into the quilt.

There's a moment of reprieve before whoever it is leans on the intercom buzzer and a horrendous noise booms around the flat, causing pain to shoot through my skull.

Who the…!

I practically do a forward roll to launch my sluggish body from the bed, and then ricochet between three walls as I make my way unsteadily towards the intercom. Whoever's downstairs is going to regret landing on my doorstep uninvited this morning. I'm in no mood for visitors.

I snatch at the intercom and growl 'What?' into the receiver.

'Hi, honey. It's the welcoming committee,' Simon's far too cheery voice sing-songs loudly into the flat.

I roll my eyes. Of course it's Simon. Sophie would know better than to call around unannounced on a Saturday morning.

'Simon, it's too early,' I protest.

'Don't be rude, Emmie. Let me in. I brought coffee and breakfast.'

Alright. That's different then. I'm pretty sure my body could use a caffeine hit right now.

I press the button to release the external building door and then, realising that I'm completely naked, I go in search of my dressing gown.

Simon holds out a brown paper bag and a takeaway coffee cup as I let him in moments later. 'You look like crap.'

'Gee, thanks, Simon. Have I said how nice it is that you thought to pop around at this unearthly hour on a Saturday morning?' I close the door quickly behind him usher him through to the lounge conscious that my new neighbours don't need to catch a glimpse of me half-dressed and looking slightly, okay very, worse for wear.

'Unearthly hour? It's eleven a.m.'

Oh.

'Well, that used to be early for you. I remember when you used to party for twelve hours straight and only go to bed at eleven a.m.'

'Those days are gone, Em.'

'How come?'

'I grew up.'

'No, seriously?'

'Cheeky.'

He swats my arm, nearly causing me to wobble over due to my lack of balance this morning, which I fear has been caused by a liquid imbalance in my body: i.e., I filled it with far too much vodka last night.

'I'm in love, Emma. I no longer spend my evenings drinking myself into a stupor and surviving on three hours' sleep. Unlike some.' He looks judgingly at me and takes a drink of coffee.

Yes. Well…

I open the brown paper bag and inspect the contents, as a distraction from Simon's obvious attempt to get me to explain my bedraggled appearance.

'What are you doing here, Simon? You only left this flat sixteen hours ago.'

'Yes, but I feared as I did so that your sunny disposition was actually fake, and that the moment Sophie and I left you protesting your happiness you'd descend into a drunken mess.'

I stare down, fumbling with the paper bag. Damn him, how does Simon read me like a book?

'So, am I going to have to drag it out of you?' Simon asks.

I pull a chocolate twist pastry from the bag, take a large bite and chew, buying myself a little time before answering. Finally I decide honesty is the best way forward.

'I drank too much vodka.' I shrug nonchalantly.

'No kidding.' Simon retrieves the paper bag from me and takes out the second pastry. 'Any particular reason for that?' He raises his eyebrows, but I suspect he already knows the answer to his question.

'I was sad.'

'About Joe?'

'About everything.' I take a swig of coffee deciding I'm not ready to divulge the fact that I mustered up the courage to call Joe last night (admittedly some drunken courage was involved) and that a girl answered his phone. Oh god, it hurts so much to even think about that. 'I thought I was ready to get my own place. I thought I was dealing with the fact that my relationship is over.'

'And?'

'And it turns out I'm not dealing with it very well at all, and living on my own gives me far too much time to think about things. And by think about things, I mean dwell miserably on my failures. Plus there's no one to police how much alcohol I pour into my body. Living alone means relying on self-control, and let's face it, that's never been my strong point.'

'Mine either.' Simon giggles and takes another bite of his pastry. 'You know what you need?'

'Three wishes and a magic lamp?'

'Hair of the dog.'

'Simon, I told you only a moment ago that I drank my body weight in vodka last night, and I'm currently swallowing this coffee and pastry with trepidation, and you want me to drink more alcohol? Are you crazy? Okay, stupid question.'

'It's only due to your fragile state that I'm going to let that comment pass; however, I'll file it away for future reference. Anyway, it's proven by scientists that a beer settles your stomach and perks you up a bit when you're hungover.'

'Scientists? Don't you mean alcoholics?'

'Just get in the shower and put some clothes on. We can eat food as well as have a beer or two. But then that's it.'

'What's "it"?'

'You need to get on the wagon – the sober one, that is.'

'Hmm. Where's James today? Why are you here disrupting my plan to wallow in self-pity under the comfort of my quilt for the entire weekend?'

'James is at work, but I'd have come around anyway. I know you too well, Emma, and I could have predicted that this is the exact state I'd find you in. My only fear was that I was going to have to kick the door down to get in, and you know brute force isn't my forte.'

I laugh then, really laugh, at the thought of Simon trying to barge down the door to my flat, all gangly, skinny arms and legs flailing around.

'Oh, that's funny, is it?' Simon looks hurt, but I'm laughing too hard to try to console him. 'Okay, so maybe it is,' he concedes. 'But you could have paid me the courtesy of pretending otherwise.'

'I'm sorry, Si,' I manage between gasps of air and giggles, 'and I appreciate your concern for me, I really do.'

'Well, you're going to have to come for that drink now with me, given that you've hurt my feelings.' He stands and puts his hands on his hips.

'I'll get in the shower,' I mumble and I trudge from the lounge.

'I hate to admit it, Simon, but I'm starting to feel a little better.' I stuff another chunky chip in my mouth and wash it down with a mouthful of beer. Either those "scientists" are right or I'm simply topping the alcohol in my system back up and getting drunker by the minute.

'Told you.' Simon looks all righteous.

'So, how are thing's going with you and James? I haven't seen him for ages.'

'It's all good, Em. For some reason, James thinks I'm amazing and he loves me for who I am. I'm lucky, I guess; I found my Mr Right.'

I gulp in air.

'Oh, I'm sorry, hun. Me and my big mouth. What am I saying?'

'It's alright, Simon.'

'No, it's not. You don't deserve to be on your own, Emma.'

'Maybe I do. I mean, let's take a look at my relationship history.'

'Oh no. Really? I'm not sure that's a good idea,' Simon says jokingly.

I continue regardless. 'I mean, take Chris, for example. I spent two years cultivating our relationship to the point where I thought he was going to propose to me, and it turned out he was actually cheating on me with some girl ten years younger than me.'

'He was a bit of a shit.'

'And then I had a one-night stand with Connor, who turned out to be Sophie's new boyfriend and also a complete psychopath.'

'That's unfortunately true.' Simon nods.

'And then I met Joe. Joe, who actually did propose to me and want to spend the rest of his life with me. And now I'm here, all alone again, living on vodka in solitude in my new flat.'

'So what's wrong with Joe then?'
'Me, Simon. I'm what's wrong with Joe. It's all me.'
'I think we need another beer.'
'Men rrr rubbish.'
'Women worse, def worse.'
'You no like wwwmen anyway.'
'Not true. Lllike you.'
'Ah. Luv you.'

Chapter Nineteen

Oh my God! There's a man in my bed! There's a man in my bed!

As I roll my head to one side, feeling the hangover slide across my forehead, I stare with blurry eyes at the male arms protruding from the quilt. The rest of him is buried under masses of cover, but there's no denying it – that arm belongs to the male species.

How did this happen? How the hell have I managed to have yet another unexpected encounter with a man I can't remember? The last time this happened, I woke up in bed with Connor and – no, don't even think about that. I shake my head to dismiss those horrible thoughts, but instantly regret it as a wave of nausea sweeps over me and I reach my hand up to rub gently at my throbbing temples.

I daren't even look across to the other side of the bed. It's too much to comprehend in my current state of hangover/still drunkenness. I don't even remember meeting a guy last night, so how did I end up in bed with one? I'm a terrible person, a terrible, terrible person, with a serious one-night stand problem.

Or maybe I'm a terrible person who has a problem with alcohol.

Hmm. I close my eyes, trying to recall last night's events, but I'm at a loss. It's a fuzzy blur. What the hell was I drinking last night? More to the point, where the hell was I drinking and with whom?

'Emma?'

Shit!

I sit bolt upright and swallow down the urge to throw up as what feels like a bag of wet cement moves from one side of my stomach to the other. I shoot a glance at my neighbouring pillow.

'Simon!'

Simon crawls out from under the covers, rubbing groggily at his head.

'Simon! Thank God for that!'

'What the hell did we drink last night, Em?'

'Never mind that! You're not a strange man in my bed!'

'What? And can you take it down a notch or two. I think my head might actually explode.'

Oh, what a relief. I don't have to try to remove some unwanted man from my apartment while I turn scarlet with embarrassment, not only at the fact that I ended up in bed with a stranger (again!) but also that

I didn't even remember meeting him. That would have been, well, a disastrous start to a Sunday morning.

I lie back down, allowing the cement to slide to the back of my body as I squash myself into the comfort of my pillow.

'I hope you have bacon,' Simon mumbles.

Bacon? Mmm, that sounds good. But alas, I'm not an organised weekly food shop kind of girl, so there's no bacon…or eggs…or bread for that matter.

Damn it. I'm going to have to drag myself to the corner shop to forage for food.

Simon leans up on his elbows and whines in my face, 'Em. I need bacon. Please bring bacon.'

Grrr!

'Alright.' I fling the covers off and slide precariously to an upright position. At this rate I'll be lucky to make it to the corner shop and back in one piece. 'I'll fetch bacon from the shop on the proviso that you cook it for us.'

'Deal.'

'Okay.' I stumble across the bedroom. 'Let me find some clothes.'

'Bring juice too.'

Honestly!

Dressed in jeans and a sweatshirt, I stare at the horror show reflection in the bathroom mirror. I have no idea what's happened to my hair, but it no longer resembles anything I've ever seen before. Chunks of it are flicked out in random directions and no amount of application of water appears to be helping. Never mind. I'll wear a hat.

I'm not prepared for the bright sunlight and I slope down the street squinting and fearing for my corneas. Once in the convenience shop, I grab the essentials for breakfast to bring both Simon and I back to life, and unload my basket with wobbling hands, ignoring the smirk of the shop assistant as he eyes my beanie hat. Back in the comfort of my own four walls, greeted by a fully dressed Simon, the fog I woke up in begins to disperse. He starts to prepare breakfast and the delicious scent of sizzling bacon wafts around the kitchen.

'So, what now?' Simon hands me a bacon sandwich.

'Now?' I mumble through a huge mouthful.

'Yes, now. Are you going to be okay living here on your own? I don't want to have to ring you every hour to make sure you haven't drunk so much that you've fallen over and banged your head and will be lying there for days until it's too late.'

'Too late? Oh, I see.'

A horrible image fills my mind: me dead, alone in my flat, surrounded by empty vodka bottles and photographs of me and Joe. I realise that things have to change. I have to get over him and start living a normal life, or I'm only going to descend into a depressing existence. I feel like I'm nearly at the end of that slippery slope and I only have a very small window of opportunity to pull back from it.

'You know what, Simon? I think I've reached the bottom. Things can't get any worse, and so I simply have to start being positive. I'm going to throw myself into my college work as a distraction, I'm only going to drink wine at the weekends and I'm not going to think about Joe.'

'Sounds like a good plan, honey.'

'Thursday counts as the start of the weekend, though. Right?'

Simon laughs at me and takes another bite of his bacon sandwich. As I drink a mouthful of my coffee, I feel optimistic. This hangover might even pass before lunchtime now too.

Chapter Twenty

'Hi, Carly.' I've arrived early for class tonight and Carly looks at me with surprise as I bump into her in the car park.

'Hey, Emma. How are you?' She cocks her head to one side and frowns.

'What?'

'You look different somehow. Is everything alright?'

I didn't tell Carly when Joe and I split up, and for the last two weeks I've been pretending everything's fine while we've been at college. It was just too raw to speak about with a friend I haven't known for that long.

'Um, well, actually...'

Get the words out, Emma. Once you've said them out loud a few more times, it'll stop feeling like a knife is being plunged between your ribs.

'Joe and I have sort of separated.'

'Separated?'

'Well, broken up. Called off the wedding. Our relationship is over,' I state a little bluntly.

Carly's response is open-mouthed silence.

'Look, I didn't mean that to sound so...I'm having difficulty talking about it without descending into a quivering mess, that's all.'

'Of course.' Carly nods slowly. 'How did it...I mean, what happened?'

'A mixture of everything and nothing, I guess. It's hard to explain.'

'I'm so sorry, Emma.' Carly pulls me into a hug and it takes all my inner strength not to cry right there in the car park.

'Come on.' I pull away from her, sniffing back tears. 'We're going to be late.'

As we walk towards the college building, a heavy sadness hangs between us.

'So, what have you been up to?' I ask brightly to break the awkward tension.

'Oh...' Carly starts to reply but then stops.

'What is it?'

'I don't feel right...not after what you've told me.'

'It's okay.' I can't imagine what terrible thing she might be about to say. 'Go on,' I urge.

'I went for a drink with Tom last week after class. Just the two of us.

I would have asked you too, but you dashed off as soon as it was over.'

'He asked you to go for a drink with him?' I have no idea why this bothers me. Maybe it doesn't. Maybe I'm now turning into a selfish person who wants to spread the misery. If I can't be happy then why should anyone else be?

'Um, no, well, I asked him. But he said yes and we had a good time together.'

'That's great, Carly. I know how much you like him.' I'm a little surprised as Tom's never shown much interest in Carly, but then again, what do I know? 'Are you going out on a second date?'

'I'm not sure you'd class it a date.' Carly blushes. 'I mean, there was no kissing or anything intimate – just a drink, that's all.'

'Well, ask him out again. Then you'll know.'

'I guess you're right.'

We've reached the classroom door. As we filter in and find our seats, I can already see marked essay papers lying on the desks and my stomach does a flip. I got the top grade on my first two essays and I'm praying that my the hard work I'm putting in continues to pay off. I slide into my seat and discretely flip the paper over, and I'm relieved to see that I scored a high merit. At least this there's some consistency in this part of my life, while the other aspects fall spectacularly apart.

I decide to call at Sophie's on my way home from college to give her the good news about my essay. I know she's been worried about me. Thankfully Simon promised not to tell her about my weekend dowsed in vodka, as it would only fuel her notion that I'm not coping. Alright, I wasn't coping, but now I've had a serious talk with myself and I'm determined to get on with things regardless and to try to see the positive in something each day – and today that's my essay grade.

'Soph? Hey, Sophie?' I call as I knock on her front door and it open simultaneously. I head towards the lounge. 'Hey,' I say, pushing the lounge door open and swinging in front of me the box of chocolates that I bought on the journey for us to celebrate my new-found karma (see – no alcohol. My conscience is happy). But as I enter the room Sophie greets me with a look of fear and…is that guilt?

'I didn't expect you tonight, Emma.' She's all of a fluster, and then I see why as I notice the figure on her sofa.

'Matt, what are you doing here?' My voice is high from surprise at finding Joe's younger brother looking far too relaxed in Sophie's house with a bottle of beer in his hand. I clear my throat.

Matt looks uncomfortably at Sophie and then back at me.

'It's not what you think!' Sophie states, waving her hands around in a dramatic fashion that I instantly recognise. It's her "tell". When she's lying, she has a tendency to overdramatise.

'Really?' I feel my eyebrows shoot skywards. 'Because from where I'm standing it looks like I've caught two people in "the act" - the last two people I ever expected to find together.'

I put the box of chocolates down heavily on the coffee table and place both hands on my hips as I await some sort of explanation, any explanation but the one I'm dreading: that Sophie has been carrying on with Matt behind my back.

'Okay, so maybe it is what you think.' Sophie cringes and hangs her head.

'Sophie! How could you?!' I snap, feeling a rush of anger, shock and betrayal all at once.

Matt leaps to her defence. 'It's not Sophie's fault. We both knew what we were doing.'

'And what exactly is it that you're doing, Matt?' I'm shouting now; whether I have any right to or not, I simply don't care.

'We didn't want to tell you until we were absolutely sure there was something to tell,' bleats Sophie.

'And is there? Is there something to tell?'

They both look at each other sheepishly and I realise that this is for real. Sophie and Matt are more than two people enjoying a friendly beer together one evening. He's here in her house, and this looks like it's serious.

'I mean, how did this even happen?' I say, trying to keep my voice a little calmer and swallowing my urge to yell at them both for being so, I don't know, disrespectful.

'Well, as best man and chief bridesmaid we started meeting up to discuss and plan things for your wedding to Joe.' Sophie starts.

'It was all innocent at first,' Matt interjects.

'And then we had a few glasses of wine, and one thing led to another.' Sophie shrugs.

'So this is actually happening? You two are an item?'

They nod gently in unison and my stomach does a little flip - no, make that a big flip. I feel an unusual tightening in my chest. Perhaps it's the onset of a heart attack that will end my misery once and for all. My earlier excitement at doing well on my course and my positivity have burst like a popped balloon, and all that's left is the overstretched, floppy latex, a parody of my current life, lying forlornly on the floor.

Sophie takes a step towards me. 'Emma, if you could –'

I hold up my hand to silence her. 'You know what, Sophie? I need to...to leave.'

'I want you to hurt too. I want you to feel the pain that I've felt.'

Chapter Twenty-One

I turn quickly and hurry out of the room and out of Sophie's house, ignoring her calling my name. Once outside I realise it's cold and I pull my coat tighter around me. I clamber into my car, start the engine with shaking hands and drive off. I don't know where I'm driving to and I don't care, anywhere away from this situation that I'm absolutely not ready to deal with. I mean, this is Joe's younger brother – Joe, my ex-fiancé. Aren't there enough young single men out there for Sophie to date who don't happen to be explicitly connected to my own disastrous love life?

Hmm…I've tried and tested this theory, and maybe not. There appears to be a severe lack of attractive, eligible, single men once you reach your thirties. Regardless, I could kill her for this. Lack of choice is simply not a reasonable excuse for dating your best friend's former fiancé's brother. It's just not. It's not. She's bang out of order.

I don't know how but I've ended up outside Henry's wine bar on the high street in town (perhaps it's like a homing beacon, calling to me). I've no recollection of driving here – I must have been on automatic pilot, drawn by the need for a large drink in familiar and comforting surroundings. I pull the car into the car park and head into the wine bar. I'm greeted by a rush of warm air mixed with casual chatter and soft R&B music. Glancing at my watch, I notice it's nearly eight thirty. I head straight to the bar to buy a drink.

The barmaid smiles welcomingly. 'What can I get you?'

'Um, a glass of sauvignon blanc, please,' I stutter, struggling to speak. My whole body is still in shock.

'Large or small?' She waves two different glasses at me.

I pause for only a second.

'On second thoughts, I'll take the bottle.' I push Simon's comments about me getting on the sober wagon to the back of my mind.

The barmaid nods and hands me the larger of the two glasses and a chilled bottle of Pinot Grigio. That should be enough to blot this evening out.

I hand over payment before taking refuge at a corner table towards the back of the bar. In any other circumstances I'd have thought drinking alone in a bar to be sad and pathetic. Perhaps that's what the other punters are thinking about me right now. Maybe they're nudging each other and whispering. But tonight I don't care. Maybe I am sad and pathetic. I pour wine almost to the brim of the glass and take a large gulp, closely followed by another, and another.

Oh God, what if Sophie and Matt are actually meant to be together? We're all supposed to have a soul mate. What if Matt is Sophie's? What if they stay together and they get engaged and, in a cruel twist of fate, I end up planning their wedding?

What if they then have children?

I down the rest of the glass and quickly refill it. Glancing around, I note that my surroundings have become a little blurred already and I rub at my temples to clear the haziness.

What if they get married and have children?

I'd be forever linked to Joe, who would only ever be my ex-fiancé, nothing more. It would be awkward and uncomfortable at every family event, where we'd be thrust together to mark little Sophie's or little Matt's christening or first birthday.

I couldn't bear it. I couldn't bear it.

Seeing him but not being able to be with him, to touch him, to kiss him – it would kill me slowly until I'd completely died inside.

I swill down the remainder of the second large glass of wine now as an even worse thought pushes itself to the forefront of my mind. The only thing worse than being constantly thrust into Joe's company would be having to watch from the side-lines as he lived his life with someone else. The perfect woman. The one he's sure to find. The one who can balance everything in her life with ease and grace, instead of lurching inconsistently from day to day. The one who can be the person that Joe needs, wants, her to be. The one who can give him everything I couldn't.

The person I couldn't be. The person I failed to be.

Oh God...what if he's already found her?

I can feel wetness on my cheeks and taste salt. Wiping away the tears with the back of my hand, I down the rest of the wine and signal for the barmaid to bring over another bottle. But as the barmaid moves towards my table I see a fuzzy figure intercept her.

A familiar voice penetrates the slightly drunken (okay, very drunken) fog. 'I'll take that, thanks, and could I possibly have another glass, please?'

97

'What are you doing here, Sophie?' I huff like a teenager, trying so very hard not to slur my words. 'I'd have thought you'd have realised that I want to be alone and that you're the last person I want to see right now.'

'We need to talk, Emma.' Ignoring my words, she places my second bottle of wine that she took from the barmaid on the table and plonks herself down next to me.

'Thank you.' She says as the barmaid appears with another wine glass. Then Sophie proceeds to help herself to a glass of my wine. At least she has the courtesy to top up my glass too.

'How did you even know I'd be here? I could have been anywhere.'

I lean my forehead on my hands, willing her to go away. I'm not ready to deal with this yet. I need to crucify myself with a lot more disturbing thoughts of my desolate future before I can even think of talking about Sophie and Matt, let alone accepting that they're a couple.

'Yeah, remember how after the whole Connor thing, for safety we downloaded an application on our phones that tracks our GPS signal?'

'Oh.' I do remember. Damn stupid technology.

'I knew you were here for the last half an hour, but I thought I'd give you some time to...' She struggles for the right word. '...think.'

Not the right word. I've been doing nothing but that since I left Sophie's house, and all it's done is produce too many thoughts for my brain to process, most of them torturous.

'Do you love him?' I hear the slur in my speech but I no longer care about trying to keep up a pretence that I'm not drunk. I take a gulp of wine to numb the pain from the answer I know is going to come.

Sophie takes a sip of her own wine before answering. 'I don't know.'

I nod, knowing there's a "but" coming.

'But I do like him...a lot.'

I press my lips together, wondering what the right response to this situation is. I'm not sure that there is one.

'I'm sorry, Emma.' Sophie's voice is small and she avoids my gaze.

I shake my head, causing the blurriness around me to intensify. 'Don't be. And I mean it. We can't help who we fall for.'

I can't believe my own words. I'm angry at her, but I know in my heart of hearts that she hasn't hurt me on purpose. She's my best friend and she wouldn't do that.

'And I'm sorry that that's how you had to find out,' Sophie continues. 'I should have spoken to you about Matt as soon as I realised that we had feelings for each other.'

'Yes, you should.' I see a flash of guilt across Sophie's face. 'But I can't say I'd have reacted any better.'

I down the remainder of my wine, feeling it slosh deep down in my stomach, topping up the vat of wine that's already swilling around in there. 'It isn't your fault I made a right cock-up of things with Joe. It's just still raw, I guess.' I fiddle with the stem of my wine glass. 'I think I've had too much wine for tonight.'

We sit there for a moment in silence.

'Have you slept with him?' I know I shouldn't be asking, and I'm not sure either answer makes any difference, but the wine is prompting me to desire further information. Sophie's cheeks flush crimson and that says it all.

'Wait a minute.' A surprisingly clear thought pops into my mind. 'I lived with you for two weeks and you were seeing Matt the whole time? How come I never saw him? Am I really that dumb, or were you hiding him in the wardrobe or the cupboard under the stairs?'

Sophie looks down at the floor before answering. 'We had to meet at a hotel in our lunch hour so you wouldn't notice me sloping off to his flat in the evenings.'

'Oh...' I ponder this for a moment. 'You met in a hotel for lunch-time sex?' I slur. A giggle escapes as I imagine Sophie sneaking into a hotel foyer dressed in disguise for her romantic interlude, all because I was camping out in her living room. The giggles worsen and a drunken snort erupts. I clamp my hand over my mouth, silencing any further embarrassing bodily sounds, but my shoulders still heave silently. It's as though I've been storing up all my laughter and now it's set free and is out of control.

'Are you going to be okay with this?' Sophie asks tentatively. I realise that I sound like I'm bordering on hysterical.

I take a second to compose myself before answering. 'I want to be.' I reach over and squeeze her hand.

'Let's get you home.' Sophie stands up and pulls me to my feet. 'I'm guessing you have work tomorrow.'

Oh crap. I'm going to have a raging hangover in the morning and turn up at work looking like road kill (and not for the first time since Joe and I separated). That will result in a warm-hearted telling-off from Jenny again, which I can tolerate, but it will also fuel the hatred that Julia Bamford seems to possess towards me. She won't be the slightest bit impressed. I vaguely remember telling Simon that I wold only drink alcohol at weekends. Epic fail so far given it's mid-week and I've consumed the best part of two bottles. Must try harder, although to-night's circumstances, I think, would send the most alcohol conscious person to reach for a bottle of wine.

Chapter Twenty-Two

What the hell is that noise?

I peek my head out from under the quilt. My bed has become my safe haven for the last thirty-six hours. I arrived home from work on Thursday night and took up residence in my bedroom with a vodka and tonic for company, and since then I've only got up when in danger of having a bathroom emergency. Adjusting to living on my own, which I have to admit I haven't done particularly well, and then finding out about Sophie and Matt's secret relationship has simply proven too much for me to cope with, and I've experienced emotional meltdown and sought solace in numbing my brain with vodka. I am well aware of my promise to be more conservative with my alcohol intake but right at this moment I don't care. I need an emotional crutch to see me through this dark faze of my life.

The strange noise presents itself again. It sounds like a burglar. I'm being burgled already and I've been here for less than a two weeks. Damn that stupid estate agent with his cheerful 'No, there's no crime around here; it's totally safe for a...er, young lady living on her own' speech. Totally safe, my arse.

I hear a fumble of what sounds like keys and then a woman's voice. Is that...? No...It can't be....

Suddenly the door clicks open and I hear two familiar voices getting louder and louder before my bedroom door is pushed open and my fear becomes a reality.

'Mum! What are you doing here? You live in New York. And Sophie, that spare key was for emergencies. What's your emergency? Because I'm pretty sure I didn't call you to say that I had one.'

Sophie has the decency to look contrite. My mother, on the other hand, just looks at me and shakes her head in that disappointed manner that all mothers perfect.

Mum addresses Sophie. 'It's worse than we thought.'

Worse than who thought about what?

'Um, hello? I'm actually here, you know,' I snap, feeling the after-effects of last night's vodka, and the previous night's – oops. 'And can you explain to me why you've broken into my new flat and appeared in my bedroom, disrupting my sleep?'

I reach up and realise that my hair is in a strange shape, squashed flat on one side where I've slept on it, while the other feels like it's trying to escape from me as it sticks out at a right angle. I try to pat it down but fail due to the lack of coherent communication between my body and mind.

'Sleep?' Mum raises her eyebrows skywards. 'It's two thirty in the afternoon, Emma.'

'So?' I realise that I sound like a petulant teenager, but that appears to be how I'm being treated.

'And how long exactly have you been wallowing in your bed?'

I scowl silently, refusing to answer this hostile question during such an unprovoked attack on my own territory.

Mum continues her sergeant major interrogation: 'When did you last go to work?'

'Yesterday,' I retort.

Mum's eyebrows rise even further.

'Okay, the day before,' I huff, not wanting to admit that I called in sick yesterday. I feel horribly guilty for leaving Jenny in the lurch, but I really wasn't in any fit state to stand up all day and serve customers. My "illness" was completely self-inflicted, of course, and I swore to myself that I'd never do that again.

'Why were you not at work today?' Mum demands, standing with her hands on her hips.

'It's my day off,' I state flatly.

'And what was yesterday?'

'Urgh!' I flounce up into a sitting position, keeping the quilt wrapped around me as a defensive barrier. 'Yesterday was my day off too, okay? Jenny let me have a few days off to settle into my new place,' I lie.

'And this is settling in, is it?'

'Argh! Mum, I'm thirty-three years old. Why can't you treat me like an adult?'

'Because you're not behaving like one!'

I see Sophie retreat towards the bedroom door with a look of horror on her face, like she's realised the cute little monkey she's just let out of its cage is going to rip the faces off all the cooing visitors at the zoo. I guess she was expecting the tea and sympathy routine from my mother. She should have known better. And I'm still unaware how, and why, my mum is here in my flat in England and not at home in New York, but she doesn't seem to be very forthcoming in offering an explanation for that.

'What is this anyway?' I glare from Sophie to Mum.

'Well, you see darling…we're just worried about you, that's all.' She begins.

'Worried about me?' I snarl.

'About your drinking.' Sophie interjects.

'My drinking?'

'We've all noticed that you've been, um, drinking a lot more alcohol than usual.' Mum treads carefully.

I'm embarrassed, and a little shocked. I didn't realise it had become so apparent. Maybe I have been hitting the bottle a little too much lately and so what if I've spent more on wine and vodka than food in the last month. How dare they…I can feel defiance take over.

'And how exactly have you noticed that I've been drinking heavily Mum? You live in New York which, if I'm not mistaken, is several thousand miles away.' I know I sound petulant but I don't care. 'What I'm guessing has happened is that my 'oh so good' friend has taken this opportunity to tell tales on me.' I shoot an accusing glare at Sophie.

Mum gives me a disapproving look 'You can drop the attitude Emma. We're doing this for your own good.'

'Doing what exactly?' I snap.

'It's an intervention Emma.' Sophie says.

'An intervention? You make it sound like I've got a major drinking problem.'

Sophie just cocks her head to one side and I'm met with silence from both of them.

'I've gone through a very rough time.' I protest.

Still a wall of silence

'The breakdown of a relationship isn't something that you get over with a few cups of coffee and a blueberry muffin!' My voice raises a few octaves.

'Emma' It's Sophie's turn to try to reason with me 'We just don't want you to end up on a slippery slope to a dark place, that's all.'

I think that ship has sailed. I already feel like I'm at the bottom of said slope and I'm drowning in sludgy brown stuff. If I'm honest with myself then I the reason that I'm being so defensive is that I realise that my drinking has become out of hand I just haven't wanted to admit that. To me someone who uses alcohol as a crutch is weak and in need of help but maybe that's not true, maybe that person is just sad and trying to mask their feelings with alcohol so they appear fun and happy on the outside even though they're hurting on the inside.

'Okay….'

'Okay?' Mum glances at me, then Sophie.

'You might be right after all.' I exhale as though admitting the truth has actually taken some physical exertion 'perhaps I do need to stop drinking as much.'

This is met with slightly wary expressions.

'But you need to stop inviting me out to places where I can drink freely.' I point at Sophie 'and you and Simon need to stop turning up at my flat armed with Sauvignon Blanc.'

'Deal.' Sophie smiles satisfyingly clearly realising that their mission is accomplished and I haven't reacted too badly to her and mum's blatant coercion or the fact that she "told" on me to my Mum and the two of them ganged up on me.

'So we're all good?' Sophie asks.

I contemplate making her suffer a little but decided against it 'Yes Sophie, we're good.'

'Why don't you try simply getting up and going in the shower, darling?' Mum's taken on a calmer tone, trying to reason with me now instead of challenging me.

I'm in no mood to argue further. I'm hungover and exhausted and this is taking up energy that I simply don't possess. I take a moment to consider what I must look like. I've been thrashing around in a disturbed fit of nightmares of the current reality and the occasional nice dream of Joe and I still together. I can't help but wonder whether the amount of vodka I've drunk has strengthened the darkness within. My appearance must be borderline "scaring young children" or perhaps as bad as "commit me to a padded cell".

'Alright,' I say, still in a slight grump, 'I'll get in the shower if you'll stop all this judging. I am in the throes of depression, you know.'

'I know.' Mum nods solemnly. 'And I promise no more judgmental tone.'

'And please get my spare key from Sophie.' I scowl, dragging myself from my bed with some difficulty. 'I no longer care about a potential emergency that might require her assistance. She can no longer be trusted with its possession.'

'Of course.' Mum tries not to smile, and I see Sophie turn away as she attempts, and fails, to supress a giggle.

It actually feels quite nice under the hot shower, almost like it's washing the vodka hangover off me and sending it swirling down the plug hole. I reach for the expensive shower gel, an extravagant impulse buy which I usually use only on special occasions, and lather myself in it, enjoying the rich floral scent. I don't know how long I spend in there, but by the time I emerge, towel clad with my hair wrapped in a turban, Mum and Sophie are standing and talking quietly in the kitchen like co-conspirators. I wonder what else they're planning together in addition to this intrusion.

'Ah, there you are, darling,' Mum says brightly.

Sophie looks at me from under her eyelashes, still a little wary.

'When did you last eat something, Emma?' Mum's opening cupboards with what I can only presume is optimism, as she knows my idea of cooking is calling for takeout food and as such all cupboards are bare except for crackers to accompany my cheese and any wine that may remain in the fridge.

Undeterred, she's now bending over to inspect the lacking contents of the fridge. She announces with a hint of dismay, 'There appears to only be an empty wine bottle, a trickle of vodka, the dregs of some tonic water and some…cheese.'

See ¬– at least I'm true to form.

'Right.' Mum closes the fridge door with a clunk. 'I suggest you get dressed and then we can all go out for a spot of late lunch before a well-needed visit to the supermarket.'

'Are you judging me again?' I sniff.

'Absolutely not, Emma.' Mum's expression remains blank. 'I'm merely offering to take you and Sophie out to lunch and then to replenish your food cupboards so you won't starve to death.'

'Why is it you're here again, Mum?' I bite my lip to stop tears forming over the fact that someone cares about me. Well, and to hold in my annoyance that I presume Sophie has called Mum after fearing I'm about to implode and Mum now feels it necessary to babysit me. Maybe I do need looking after like a small child. At the moment I'm not doing such a great job of taking care of myself.

'Go and get dressed, darling.'

I start to protest further, but then stop myself. I can't actually remember the last time I ate proper food. If Mum had riffled through the contents of the bin (at one point I feared she might), she'd have found a Mars bar wrapper and an empty packet of roasted peanuts which constituted lunch and dinner yesterday. I realise I'm ravenous and in fact lunch sounds like a very good idea.

As I turn to walk back to my bedroom to get dressed, I catch Sophie's eye.

'I'm sorry,' she mouths silently.

'It's alright,' I mouth back.

'So how long are you here for, Mum?' I ask once we're back at my flat later that day, having eaten filling pub food and visited the supermarket for supplies. Although that was more challenging that I expected it to be. It would appear that my idea of "nice food" that I'd like to consume varies hugely from the type of food my mother thinks I should be eating. In the end it was simpler to just agree with her and let her fill my trolley with random vegetables and things like couscous.

'I fly back tomorrow morning at eleven thirty.'

'So you flew all this way for twenty-four hours?'

'You needed me, Emma, even if you didn't realise it, and that's what mothers do.'

'When did Sophie call you?' I glance over at Sophie.

'I rang your mum after Jenny sent me a text to say you'd called in sick. She was worried about you. We all were…are.'

'There's nothing to worry about. I'm fine, honestly.'

Sophie looks at me sceptically. 'Honestly? We found you buried under your quilt, unkempt and unclean, with a scent of vodka emanating from you.'

That's a bit harsh, isn't it?

'I had a moment, that's all. I temporarily lost my mind and now that's over. It's done. I'm focused and back on track.'

'Focused on what exactly, though?'

'My college work. I'm focused on that and…oh crap!' In the depths of my despair I forgot all about the essay that's due this week. How on earth am I going to be able to complete that in time?

Chapter Twenty-Three

Hmm. I stare at a textbook the size of War and Peace and then at the half-finished essay I've been battling with for the last few hours since Mum left in a taxi for the airport. Maybe I'll just Google a few things first. I mean, this is the twenty-first century. Surely we should have evolved past textbooks by now anyway. My fingers hover over the keys on my laptop. My conscience gives me a jab: No. No. Come on, Emma. You wanted to do this course, and you're going to do it properly.

I flick open the textbook and scan the first few pages, then go back to the laptop and load up Google. Maybe a combination of two methods is the best approach.

After half an hour (but what feels like an eternity) I'm relieved to hear the intercom buzz, which means I can be distracted from my studies guilt free. It isn't my fault that a visitor has decided to arrive unannounced.

'Hello?' I call into the receiver.

'Hiya, babe. It's only me. I'm checking that you're still alive.'

'Hi, Simon. The door's open.' I press the release button, a grin already spreading across my face.

'Hey.' Simon greets me with a big hug. 'I'm part of the "care in the community" club that Sophie's drafted in.'

'Very funny, Simon. I take it you, my mum and Sophie are all in this together?'

'Well, Sophie did mention something about you having to be practically forced from your bed and dragged back into the land of the living.'

It wasn't quite like that…

'I needed some time to gain some…um…composure, that's all.'

'Oh, right.' He scratches his head thoughtfully. 'Anyway, I brought you a present.' He glances around the kitchen. 'Shall I put the kettle on? It looks like I've interrupted you.' He points to the laptop and textbook.

'It's fine. I was about to take a break anyway.' I bite my lip awkwardly, realising I've technically been having a break for the last half an hour while I've been googling then staring blankly at the laptop screen. 'You didn't have to check up on me. Mum only left this morning, and I'm sure you must have got an update from her or Sophie on my wellbeing.'

'So you're not going to descend into a dark depression seeing as you managed to let the one good man you've ever dated slip right through your fingers.' He shrugs humorously.

I glare at him. 'Is there anything less constructive that you can think of to say, Simon?'

'Oh, babe, I was just trying to make light of the situation, that's all. I know you're hurting.'

I sniff back the onset of tears and simply nod. Must not cry. Must not cry. Need to keep up the pretence of normal behaviour not complete lunacy.

'Come here.' He pulls me into another hug. 'I'm sorry. I'm an idiot. Forgive me?' He kisses the top of my head.

'You are an idiot,' I mumble into his chest, 'but I forgive you. You can't help it that you're an arse sometimes.' I find myself giggling into his jumper.

'Under the circumstances I'll let that one go,' Simon says in a mock-hurt tone.

'Anyway...' I pull away from him. 'I thought you said you'd brought me a gift?'

He holds a bag out and I take it.

'Simon, this is a bottle of non-alcoholic wine.'

'I know.' He grins. 'But it sounds like you've drunk enough alcohol lately to sink the Titanic all over again, so I thought we'd best take it easy.'

'Should I take this moment to remind you that you were in fact my drinking partner only a week ago and you were so drunk that you didn't make it home and ended up in my bed?' I admonish.

'It's not the first time that's happened.' He chuckles. 'Shame you're the wrong sex.'

'Let's hope it's the last time you get so drunk you end up in someone else's bed. James deserves your monogamy.'

'You're right, Miss Sensible,' Simon says in a sulky voice. 'Come on, we'll have a cup of tea.'

I walk over to the kettle and switch it on before taking some mugs out of the cupboard.

'Got any chocolate biscuits?' Simon asks.

'Sure.'

The cupboards are brimming with food that Mum bought yesterday. Chocolate biscuits included, although I did have to sneak them into the trolley while she wasn't looking.

When I bring the tea over, Simon has already sat down at the small kitchen table and he's looking at my laptop screen.

'What's this?' he asks and takes a slurp of tea.

'Um. An essay for college.' I try to turn the screen away from his gaze. 'I'm struggling with it a bit, I guess.'

I shove a packet of double-chocolate-chip cookies in his direction, hoping it will act as a distraction. I'm conscious that Simon's aced every essay he's ever written. The biscuits seem to meet with his approval as he instantly devours two.

'What's it about?' he says between munches.

'Nothing you'd be interested in.' I take hold of the laptop.

'Honey, show me a gay man who isn't interested in fashion, and I'll show you a liar.' He holds out his hand.

'Okay,' I concede, and put the laptop back down on the table. 'But it's not finished yet, so don't judge me.'

Simon shakes his head at me and turns the laptop screen around to face him. I drink my tea nervously as he starts to read and then reach for a biscuit and begin to nibble at the edges.

'It's not that bad,' he says a few moments later, 'but I think you could make some improvements. Come here.' He pats the chair next to him and I sit down as instructed.

And there we stay for the next hour. I'm transported back to being thirteen years old as Simon helps me with my homework just like he used to then.

Once the essay is completed we celebrate with a glass of non-alcoholic wine.

'This is disgusting.' Simon pulls a face, handing me back his glass still mostly full.

Chapter Twenty-Four

I grab the mail from the mat as I step through the door and chuck it dismissively on the kitchen table. Then I open the fridge door and pull out a chilled bottle of Sauvignon Blanc – it's Thursday, after all; the weekend starts here, so I can surely have one guilt free glass? The first sip instantly takes the edge of yet another fretful day at the shop. I'm seriously wondering how much longer I can take working with Julia Bamford. I like Jenny's mature attitude of taking the moral high ground, but the reality isn't so easy to achieve. I spend most of my days visualising stuffing Julia into the store room and padlocking the door shut.

As I take a second sip of wine, something catches my eye. The envelope on the top of today's mail is blank. There's no stamp on it, no name or address, yet here it is along with my other post. Maybe someone hand delivered it. I pick up the envelope and eye it with some suspicion. It's probably some local advertising crap or an appeal for charity. I'm tempted to simply discard it in the bin without giving it a second thought, but curiosity gets the better of me. I have another mouthful of wine before placing my glass on the kitchen table and sliding my forefinger under the flap of the envelope.

As I pull out piece of paper and unfold it my breath catches in the back of my throat and my heart leaps up into my chest. I read the words over and over again. This is surely a joke. But as I turn the envelope over with shaking hands to check again for a postmark or anything that signifies the origin of the letter, I realise that this might actually be for real.

With Whitney Houston trying to escape a psycho stalker in The Bodyguard flashing through my mind, I stare at the letters, which have been cut from a newspaper and spell out: You deserve everything that you get.

Maybe I'm overreacting a little here. I mean, it's not exactly a death threat, more like the kind of statement you get in a fortune cookie. But what does it mean? And more importantly, who would send me something like this?

I stare at the piece of paper.

It may not be a death threat but the fact that it's newspaper cuttings and not typed or something is in itself weird. It's old school. I thought people got "trolled" on social media nowadays, a much easier way of threatening somebody anonymously. But I'm not really on social media. I mean I am, but I have only four friends: Simon, Sophie, Jenny and Lola.

I grab the wine glass and take a gulp. Someone obviously wanted me to receive this letter. They've posted it directly through my front door. It's creepy, really, really creepy.

Wait a minute – maybe it's not meant for me. There's no name on the envelope, no "Dear Emma" on the letter. I only moved in recently. Maybe this was intended for the person who lived here before. I have no idea why anyone would want to send such a disturbing message to an apparently lovely couple with a new baby, but who knows what really goes on behind closed doors? Maybe they were part of a gang or something. Maybe they were involved in some torrid love triangle. Now I sound crazy…

Why would someone send a horrible stalking-type letter?

Is this stalking? What constitutes stalking anyway? People follow every aspect of each other's lives on social media and no one seems to care about that or think it intrusive. In fact, people seem quite willing to share every moment of their lives on social media nowadays.

You know what? I reason with myself; you're worrying about nothing. I decide to put the letter in the kitchen drawer for safe-keeping, in case I ever need it for future reference, and then forget about it.

I close the drawer and stare at it, waiting for it to fly open and for the letter to jump out at me.

Emma. You're being ridiculous. This is a piece of paper, not a poltergeist.

I double check that the drawer is firmly shut and walk away.

See…Done. Forgotten.

I have the pleasure of forgetting about the unpleasant threatening letter for all of one week. Then, exactly seven days later, I'm greeted with a similar plain white envelope as I get home from college. I hate to admit it, but my gut reaction is that this is no mistake. Someone is purposely sending these letters to me.

I scoop up the envelope with a shaking hand and try to quell the uneasiness that's spreading through my whole body as I walk into every room, switching on the lights as I go. Perhaps I've seen too many horror movies for my own good, but I'm taking no chances; I even check under the bed and in the wardrobe for the bogeyman. The last thing I want is some maniac coming out from his hiding place under the cover of my hanging clothes to stab me to death in my sleep.

Once I've carefully inspected every crevice in each room and found nothing suspicious, I head back through to the kitchen, leaving all the lights on in every room so the flat is lit up like a Christmas tree. Throughout I've held the envelope at arm's reach, as though it's a bomb that might explode at any minute, and now I place it on the worktop and reach into the cupboard for the remnants of a bottle of vodka I know are still lurking there. I need more than a cup of tea to steady my nerves before viewing the contents of the latest letter. I pour a generous measure and down it in one without bothering to add ice or tonic, then immediately refill the glass.

I bite the side of my mouth in consternation, ignoring the pain, as I stare at the white envelope that's taunting me, daring me to open it. Maybe it won't be anything bad at all and I'm imagining something a lot worse than the reality. But I know this isn't true. Although the last letter wasn't threatening as such, it's definitely something to worry about. At what point should call the police and report this? Report what exactly, though?

I snatch the envelope up and roughly rip it open. As I slide out the sheet of paper I can already see the newspaper letters on it and my heart starts hammering in my chest. Slowly I flip the paper open and the words dance across the page: Your life as you know it is over.

Holy shit.

I drop the letter like it's a burning-hot poker and rush to the front door, where I discarded my handbag earlier. I rummage around for my mobile phone, find it, hit speed dial once and try to calm my breathing as I listen to the ringing tone.

'Hey, Emma. How's things?'

I've never been so relieved to hear Sophie's voice.

'Hi, Soph.' I'm surprised by how normal my voice sounds. 'Are you doing anything tonight?'

'Erm, no. Why?'

'Could you come over by any chance?'

'Sure. Is everything okay?'

'Yes, everything's fine. I just feel like having some company tonight, that's all.'

'Sounds good to me. Give me fifteen minutes and I'll be there. I'll bring wine.'

I glance at my watch and realise it's nearly half past eight. 'Are you sure, Soph? I didn't realise the time.'

'Emma, we're thirty-three. I'm sure we don't have to be in bed yet, even on a work night.'

'Okay, thanks, Soph. See you in a bit.'

I hang up the phone and then walk around the flat again, reopening every cupboard and drawer and inspecting each with care, half-expecting a balaclava-clad monster to jump out at me at any moment. I even look under the sofa, although I'm pretty sure it's physically impossible for a human being to fit under there. As it happens I find nothing other than a discarded sock. I'm driving myself crazy, increasing my fear and irrational thoughts, but right now it doesn't feel like there's anything else to do but keep checking. And is it really irrational to imagine a crazed person hiding in your home when you've been sent disturbing correspondence that sends a huge chill up your spine?

I stand right next to the front door, hovering on tenterhooks as I wait for Sophie to arrive, and the loud buzz of the intercom makes me jump.

As I reach for the intercom my hand freezes. What if it's not Sophie? What if it's the crazy person who's sending me these macabre notes?

I glance at my watch. It's eight forty. I'm overthinking things. It must be Sophie.

'H…h…hello?' My voice is cautious and stuttering as I speak into the receiver.

'It's me, Emma.' Sophie's voice fills my ears and I exhale with relief.

'Of course. Come up.'

I press the door release and hang up the receiver, then lean against the wall to try to quieten my thudding heart. My whole body feels jittery and on edge.

Sophie waves a large bag of crisps in her hand as she walks through the door a few seconds later. 'I brought nibbles. I presume you haven't bothered to eat?' She raises her eyebrows questioningly.

'I ate earlier, before college,' I lie. Right now food is the last thing on my mind. My stomach is twisted into a thousand knots.

Keeping up my pretence that all is well, I take the crisps and the promised wine from Sophie's grasp and busy myself pouring two glasses (one glass of wine won't hurt. See I am being more conscious of my alcohol consumption. I have put the vodka away), I justify to myself as I tip the crisps into a large bowl. But Sophie isn't fooled. She watches me in silence, a frown lowering her perfectly shaped brows.

'What's wrong, Emma?'

'Why would anything be wrong?' I say dismissively. Although I'm totally freaked out, I don't want to appear that way to Sophie. I want her calm and methodical advice on what I should do with these letters.

'Other than you calling me over at eight thirty on a Wednesday night?'

'I thought you said we're thirty-three so eight thirty isn't late?' I protest.

'And you're a sickly white colour...'

Oh.

'And your hands are shaking.'

Crap. I hadn't noticed that they still were.

'So you can stop pretending that you're okay and you can tell me what the hell is going on.'

'It's nothing. Well, it might be something. But nothing really. It's –'

'Emma!'

I walk over to the drawer and retrieve the two white envelopes containing the letters and hand them to Sophie.

'What are these?' She looks down and then back up to me.

'Just open them,' I say quietly.

I watch as Sophie takes the first of the two letters out of its envelope and see the expression on her face change.

'What the...?'

She quickly opens the second one and roughly pulls out the piece of paper. Her mouth opens in shock as she stares down at the uneven letters splayed across the page.

'Now can we drink the wine, please?' I pick up the glasses and offer one to Sophie before taking a gulp from my own.

'When did you get these?' Sophie asks as we make our way into the lounge.

'I got the first one a week ago,' I say as I perch on the edge of the sofa.

'A week ago? And you're only telling me this now? Emma!'

'Calm down, Sophie, and sit down, please. You scare me when you hover.'

She huffs loudly but takes a seat next to me.

'I thought it was a joke or something.' I take a sip of wine. 'Or that it was meant for the previous tenant. I didn't really think it was that serious.'

'And when did the second one arrive?'

'Today. It was on the doormat when I came home from college.'

'So it was posted directly through your letterbox?'

'Yes.'

'Which means whoever it is has access to your building.'

'I realise that, but they could have also waited outside until someone left through the main door and then grabbed the door before it closed. They wouldn't have had to buzz someone's flat to get access.'

'I guess not. But it's still worrying that whoever sent this was right outside your front door.'

'Not helping to calm my hysteria, Soph.' I give her a gentle nudge.

'I'm sorry, but I'm not trying to.'

'What?'

'I think this is serious, Emma, really serious, and you need to call the police.'

'I thought about that, but maybe I'm overreacting. I mean, they haven't actually threatened me or anything. It might be someone playing a practical joke.'

'This is no joke, Emma. Either you call the police or I'll do it myself right now.'

I know Sophie's right. It's better to play it safe and report it just in case I'm in danger. That seems ridiculous, though: who would want to hurt me, and why?

'Okay,' I concede, 'I'll call the police.'

Chapter Twenty-Five

An hour later, after much floor pacing from the two of us, two police officers file into my living room, which instantly feels crowded. They sit down on the sofa, Sophie sits on a beanbag and I carry on wearing out the carpet.

'You received the first of the two letters a week ago?' asks the older of the two police officers while adjusting his considerable bulk into a more comfortable position. How he could ever catch an offender on the run is beyond me. I think even I could outrun him, and that's saying something given that I never run.

Suddenly I'm plagued with a vision of Sergeant Bulky hurtling after a suspected criminal, leaping over whatever may be in his path, and I have to try hard to supress a giggle. I think it's my mind's way of coping with this surreal situation. I always imagined having a police officer present would be sexy; the allure of a man in uniform. I'm disappointed to find that it's neither and I actually feel like I've done something wrong.

'Yes,' I confirm, my voice steady without a hint of the giggle that was threatening. 'I got the first letter last Wednesday.'

Sergeant Bulky scribbles furiously on his notepad and I try to sneak a look at what he's writing. His handwriting is inelligible from my upside-down perspective, although I suspect it would be regardless.

'Can you think of anyone who might want to cause you harm?' I glance over at the second police officer, whose voice is soft. He's slightly younger and painfully thin and has a kind smile: still nowhere near the image of my ideal policeman.

'Anyone who would want to hurt me? Um…no.'

'No ex-boyfriends? No recent relationship issues? No arguments with any female friend's? Any new people in your life who may have recently injected themselves into your work or social life?' This from Sergeant Bulky.

'A new man in my life? If only,' I joke, but this is met with a stern stare from Sophie and blank expressions from both policeman. Clearly this isn't the time for jokes.

'I mean, no. Um, yes,' I stutter.

'Yes to which part?' Sergeant Skinny prompts.

'Well, technically all three. I have an ex-boyfriend, Chris, but I haven't seen him for ages, and he's more sulky and obnoxious than terrorising. Then there's Joe, my ex-fiancé.' I gulp at the mention of Joe's name after trying so hard not to think about him since…since I left our home that day and we said goodbye forever.

'Miss?' Sergeant Bulky's voice jolts me back into the room.

'Sorry. Where was I?'

'Your ex-fiancé?'

'Ah, yes. Joe. No, it's not him.'

'How can you be sure? We shouldn't eliminate anybody at this stage.'

'I'm sure,' I state a little too firmly considering I'm addressing police officers. 'It's not Joe. He would never do this to me. He's…he's a good man.'

The best. He's the best man I'm ever likely to meet. Oh God, this is so depressing. I'm alone and single, and now some stalker wants to target me. Could it get any worse? No, I shouldn't tempt fate by asking that, or who knows what other hideous scenario could present itself.

'And anyone new in your life?' Sergeant Bulky looks up from his notepad scribbles.

'I've recently started college so I've met lots of new people there, but…' I really can't imagine one of the nineteen-year-old students I attend college with bothering to stalk me, plus they have absolutely no reason to.

'What about that guy you went for a drink with from college?' Sophie drops into the conversation.

'You mean Tom?'

'Yeah, that's him.'

'What's Tom's full name and address?' Sergeant Bulky has his pen poised.

'Um, I don't…he's just Tom.' I wrack my brain, knowing at some point Tom must have mentioned his surname, but for the life of me I can't recall it now I'm under pressure. 'And I have no idea what his address is. He lives somewhere on the other side of town, I think, on the estate behind the retail park.'

Sergeant Bulky scribbles more ineligible notes.

'But it's not Tom. It can't be him,' I protest.

'It has to be someone, Miss Story.'

Sergeant Skinny is stating the obvious. But until now it hadn't really registered that it was a real person doing this; it felt like a fictional situation. Now it dawns on me that someone –potentially someone I know

– isn't just going to great lengths to terrorise me, but might actually be enjoying doing it.

Chapter Twenty-Six

'Emma, I'd like you to meet James.'

Simon beams at James, who's standing next to him, looking slightly bemused. I try to forget the fact that James and I met for the first time months ago, when I let myself into Simon's flat and walked in on them in a compromising position. I've spent plenty of time with Simon and James since, and the specific details of that initial meeting are never actually discussed, yet Simon seems intent on repeating this little charade every time the three of us meet up.

'You know James and I have seen each other on a number of occasions, Si.' I elbow him none too gently.

'Oh yeah, I forgot. You've seen more of James than most.' Simon giggles, and that sets us all off and I collapse on the sofa next to them both. It's Saturday afternoon and we're in the White Bear pub on the High Street in town.

'So what are we drinking?' I manage once I've regained my composure.

'Just coke today Hun.' Simon answers

'Good idea, Si. The first round's on me.'

As I walk toward the bar, I turn to look back over my shoulder and see Simon and James snuggled together, Simon's hand placed lovingly on James's knee. They look so happy and in love that I feel tears spring to my eyes and I swallow hard. It seems like everyone is finding happiness at the moment; everyone except me, that is. Sophie and Matt are getting serious. I know Sophie's trying to pretend that it's only causal between them for my sake, but I can tell she's falling hard. How ironic that Sophie should find love with Joe's brother just as things between Joe and I fall spectacularly apart.

A voice permeates my thoughts: 'What can I get you?'

I hadn't realised I'd made it to the bar.

'Um, three cokes, please.'

'Large?'

'Yes please.'

I take the drinks back to the table and seat myself next to Simon.

'Is there something you need to tell me?' Simon asks, taking hold of my hand, which I find a bit unnerving.

'I don't think so.' I pick up my glass and take a sip.

'So you don't want to tell me about the psycho letters you've received.'

I'm going to kill Sophie. Can't she keep anything to herself any more?

'Now don't be mad at Soph. She worries about you. Plus I have a right to know if my friend is in danger.'

'I'm not in any danger, Si. It's just a crazy note or two that's been put through my door.'

'Is that why the police were round at yours the other night?'

'Oh my God – can't I have any privacy!'

'No, not when you're my best friend and someone is trying to hurt you.'

'Simon, I'm fine, honestly. Nobody is trying to hurt me. Someone's simply playing a stupid game to frighten me.'

'But who would do that?'

I bite my lip, thinking about this for a second.

'That's the really scary bit, Simon. I've no idea.'

'Do you want me to come and stay with you so you're not on your own? James wouldn't mind, would you?' Simon glances over at James.

'Of course not.' James smiles kindly. 'We want to make sure you're safe, Emma.'

'Thanks, both of you. That's kind, and I really appreciate it. But honestly, Simon, I don't want you confronting some potential nutcase.'

'Why? You don't think I can be scary too? I can be scary if needed. I can protect you.'

'I know that.' I press my lips together to hide the laugh that's building. For some reason, the image of Simon dressed as a ninja has popped into my mind and it's incredibly funny.

'You don't think I have it in me, do you? But let me tell you, I can be fierce.'

Simon has such a serious expression on his face. I glance at James and see he's trying not to laugh too, but as our eyes meet he falters. Then I start laughing so hard that my shoulders are heaving and tears are streaming down my face. James is in hysterics too, and Simon just looks at us both, bewildered.

'Honestly, you too,' he huffs. 'A guy could be seriously insulted.'

'I'm so sorry, Simon,' I manage between gulps of air. 'I really don't mean to insult you.'

I've never thought of Simon as the strong protector type. My drinking buddy with a sympathetic ear, yes, and someone who'll always tell me the truth, but if it's protection I need then my money would be on Sophie. That girl has a mean right hook.

As the three of us leave the bar an hour later, my mobile phone rings incessantly in my bag.

'Wait a minute, Si,' I call as I stop to locate the phone in the depths of my handbag and Simon and James stroll on ahead of me then stop as they realise I'm lagging behind. I see Mum's number flashing on the screen and my heart sinks a little. I've been dodging her calls since the episode the other week where she flew thousands of miles around the world to find me wallowing, unkempt, in my bed.

'Hi, Mum,' I say brightly into the receiver.

'Oh, you've deigned to answer my call now, have you?'

I ignore her sarcasm. 'How are you?'

'I'm very well, darling, which is a good thing seeing as you haven't taken my call the last three times I've rung you.'

I cringe. 'Yeah, sorry about that. I've been...busy.'

'Actually busy I hope, Emma, and not busy lying in bed and ignoring work.'

'No, Mum. I've been going to work. In fact I'm feeling much better about things.'

'That's great, Emma. Now, have you thought about your plans for Christmas?'

'Christmas? As in, like, two months away?'

'Yes.'

'Um, no.'

'Well, we need to decide what we're doing, whether you're coming here to see me or I'm coming to you.'

'Coming to me?'

'Yes, Emma, I'd like to see my only daughter at Christmas.'

'Of course, Mum.' I wave to Simon, who's beckoning to me from where he and James are standing shivering. 'I really have to go, Mum. Simon's waiting for me.'

'But you'll think about Christmas.'

'Yes.'

'Okay then, enjoy yourself with Simon and we'll speak next week.'

'Bye, Mum.'

I end the call and stare at the phone. Christmas? The realisation hits me: I'm going to be alone at Christmas with no significant other to share it with...My heart sinks. Great – I was just starting to feel better about things.

Chapter Twenty-Seven

I'm looking forward to Sophie coming over tonight; I'm ready for a good gossip. It finally feels like I've turned a corner. I'm on top of my studies and getting good grades. Even work has become much more tolerable. Julia Bamford has taken to flitting between our shop and the one in London where her aunt, and the business owner, Marissa Bamford spends most of her time, so Jenny and I get on with running the shop on our own, which works pretty well; in fact, we're a lot more productive without being constantly on edge for fear of being reprimanded for some minute offence such as not putting the scissors away. And, even better, no more creepy letters have landed on my doormat.

I take the chilled Sauvignon Blanc from my fridge and pour two glasses. Sophie will be here in a minute so I might as well have a sip. Mmm. There's nothing quite like the first taste of alcohol on a Friday night, signalling the start of the weekend.

By the time the intercom buzzes I'm halfway through my glass of wine and starting to feel quite merry as the alcohol takes effect on my empty stomach. Oops. I hope Sophie's brought a bottle or we'll have to go down to the off licence again. Up until a few weeks ago that was becoming too much of a regular occurrence. I had to start walking to the shop five streets away and alternating between the two, as the frowns of disapproval from the shop assistant were becoming far too frequent. Which is quite hypocritical really: it's their job to sell alcohol to people so they shouldn't judge repeat customers. It's rude and…whoops. The intercom buzzes more persistently and I reach for the handset.

'Sorry,' I call into it, pressing the door release button.

'Hey, Soph.' I thrust a glass of wine at her as the front door opens.

'I'm late,' she states, taking the glass from me and closing the door behind her.

'No, you're not. I thought we said seven?'

'No. No. Not that kind of late.'

'What are you going on about?' I walk through to the living room and flop down on the sofa. 'Sit down and have a drink.'

Sophie lowers herself onto the sofa next to me and eyes the glass of wine in her hand, but she makes no attempt to put it anywhere near her mouth.

'Holy shit, Sophie!' I take a large gulp of my own wine. 'You're pregnant?!'

She blanches. 'Yes. No. Maybe.'

I stare at her, dumbfounded, and then realise that this probably isn't the reaction she needs from me in this time of crisis but I've never been able to hide my emotions from Sophie.

'Okay, okay, let's just calm down a little,' I suggest in an even tone,

'Calm down?' Sophie practically shrieks.

I cringe. 'I said a little.'

This is worse than I thought. Usually Sophie is the epitome of calm, even when faced with the most trying of situations. If she's flipping out then this is real. She might actually be pregnant.

Sophie goes to take a drink but stops herself as the glass of wine meets her lips. She thrusts the glass at me. 'Take this away from me, please.'

I take it from her gratefully. I think I'll need the extra wine myself at this rate.

'How late are you?' I ask tentatively.

'Two weeks.'

'I don't understand, Sophie. How could this happen?'

'Do you want me to draw you a diagram?' Her voice is still slightly out of control, bordering on unhinged.

'No, of course not. I know how this happens. I mean, how could this happen to you? Didn't you use protection?'

'I'm not an idiot, Emma.'

'I know that, but people can get...caught up in the moment.'

'Well, we didn't get caught up in the moment. I mean, we did, but we used protection. This shouldn't be happening.'

'Alright. I get it. You haven't been irresponsible, but sometimes a person does everything they're supposed to do, protection wise, and for whatever reason something doesn't work.' I'm rambling nervously, and Sophie glares at me.

Okay, moving swiftly on. 'Have you done a test?' I try to keep the anxiety from my voice, but two weeks is quite a long time.

Sophie pulls a paper bag from her handbag and puts it on the coffee table in front of us. 'I'm scared, Emma,' she whispers as a tear slips silently down her cheek.

'I know you are.' I pull her into a hug. 'But you need to do the test to make sure. You could be worrying about nothing. I'll be right here with you, okay?'

She nods solemnly.

'Go and do it now and get it over with, and then we'll at least know what we're dealing with, if anything.'

Sophie takes the paper bag and heads towards the bathroom. She hovers at the door and glances back at me hesitantly.

'Go into the bathroom, wee on the stick and come back out,' I state simply. 'We'll wait for the result together.'

Sophie bites her lip.

'I'm right here, Sophie.'

As she closes the bathroom door behind her, I down the contents of my wine glass and Sophie's too, trying to calm the leaping of my heart. Jesus Christ. What if she is pregnant? What if Sophie is pregnant with the love child of Matt, Joe's brother? God, this is a hideous situation – from a completely self-centred point of view, I realise. It was bad enough when I was forced to accept the reality of Sophie and Matt dating, but a baby? Oh no – Sophie will ask me to be godmother, and what if Joe's the godfather? We'll be irreversibly linked for life through Sophie and Matt's child.

Why…why would this happen…?

I'm a horrible, selfish person. Sophie might be carrying a child that wasn't exactly planned, and I'm more concerned about how this will cock up my own life, not hers.

I hear the creak of the bathroom door opening. As Sophie makes her way back to the lounge, I exhale deeply, trying to remain composed.

She appears in the doorway, her face milky white, and places the paper bag on the coffee table with the plastic stick staring at us. Neither of us speak; we both look at the stick with trepidation, awaiting confirmation of Sophie's fate.

In all honesty I've no idea what I'm looking for; I forgot to ask whether one blue line or two means she's pregnant. Now doesn't seem the time to start asking questions, so I remain focussed on the stick, trying to ignore the fact that Sophie's wee is almost in contact with my coffee table. I have antibacterial spray, it's fine…

Suddenly Sophie lurches forward, grabs the stick and bursts into tears. Oh no, this can't be good.

'Soph, Sophie, don't cry.' I put my arms around her heaving shoulders. 'We'll work it out, I promise.'

'No, no, it's alright. It's negative. I'm not pregnant.'

'Oh, thank God for that…um, I mean that's good, right?'

'Yes, yes, these are tears of relief. I've only been seeing Matt for a few months. I'm not even sure how serious we are. It's definitely not the right time to be having a baby together. I don't even know if he wants children.'

'Of course, of course.'

I pat Sophie's head in a motherly fashion, not knowing what else to do under these alien circumstances. Having a baby seems far too grown-up and responsible (although I admit an unplanned pregnancy might not be perceived as entirely responsible). Surely we're not old enough or mature enough to be bringing children into the world. I can barely look after myself sometimes, without having to keep another small human being alive as well. I certainly don't feel responsible enough for that; in fact, most days I still feel like I'm eighteen not thirty-three.

'Can you get me a drink now, please?' Sophie sits upright and I glance at the two empty wine glasses on the table. Whoops!

Sophie giggles at me, her whole demeanour now relaxed. 'I must have given you quite a scare.'

'You could say that.'

'Me too.' She exhales.

'I have vodka,' I offer.

'Sounds good to me.'

An hour later and we're both starting to feel the relaxing effects of the vodka. It seems to have taken more of an impact following the spike of adrenaline.

'Do you see yourself having children?' I ask, propping myself back up to a seated position after being somewhat slumped in the corner of the sofa. Is my brain playing tricks on me, or did I just slur my words a bit? So much for reducing my alcohol intake! It's not my fault though that there always seems to be some catastrophe of epic proportions to deal with.

'Um, yes, um, definitely. I think,' Sophie slurs back.

'You don't sound convinced.' I reach forward and pick up the half-empty vodka bottle from the coffee table and slosh another measure into each of our glasses, then top them up with a dash of tonic.

'Well, it's a very big decision. I like the idea of it in principle, but the reality scares me shitless.'

'I agree.'

'Really? I was never sure whether you actually wanted children. I mean, I know you've always said you thought you would but...'

'What? I don't seem to be the maternal type?' I swing my glass of vodka to my lips and take a sip.

'Of course not.' Sophie gulps from her own glass. 'Did you and Joe talk about having kids?'

Ouch. It hurts, it physically hurts, to think back to the conversations we had about our happy married life together.

'Yes, yes we did.'

I hear my voice break a little and I down the remaining vodka. I should have stopped drinking about three shots of vodka ago. I'm drunk, very drunk, but I don't care. It's a week night and there's work in the morning but I'll have to deal with that, well, in the morning.

Three weeks later, it seems like the god of relationships has decided to hunt me down and maim me. Not kill me outright, which would be the humane thing to do, but let me die a slow and painful death while I reflect on my self-inflicted misery at the failure of my relationship.

Okay, so that might be a bit melodramatic, but still. Upon being summoned to brunch with Simon and James, I find myself in Henry's at eleven thirty on Saturday morning and presented with Simon as excitable as I've ever seen him, bouncing at the table like a puppy.

'Hey, Emma.' He greets me with a huge bear hug that nearly topples me over completely.

'Hi Simon, James.' I smile across the table once I've extracted myself from Simon's grip. 'What's going on?'

'Ah, everyone's here now.'

I turn around to see Sophie and Matt walking through the door and heading over to our table.

'I didn't know you were going to be here.' Sophie hugs me too.

'I wanted you both here,' Simon announces as we all sit down around the large wooden table. 'I wanted my two best girlfriends to be the first to know.' He grasps James's hand and squeezes it tightly as we all wait with anticipation. 'Last night...' He exhales. 'Last night, James asked me to marry him and I said yes.'

'You're engaged!' Sophie squeals, jumping up. She launches herself at Simon first and then James, squishing them into tight embraces.

I watch the scene before me unfold and it takes my brain a second to catch up. I'm torn between two thoughts. The first: this is really good for Simon. He's struggled with monogamy for a long time and James has been his first long-term partner. It's sweet that they've found each other and are totally in the same place. The second: even my gay friend is getting married before me.

I sense someone's eyes on me and as I glance sideways. Matt is watching me and, as though reading my thoughts, he half-smiles with what I take to be pity. Even he's aware of my pathetic emotional state; although we're very careful when in each other's company not to talk about the elephant in the room – Joe. But this isn't the time for self-indulgence. I'm a better friend than that. So I swallow down my thoughts and plaster a huge grin on my face.

'Congratulations.' I fling my arms around Simon. 'I'm so pleased for you both'. And I am, I really am.

'Thanks, honey.' Simon kisses my cheek. 'I can't actually believe that I'm getting married.'

'It's fantastic, but I can. I knew you'd meet Mr Right eventually.'

Chapter Twenty-Eight

'Here's to your last week as a single man.' I raise my glass of vodka and tonic and clink it against Simon's. It's Friday night and we're curled up on my sofa.

'Who'd have thought it, babe? I thought I was destined to be alone, lurching from one-night stand to one-night stand for eternity, or at least until I could no longer get it up.'

'Simon!' I jab him on the arm but I can't help laughing at his words. 'You and me both, though.'

'Cheeky cow!' He whacks my arm and I feign hurt.

'I'm only kidding, Si. I always knew you'd find Mr Right one day. You just made sure that you enjoyed the hunt first.'

'That's true. I've had a good run at being commitment free.'

'A very good run.' I drink the last of my vodka. 'Refill?'

'Okay.' Simon empties his glass. 'But don't let me get too drunk tonight. I want to enjoy my last weekend as a single man without a raging hangover. I'll be drinking enough at my wedding – once the ceremony is over, of course.'

'Of course.'

'And I need you coherent enough on the day to make your speech. I don't want you slurring your words while you tell everyone how amazing I am.'

'You've clearly not read my speech.'

'Emma Louise Story, you'd better be only saying nice things about me. No drunken tales about catching me and James in a compromising position, none of that.'

'Spoilsport!'

'My parents will be in the room!'

'Fair point.' I wouldn't want my parents to receive a documentary of the life I shield them from.

'Then we need to get you sorted.'

'Get me sorted?' I walk over to the fridge and take out more tonic and vodka, and refill our glasses with generous measures.

'You know, find you your Mr Right.'

Oh.

I glug my vodka.

'I found my Mr Right, Si, and then I chased him away.'

'You mean Joe?'

'Yes, I mean Joe.' I sigh heavily. 'And then Sophie fell head over heels for his brother, which acts as a constant reminder of the love I lost – or systematically destroyed with my emotional crap.'

'Oh, Em.' Simon stands up and pulls me into a hug. 'Does it really bother you that Sophie's dating Matt?'

'Yes…No…'

'I'm not judging. I can totally understand what a mixed-up scenario this is.'

'On one hand, I want Sophie to be happy. I love Sophie, and she deserves a good man. But…it's…oh, you couldn't make this up! Of all the guys in the world, she ends up in love with Joe's brother. But Matt's a lovely guy, and he and Sophie are so cute together.'

'It's pretty bad luck for you, though.'

'But then I think about it, and maybe the pool of single, eligible men in their thirties is actually smaller than we'd all like. If not, I wouldn't still be single.'

'Is that so?'

'No, that's a lie. I'm not looking for a relationship. I'm not ready.'

'I don't know, babe. It's been a while since you and Joe broke up.'

'I'm not ready.'

'Okay.'

I drink the rest of my vodka and tonic and decide that's enough for tonight. I don't want to end up drunk and over-emotional.

'You're still in love with Joe, aren't you?'

'No.' I shake my head defiantly, starting to feel slightly tipsy from the vodka. 'Of course there are still feelings there, a mixture of feelings. But that's normal, isn't it, when people break up? You feel conflicted.'

'I guess so.'

'So…' I'm keen to get off the subject of my lingering feelings for Joe. 'Are you prepared for a committed, monogamous relationship, Si?' I glance at my watch. 'Because you've only got about six days and twelve hours to change your mind.'

'No, Em babe, I won't be changing my mind. I've found what I've been looking for in James, and he makes me happier than I ever thought I would be.'

I gulp down the mountain of emotion that's filling my chest, realising what an empty void I've created in my life.

'I'm so excited, honey. I don't think I'll be able sleep the night before,'

Simon says into the darkness a while later as we snuggle under the quilt in my double bed.

'I really am happy for you, Simon. Although I'm a bit nervous about my speech.'

'Don't be, Em. You'll be great.'

'No, I won't – I'll be like Bridget Jones, saying totally random crap and going completely off point. But I'll do it anyway, because I love you.'

'I love you too, Em.'

'Goodnight, Si.'

'Goodnight.'

Within moments I find myself listening to the soft muffled snores of Simon deep in sleep. But the thought of the lack of marriage on my horizon, or of any meaningful relationship at all, goes round and round in my head like a stuck record, repeating my failure, and keeping me wide awake for a good few hours.

Along with having a traditional stag do, Sophie and I have convinced Simon to have what we've christened a "hag", which is basically Simon, Sophie and I going out and getting absolutely sloshed to celebrate his upcoming nuptials. This seemed like such a good idea at the planning stage, but none of us took into account the fact that we haven't been out just the three of us for ages, so we're a bit overexcited.

We spend a long time reminiscing about the numerous times in our younger years that we had top nights out together, most of which we couldn't remember the following morning. But they're the best ones, right?

Now we're all in our thirties, our tolerance to alcohol appears to have dimmed, and far too many shots of multi-coloured concoctions of who-knows-what alcohol take their toll. Sophie is throwing out some moves on the dance floor that are unrecognisable and I'm propping myself up on a high table, unable to move through fear of collapsing into a drunken mess on the floor. I've no idea where Simon is; the last time I saw him, he was chasing some unfortunate boy around the dance floor, but now the sea of bodies in front of me has become a blur.

It's only one a.m. Well, I think it's one a.m. That's an educated guess – in fact, a befuddled guess, as my eyes will no longer focus enough for me to tell the time on my watch.

'Water?' I shout across at Sophie when I finally catch her eye.

'Water is for wimps.'

Simon appears from nowhere at my side and flings his arm around me, knocking me off my perch so that I have to cling to him for dear life.

'Let's have more shots!' he declares.

I falter for a moment, before shoving the sensible part of my conscience to one side.

'Okay, one more round should be alright. I'll grab Sophie.'

Simon moves away and I lurch and grab the table again for support. Once stabilised, I wave to Sophie.

'Did you see that cute guy I was dancing with?' she shouts at me as she zigzags off the dance floor, ricocheting off a couple of innocent revellers.

'Cute guy? Don't you have a boyfriend?'

'It was only dancing,' she protests. 'Where's Simon?'

'Gone to get another round.' I nod towards the bar, but instantly realise my error as the room sloshes from side to side.

'Great. I need another drink. All that dancing's made me really hot.'

'Hmm. I think I've had enough alcohol.' The truth is that I'd had enough a few hours ago. I've now reached the "had far too much to drink and is insanely drunk" level of incapacity. Now, my main concern is how I'm going to get myself to the taxi rank and home in one piece without taking this table with me as a crutch.

Chapter Twenty-Nine

I smell bacon.

That's good.

Or is it? My stomach does a weird little flip.

'Emma?' I hear Sophie's croaky voice from somewhere in the near vicinity and I open my mouth to respond, but no sound comes out. My throat is too dry to function properly and it feels like it's stuffed full of cotton wool.

'Emma? Are we still alive?…I smell bacon.'

'Sophie?' I push myself up to a partially seated position, swallowing repeatedly to get some moisture back to my vocal cords, and note the rolled-up quilt next to me with dark flowing curls poking out of one end.

'How much did we drink last night?' the quilt mumbles.

'Enough to mean that we probably shouldn't be alive.' I exhale, trying to get the room to come into focus.

'Is Simon cooking?'

I glance around the room and realise we're on the floor of the spare room in Simon's flat. I breathe a sigh of relief. We are, in fact, still alive, and if we're in Simon's flat then that means food and caffeine. Say whatever you want about Simon's carefree lifestyle, but the guy does his weekly food shop on a regimented basis.

At that moment the bedroom door creaks open and Simon appears, looking disturbingly spritely for someone who must have drunk the same quantity as me last night.

'Are you two getting up and back into the land of the living?' he chastises gently. 'I made breakfast.'

'Have I told you how much I love you, Si?' I squint at him through my one fully open eye.

'Come on, before it goes cold.'

Three bites into my huge bacon sandwich and I'm starting to feel marginally human again. Although trying not to giggle is proving difficult, as I sit opposite Sophie at Simon's breakfast bar. For once, Sophie's hair is in worse shape than mine. Her dark curls have taken on an excitable form and look like they're trying desperately to escape as they twist in random directions.

'I haven't had so much fun in ages.' Simon grins and takes a mouthful of coffee.

'I don't remember much after getting into that nightclub.' Sophie cringes, rubbing at her temples.

'You were dancing,' I say between mouthfuls.

'Oh yeah, dancing.' She picks at the crumbs on her plate.

'With a hot young man, if I remember correctly…Although given the number of shots we drank, I might have imagined that completely; he could have been a really unattractive old man!' I supress a smile as Sophie glares at me.

'Either way' – she waves her hand dismissively – 'let's not mention any of that, or how insanely drunk I was, to Matt. Deal?'

'You were only having a good time, Soph.' Simon clears our plates and takes them to the sink. 'That's allowed, you know.'

'I know, and I hold you entirely to blame for my inebriated state, Simon. You always were a bad influence on me,' Sophie says jokingly.

'Well, that's just charming, isn't it? Always blaming me, aren't you? You are a grown up, Sophie; you can say no.'

I nod in agreement, although I've never known anyone be able to say no to Simon, especially where alcohol's involved.

'So what's everyone doing later?' Simon asks, topping up our coffee mugs.

'I'm going home to die in my own bed.' Sophie slurps at her replenished coffee.

'How come you're so annoyingly unaffected by a hangover Simon?' I ask, in awe of his ability to consume more shots than anyone I know and then be able to function enough to not only fry bacon but do it with a smile on his face.

'What can I say, Em? Years of practice. It takes a lot of effort to make your body immune to the effects of alcohol.'

I shouldn't have asked.

'Unfortunately I have a study date with Carly later. I didn't really think that through properly. Although in my defence I didn't intend to drink so much last night. I'm not convinced I'll be able to even read the textbook, let alone write anything coherent.

Once I make it home and into my own shower, I start to feel much better, if still a little tired from our evening's exertions. By the time Carly arrives at my flat to start studying, I'm practically back to my normal self (admittedly aided by what feels like three thousand cups of coffee, so I'm probably on a major caffeine high and will collapse at some point when my coffee-induced momentum crashes).

'Do you want a drink?' I ask as Carly takes a seat at my small kitchen table.

'I'll have a coffee, thanks.'

Oh well, I might as well join her. One more coffee won't hurt.

'Did you do anything last night?' I ask as I fill the kettle and start preparing cups.

'Not much. I spent the evening with my sister and her kids, as her husband was out for the night. Her kids are great. Charlie is four and Hannah's two. She's so cute, but they're exhausting. I don't know how my sister does it.'

'I don't know how anybody does it. How do people have children and still manage to function in life – have a job, look after the house, make sure everybody is clothed and fed? I mean, that's a lot of pressure for one person to take on.' I clamp my mouth shut, realising I'm rambling either due to my caffeine overload or because I'm still drunk, which is a distinct possibility.

Carly frowns at me. 'Are you okay, Emma?'

'I'm fine.' I turn away from her to finish making the coffees. 'I'm a little tired, that's all.'

'Did you have a late night?'

Um…a vision of me clinging helplessly to the table in the nightclub flashes before my eyes.

'Yes, we had a few drinks in advance of my friend Simon's upcoming wedding.'

I dismiss the idea of going into any further details, either of my drunkenness or the fact that Simon is marrying another man. Neither are of any significance to Carly.

'I didn't see Tom this week at college. Did you?'

'No, I don't think I did.'

Carly clearly still has it bad for Tom, but hasn't mustered up the courage to ask him out on a second date yet (if the first drink together was actually a date).

'Why haven't you asked him out again?' I hand Carly a mug of coffee.

'I don't know.' Carly takes a sip. 'He might say no.'

'He might also say yes. What's happened to your confidence all of a sudden? You were going to ask him to go out with you again after you had a drink together on your own.'

'I don't know. I thought about it, and maybe he was just being friendly. It wasn't like a proper date or anything. There was no touching or kissing.'

'Did you feel a connection with him?'

'I don't know.'

'Well, you're not going to find out by not seeing him again.'

'You're right.' Carly looks defiant. 'I don't know why I'm not confident. I'm a perfectly nice person, so why wouldn't he want to go out with me?'

'Exactly. You need to go for it,' I state with a conviction that I don't hold in regards to my own actions. I'm gun shy, battle weary and too scared to put myself out there again. I don't feel ready to even think about dating someone else. The way I feel right now, I'm not sure I ever will be ready.

'What about you?' Carly's voice brings me back into the room.

'What about me?'

'Is there anyone that you like?'

'Oh…um…no.'

'Still hung up on that guy you were going to marry?' She looks at me with sympathy.

'Joe? No…it's not that,' I lie. 'I'm over him. I haven't found anyone I'm interested in, that's all.'

I cough to clear my throat; saying those words "I'm over him" caused it to constrict. What is it about Joe Stark that I can't get over? Why does it still hurt to think about what we had? Why does the mere mention of his name make my heart shudder?

'This isn't getting our assignment done.' I reach for my textbook, desperately needing to change the subject before I slip back into depression and slide under my duvet for eternity.

Chapter Thirty

Before I know it, the next week has flown by, and as the annoying bleeping of my alarm clock interrupts my somewhat disturbed sleep, the realisation that Simon and James's wedding day has finally arrived permeates my groggy mind.

Rubbing my eyes, I force myself into a seated position and sit in my bed for a moment, contemplating the day ahead. A grey cloud has hovered over me for the last few days and I've been unable to shake it off. It isn't that I'm not happy for Simon; of course I am – he's one of my best friends and I wish him only happiness. But it's a wedding, and the nagging feeling that I got so close to having one of those myself won't leave me in peace. But it wasn't meant to be; that ship has sailed, and my dream of a "happy ever after" seems to get further and further away each day.

I swallow down the lump of emotion that's formed and push back the threat of tears. This is Simon's day and I owe it to him to keep it together, to do my duty as his best friend, and to make sure that he and James have a day they won't forget.

Come on, Emma. This is no time to be feeling sorry for yourself.

Right. I fling the covers back and swing my legs out of the bed. I need a hot shower, caffeine and food, in that order.

Half an hour later, I'm failing at multitasking – striding around the flat with a mug of coffee in one hand and my curling tongues twisted through my hair in the other, already having suffered three minor burns to my head. The end result will be worth it, though, I try to convince myself as I glance at the pale gold dress that's hanging on the front of my wardrobe. It's beautiful and classy and it fits my body like a glove. Admittedly it cost more than I'd usually spend on a dress, or three month's rent for that matter, but it's important to look your best at weddings. You never know who you might meet. Who am I kidding? This is Simon and James's wedding – I'll be lucky if there's a straight guy in the whole building!

I hear my mobile phone ringing and see Sophie's number flashing on the screen, indicating that she's in the taxi outside my flat, waiting for me to appear. Damn it! I discard the coffee mug and quickly pull on the gold dress. I take one last look in the mirror before spraying most of the contents of the hairspray bottle in a toxic cloud, trying to tame the one curl that seems intent on springing out of place. I dowse my head one final time in sticky lacquer, praying that no one lights up a cigarette within a two-metre radius of me or we're going to be in some serious trouble.

After forcing my feet into very pretty but potentially uncomfortable new shoes, I grab my clutch bag and keys and head out the door. As I cling to the handrail making my way down the stairs and out of the building I silently pray that, having forgotten to wear these shoes in around the flat prior to today, they prove to be as comfortable as they are gorgeous.

'I know, I know, I'm late,' I offer as an apology as I climb into the taxi. 'Please tell me that you remembered the gift. Oh!'

I take in the huge box strapped into the centre of the car. We clubbed together to get Simon and James this ridiculous statue thing that Simon saw ages ago while we were out shopping. He whinged for a whole week afterwards that he couldn't afford it. Personally I think it looks like two naked bodies made out of charcoal entwined together (maybe that's the point – I don't know), but Simon loved it and that's all that counts. Hopefully he'll be very happy that he now has it to display in his flat. It weighs a tonne, though, so God know what we'll do with it when we reach the hotel and have to get it back out of the taxi. More importantly how on earth did Sophie get it into the car in the first place?

'Of course I remembered the gift.' Sophie chuckles, leaning around the box so she can see me. She looks impossibly glamourous, her dark curls flowing softly past her shoulders and touching the top of her strapless crimson dress.

'You look amazing,' I say in awe as I take in her nails and lip gloss, which match her dress perfectly. I reach up and fiddle with a wayward curl. It's practically rock solid under my touch, so thankfully my curls should stay intact for the whole day. At times like this I envy Sophie's natural ringlets.

'You look lovely too.' She beams. 'I'm so excited about today.'

'Yeah, me too.' I smile back, and I'm starting to get into the wedding mood. 'One question, though.'

'Yes?'

'How on earth did you get that three-foot statue into this car in what you're wearing?'

'I had Maxwell's help.' Sophie nods towards the driver, and I take in his huge, bulky frame and giant sausage-shaped arms.

'Well, he's going to have to assist at our destination too, I'm afraid. There's no way I can carry that thing in these heels.'

Once we arrive at the hotel, which resembles a stately home, Maxwell very kindly carries the huge statue into the hotel reception for us, where Sophie and I immediately abandon it with a rather confused-looking porter.

'Shall we grab a drink? I think a glass of Prosecco is in order.' Sophie starts teetering off to my right, pointing at a sign indicating the bar.

'Soph.' I hurry after her with difficulty; I can see I'm going to regret these shoes by the end of the night. 'Don't we have to greet people, or find Simon, or do something less flippant that get a drink at the bar?'

'Nope.' Sophie looks at me with a wicked glint in her eyes.

'What do you mean "nope"?'

'I know what you're like – you know, with being ready on time.'

'I don't know what you mean,' I protest, but I know exactly what Sophie means. I'm usually running out of the door fifteen minutes behind my intended time of departure. A flashback of this morning's hair-curling/multitasking disaster goes through my mind, but I'm not quite ready to give Sophie the satisfaction of my agreement. 'We're here before most people, by the look of things.' I glance around to see only a few people dressed for a wedding milling around the bar.

'I know. That's because I ordered the taxi for half an hour before we actually needed it.'

What?

'In case you were…running late.' Sophie tries and fails to supress a smile.

How rude!

'Well…I…um.'

Oh, who am I kidding? I have no right to be outraged at this sneaky tactic. If Sophie hadn't done that then there's every chance we wouldn't have arrived in a calm manner with time to spare. In fact, there's a good possibility that I'd have been running down the aisle behind Simon instead of standing at the front in advance of his arrival.

'Shall we get a drink then?' Sophie giggles.

'Yes.' I try to feign hurt feelings, but find myself giggling too. 'You know what, Sophie? A girl could take offence.'

'You love me really.' She turns to the barman. 'Two glasses of Prosecco, please.'

'Make that three,' I amend. 'I think we should go and find Simon. Who knows what state of hideousness he's got himself into this morning.'

'Good shout.' Sophie takes the glasses presented on the bar and hands them to me before paying the barman. 'Right, let's find Simon.'

As we head up the huge staircase (while I try desperately to balance in three-inch heels and carry the drinks without spilling any), I catch sight of Simon's dad hovering outside a closed wooden door.

'Hello, Mr Carter.' He's very distinguished in his black-tie suit, not appearing a day over forty-five though I know he passed that age years ago.

'Hello, Emma dear. How are you?' He kisses me on the cheek. 'You look fantastic.'

'Thank you.'

'Will you please call me David?'

'Of course.' I smile. He's been asking me to call him by his first name for years, yet somehow it doesn't feel polite.

'And Sophie, you look stunning too.'

'Where's Simon?' I ask. 'How's he doing?'

'He's in there.' Mr Carter points to the room behind him. 'And so far, so good.'

'Are we okay to go in?'

'I'm sure Simon will be pleased to see you both.'

As Mr Carter heads downstairs, I knock gently on the door.

I hear Simon's muffled voice: 'Come in.'

Sophie has to lean across me to open the door, as I realise I don't have a spare hand. I need to unload one of these Proseccos.

'Hey, Em.' Simon turns to face us as Sophie and I walk in the room. 'Wow, honey, you scrub up alright.'

'Always a charmer, Si, and here I am bringing you some bubbles. On that note I might drink them myself.'

'Come here.' He takes my face in his hand and kisses me affectionately on the cheek. 'You look gorgeous, Emma. I couldn't have asked for a prettier "best woman".'

'That's more like it.' I hand him a glass.

'You look very handsome.' Sophie squeezes Simon's hand. 'Black tie really suits you.'

'I agree.' Simon does look good in a suit. He always has.

'I'll leave you and Emma to it and go and check whether Matt's arrived.'

'How come you didn't arrive together?'

'We had an additional passenger.' Sophie winks at me. Ah yes, the huge statue!

'Oh.' Simon looks confused.

'See you in a bit.' Sophie leaves the room and closes the door behind her.

'So, how are you doing?' I ask Simon the minute we're alone.

'I'm absolutely fine.' He takes a drink of Prosecco and I do the same.

'Really?' I was expecting hysterical panic and hissy fits.

'Really. I can't wait to marry James. I finally made it, honey. I found my Mr Right, and in about an hour he's going to be my Mr Forever.'

'Oh, Simon.' I gulp the alcohol and blink back tears rapidly. 'You're all grown up.'

'Who'd have thought it?' He nudges me softly.

'Well, given your past behaviour, certainly not me,' I joke. 'No, seriously, Simon, I'm so happy for you and so proud of you.'

'Thanks for being such a great friend, Em. I love you.'

'I love you too, and the friendship goes both ways. You're always there for me when I need you, and that's been really tested over the last year or so.'

'Come here.' Simon pulls me into a hug. 'Let's get all this mushy stuff out of the way now. I don't want you getting all emotional standing next to me while I say my vows, or I'll never make it through them.'

As "best woman" I stand proudly at the front of the room across from the registrar, who gives me a warm, crooked grin. Then the first chime of music sends an immediate hush over the guests and a knot twists nervously in my stomach as I turn to see Simon walking down the aisle with his mum and dad. It's surreal, but in an amazingly good way. I'm so happy for Simon that he's found happiness with James. Simon is beaming as he strides confidently down the aisle without a hint of nervousness.

As Simon takes his place beside me, I reach for his hand and give it a squeeze and he grips my hand back. The music continues softly as James enters the room, also flanked by his parents, and the melody continues until James is standing on Simon's right, and then it slowly fades out as the registrar signals for the ceremony to begin.

'Welcome to everyone.' He smiles broadly at the guests. 'Today we're here to celebrate the love that Simon and James share.'

I glance up at Simon and note that he's glowing. I don't think I've ever seen him so happy, and that's when I realise: this is what love is. When you're standing side by side, committing to a future together. Where you're so in love that you want to share the feelings of love and happiness with those dearest to you. When it doesn't matter whether it's "boy meets girl" or "boy meets other boy"; it's just love, plain and simple. And I had this once too, but I threw it all away.

As Simon begins to speak the vows he's written himself, written and rewritten over the last week or two without letting any of us have a sneaky peek, I feel overcome with emotion. I swallow the huge lump in my throat and I listen, in awe, to Simon as he declares his love for James in front of us all.

'I feel so lucky to have found James, and for him to have accepted and loved me for who I am.' Simon clears his throat, and two single tears slip silently down each of my cheeks. I brush them quickly away, forcing back the tidal wave I know is waiting to be released.

Chapter Thirty-One

'Mmm…keep kissing there. That feels good.'

His warm, soft lips plant kisses down my neck and across my chest, causing every nerve ending in my body to become hyper-sensitive. My heart is pounding in my chest and my breath is coming in short, sharp gasps. I'm incredibly turned on.

I run my hands down his strong, muscular back and pull him closer to me, feeling him harden against my thigh. I need him to make love to me now. Thankfully he takes the hint, and as his lips find mine, his tongue gently pushing, in search of my own, he gently nudges my legs further apart. He slips inside me and I throw my head back in desire as my body melts and I start to lose my mind.

I sit bolt upright in bed and frantically scan the room.

Okay…that's new. I've not woken up all hot and bothered since, well, since so long ago that I can't even remember.

That was pretty hot. Hmm.

I exhale slowly. It's been a while since I've been with a guy. I haven't even looked at another man since Joe. He was the only one who ever led me to those dizzy heights, and I can't even imagine wanting anyone else to touch me like that, let alone letting them.

I climb out of bed feeling a little disorientated and clamber into the shower. My thoughts immediately drift back to my dream, and I can't help but wonder whether I'll ever meet anyone who can make me feel that again. A part of me thinks of course I will. We weren't put on this earth to be alone but I fear that our busy lifestyles prohibit us from bumping into potential boyfriends - plenty of eligible men are already taken, happy in relationships with wives and children. Now I've reached my thirties, it feels to me like the pool of potential partners is shrinking by the day, and the opportunities to meet people are limited solely to interaction by social media and online-dating websites.

Maybe I should join a dating site?

Knowing my luck, I'd meet Jack the Ripper's evil twin.

No, I can't join a site. Can I?

I turn the shower temperature to cool. It's an unusually warm autumn morning, causing the flat to be a little stuffy. I'm also feeling a little flushed from my unexpected dream and in need of dowsing in cold water.

Once suitably refreshed and revived, I leave the bathroom and head through to the kitchen, opening windows along the way and enjoying the soft breeze as it blows in. After pouring myself some orange juice, I stare out of the window at the park. It's still relatively early for a Saturday morning and people are strolling leisurely and basking in the unexpected sunshine.

I think I'll walk to the coffee shop to meet Sophie instead of driving this morning. It might be nice to enjoy some fresh air. I pull on some jeans and a t-shirt and apply my makeup. I have no idea what's gone wrong with my hair this morning – perhaps I should have washed it? I ponder trying to control a flicking-out bit with my hair straighteners but failing. Hindsight's a wonderful thing. Never mind, it's only Sophie I'm meeting, I conclude, and she's seen me looking much worse.

Okay, so walking was a bad idea, I realise about halfway into my journey. Yes, the warm, sunny weather is lovely, but the coffee shop is further away on foot than I thought (slight misjudgement given that I usually drive; apparently five minutes in the car doesn't equate to ten minutes on foot), so I quicken my pace from a stroll to a power walk. By the time I reach the glass door of Neptune's Coffee Bar, I'm bedraggled and sweat is pooling above my eyebrows and my lips, creating a moist moustache, and the heat feels like it's causing my hair to become fuzzier by the second.

As I push open the door and savour the welcoming smells of ground coffee beans and warm pastries, I hear my mobile phone bleep in my handbag. It's a text from Sophie: *Sorry – running a bit late. Will be there in ten mins xx*

Typical. I could have taken my time after all, instead of practically jogging here. Maybe I'll take a moment to pop to the ladies' toilet and touch up my makeup. I reach up idly with one hand and pat down my ever-increasing hair while I slip my mobile back into my handbag.

Oh crap…

As I glance up my gaze fixes on a familiar figure standing right in front of me. My eyes dart around wildly, but it's no use: there's no escaping this unfortunate situation. My ex-boyfriend, Chris, who dumped me so graciously over a posh meal, is two feet away from me, holding a takeaway coffee cup.

Why? Why would this happen to me when I'm looking the worst possible version of myself?

I don't know why I'm surprised to find myself in this situation. Although you hope that if you're unfortunate enough to bump into an ex-

143

boyfriend then the god of revenge will allow you to look your best, the reality is not so. Here I am, hot and sweaty and with giant hair.

'Hi, Chris,' I say nonchalantly in an attempt to dismiss my ridiculous appearance.

I swear I see the corners of his mouth twitch as he steps closer to me. 'Hi, Emma.'

'How are you?' I ask in an equally nonchalant tone.

'Great. And you?'

'Great,' I repeat like we're stuck in some naff sitcom with rubbish actors (sometimes I feel like I am the main character in a hideous soap opera where the most unbelievable, dire things all happen to the same girl). 'So, are you still seeing someone?'

Why? What made me ask that? I'm hopeless in uncomfortable social situations (this definitely qualifies), and I still haven't managed to train my brain to kick in before my mouth is let loose.

'Yes.' Chris smiles broadly, but it doesn't quite meet his eyes. 'We're very happy together. The wedding is coming up so we're really excited.'

'Good,' I lie. I don't particularly care whether Chris is happy or not, and I hadn't thought about the fact that he was engaged to that blond child for a while. Okay, so she's not actually a child, but she is very young.

'And how about you? Weren't you engaged to…um…' He waves the hand not holding the coffee around.

'Joe.' I clear my throat noisily, completely thrown by this. How would Chris know that I was engaged to Joe?

He nods. 'That's right.'

'Making the final wedding plans at the moment.' The words are out of my mouth before I realise it. It's not a little white lie, it's a big fat one. Joe and I aren't even on speaking terms, but I've no intention of allowing Chris to get the upper hand in this conversation.

'Anyway.' I make my tone dismissive. 'I must dash. I'm meeting Sophie.'

He opens his mouth to speak but I don't give him the chance. 'It was good to see you.' I force a fake smile as I stride past him, with as much confidence as I can muster in the circumstances, towards the toilets in the corner of the room.

I don't even bother to look back, and only allow myself to exhale once I'm safely confined to a toilet cubicle and the danger has passed. I lean against the door with my eyes closed. Did that really just happen?

I unlock the door and walk over to the row of sinks and look nervously at my reflection in the mirror. Even though no one ever looks good under a halogen bulb my fear is confirmed: I look worse than bad.

Dabbing my face with toilet paper seems to solve most of the excess moisture problem, and I quickly reapply face powder to mute the shine, followed by a sweep of pink lip gloss. As for my hair – I think it's a lost cause but I persist anyway, slapping it down with cold water and then sticking my head under the hand-dryer in an attempt to blast it into a normal shape. This seems to work, but I'm now hotter than ever.

I vacate the toilets and head back into the coffee shop just as Sophie rushes through the door. I catch her eye and she waves and then points at an empty table in the window. We both head over and she greets me with a hug.

'Hey, what's wrong?' she says into my still rather bouffant hair.

'Nothing's wrong,' I say quickly. 'Why would something be wrong?'

'Because I've know you forever and I recognise your "deer caught in the headlights" face.'

Oh. I didn't know I had one of those.

'I just bumped into Chris,' I say, slumping down onto one of the chairs.

'Oh, that's not good...is it?' Sophie's voice is hesitant.

'Does it look like it was good?' I scowl.

'I'll grab us some coffee.'

'And cake!' I call after her as Sophie heads to the counter.

Two minutes later she returns with large lattes and what I hope is lemon cake.

'So what did he look like?' Sophie hands me a plate of cake.

'He looked exactly the same,' I say flatly, 'only a lot smugger.'

'Smug?'

'He's still engaged to that young blond twiglet and apparently they're getting married soon.'

'Oh.' Sophie takes a bite of her cake before looking at me cautiously.

'What?' I shove a large chunk of sponge dowsed in icing into my mouth.

'Does it bother you that he's getting married?'

'Yes...no...well, yes, but not for the reason you think.'

'And what's that?'

'That I'm bothered because I still have feelings for him.'

'I didn't say that.'

'You didn't have to.'

'Okay, so it crossed my mind for, like, a second.'

'I wish I was still in a good place relationship wise, that's all.'

'Oh.' Sophie takes a drink of her coffee, seeming unsure of what to say to that.

'Chris knew that Joe and I were engaged.'

'How did he know that?'

'I have no idea.'

'So what did he say when you told him that you and Joe had broken up?'

'Are you insane? I didn't tell him that!'

'You told him that you and Joe are still together?' Sophie's eyebrows are dancing on her forehead.

'I may have alluded to that.' I shrug dismissively. 'It's bad enough that the god of shame saw fit to make me bump into Chris when I'm not looking my best, but –'

'You do look a little flushed.'

I ignore Sophie's comment and continue: 'But there's no way I was going to look pathetic and dumped in front of him too. It was a bit weird bumping into him. I haven't seen him since I shut the shop door on him after he turned up at my work to tell me he was getting married. I didn't expect to see him again.'

'I guess I can understand that.'

'And I walked.'

'I'm sorry?'

'That's why I look flushed. It's warm, and I walked here.'

Sophie giggles into her mug.

Charming. Like I never walk anywhere. Okay, maybe Sophie has a point.

'Right. Let's change the subject. I had a weird dream last night, well, this morning actually.' I stir my latte aimlessly and munch the last of my lemon cake.

'What kind of dream?' Sophie's raises her eyebrows.

'Um, well…um…I was kind of –'

'You had a sex dream.' Sophie puts her hand over her mouth in mock shock.

'Keep your voice down.' I glance around us, making sure the old guy sitting near the door and the barista serving coffee didn't hear that comment.

'Honestly, Emma, you're so reserved sometimes.'

'I'm not used to having dreams that are so…graphic, that's all.'

'Graphic? So what happened exactly?'

'I'm not doing details, Soph!'

'Alright. At least tell me who it was that was rocking your world.'

'That's the weird part. I don't know. I didn't see his face.'

'Okay.'

'But he had a smoking-hot body.' I bite my lip and Sophie falls into a fit of laughter.

'Well, I should hope so! Maybe it's your hormones going into overdrive. I mean, how long is it since you last had sex?'

Well...

'It must be ages. You probably just need to have sex.'

'Thanks, Sophie. That's more the response I'd have expected from Simon, not you. Since when did you become a sexual mogul? Don't answer that.' I hold up my hand to silence her as she opens her mouth. I do not need to know what an amazing sex life Sophie has with Matt. That's far too much for my poor ears to take.

'You spoiled things, though. You called the police.'

Chapter Thirty-Two

'So, you've not made up with Joe then?'

Dinner at Dad and Margaret's seemed like such an innocuous event, but clearly not. But I haven't been around as often as usual, due to work/ study/friends/life imbalance, so I guess I need to suck it up and let them say their piece.

'Um, no, Margaret. We broke up, remember? We called off a wedding. It's not like we had a fight over who cleaned the bathroom last.'

'You young ones fight about cleaning the bathroom?' Margaret looks at me, astounded.

'No, of course not.' Well, sometimes yes, but… 'I meant that we broke up over something huge, not something trivial.'

'Hmm.' She places a forkful of spaghetti into her mouth and I breathe a sigh of relief for the moment's reprieve. I see Dad give her a stern look, which unfortunately appears to be lost on Margaret.

'So, darling' – Dad turns to face me – 'how's your fashion course going?'

Thank God, a change of subject. It was starting to feel like Chinese water torture with Margaret.

'Really good thanks, Dad.' I find myself grinning. 'It's hard work and I don't always have much spare time, but I feel like I'm achieving something.'

'Good for you, Emmie. I'm pleased, and proud of you.'

'It's a good distraction.' My smile fades and Dad nods knowingly at me.

'I just don't understand what happened with you and Joe, that's all,' Margaret chirps.

Oh good, we're back to my heartbreak.

Margaret places her fork and spoon neatly on her empty plate and looks at me as though waiting for some clarification.

Well, Margaret, that makes two of us. One minute I'm basking in the loved-up feeling of getting engaged, waking up every morning with my gorgeous fiancé snuggled next to me in bed, and the next minute I feel like I'm in a pressure cooker, trying to read textbooks, plan a wedding and refrain from punching the new boss at the shop in the face on a daily basis. And now? Now I'm drowning in my own self-pity. I wake up every morning in a cold, empty bed and forget, for one second as I open my eyes, what a cock-up I've made of everything. Then I remember and my heart breaks all over again as I drag myself heavily from my bed to face the world alone.

Okay, so that might be a bit heavy for a Tuesday evening.

I settle for dismissive as I spoon the last of the tomato sauce into my mouth. 'It's complicated. Can we leave it at that, please?'

'Of course.' Dad places his hand over mine and gives it a little squeeze. 'Coffee?'

'Sure, Dad, but I can't stay too late. I've got a chapter of my textbook to read before I can go to bed tonight.' And I'm in no mood for further interrogation from Margaret.

'None for me, thanks.' Margaret waves her hand. 'Leave the plates and I'll clear the table in a moment.'

'Come with me, Emmie.' Dad stands up from the table looking almost giddy. 'I've got something to show you.'

He wags his finger and points towards the kitchen and I get up and follow him, feeling like I'm a child again and he's proudly taking me into the garden to show me his new shed. As we reach the kitchen I see a posh coffee machine taking pride of place on the kitchen side and I laugh. Dad shares my love of cappuccinos and of fancy gadgets (although I usually need an idiot's guide on how to use them from Simon).

I watch as Dad grabs two mugs and then I get to be very impressed as he pushes a few buttons and the machine starts grinding coffee beans. Wow, it's like being in my own private Starbucks.

'Margaret doesn't mean anything, you know,' Dad says quietly as we lean on the breakfast bar a few moments later, sipping what is remarkable good coffee and, dare I say it, slightly better than the coffee produced by my own pod machine. I may have to invest in one of these fandangle coffee-bean-grinding machines myself, or at least ask Santa nicely for one at Christmas.

'Then why does it feel like I'm being punished in every conversation I have with her?'

'She worries about you; we both do.'

'I wish things had worked out differently too, Dad. I really do.'

'And there's no chance of you and Joe sorting out whatever differences you have?'

'No chance.' I shake my head. 'I wouldn't know where to start.'

'There's always a way, Emmie. You simply start with hello.'

If only it were that simple.

'I'd better get going, Dad.' I drink the last of my coffee and place the mug in the sink.

'Okay, Emmie. I know you have some reading to do. But don't be doing too much, alright? You need to make sure you're looking after yourself.'

'I'm fine, Dad,' I reassure him as he hugs me goodbye.

'I love you.'

'I love you too, and Margaret most days, when I'm not having to refrain from killing her.' I grin to make sure that he knows I'm only joking.

'I'll talk to her.'

'I'll call you over the weekend.'

I grab my coat and bag from the hook next to the door. 'Thanks for dinner, Margaret,' I call through to the lounge and she appears in the doorway. I hope she didn't overhear my last comment to Dad about killing her. Whoops.

I see the blank white envelope on the mat the instant I've opened the front door to my flat and my heart leaps into my mouth thundering as it does so. This is really starting to scare me now. I instinctively glance behind me, but the corridor is quiet and empty. Stepping into my flat I shove the door firmly closed and crouch down. My hands are shaking violently as I reach out to pick up the envelope. I hover my fingers over it, not wanting to touch it, not wanting to see what threatening message it contains. But I have to do it; I have no choice.

I scoop it off the mat and slide my finger gently under the seal. I can already see the outline of the letters cut from a newspaper on the letter folded up inside. My stomach flips and I have to lean on the wall for support as my legs become unsteady. Pulling the paper out I unfold it and stare at the sea of letters scrawling out their horrible message:

'You've ruined my life; now it's my turn to ruin yours'

I gulp for air. Who is doing this to me? I haven't done anything to hurt anybody. Who would want to frighten me like this?

I breathe in deeply and exhale trying to calm my nerves and my hammering heart. I shuffle forward on wobbly legs and repeat the scan of the whole flat that I did the last time a threatening letter arrived. I open every cupboard and drawer and move the contents around making absolutely sure that no one is hiding in some dark crevice waiting to attack me; although what I'd actually do if I found someone I have no idea.

I pause halfway through rummaging through my wardrobe and wonder if it's irrational to do this given the front door was locked prior to me arriving home and an intruder would have to go to some pretty great lengths to scale the wall of the building to force a window open of a second floor flat but then I tell myself nothing is irrational if you've received threats posted directly through your front door.

I continue my check of the flat and once I'm confident that I'm alone I call Sophie.

'Hi Emma.' Her cheerful tone is in stark contrast to my own emotions.

'I got another one.' I say quietly.

'Another? Oh no Emma, another letter?'

'Yes. It's the same; it's exactly the same as the others.' My voice judders.

'What does it say?'

I read the singular sentence that's splayed across the paper "You've ruined my life; now it's my turn to ruin yours".

'Bloody hell Emma. Have you called the police?'

'No, not yet.'

'Well you're not staying there. It's not safe.'

'No one can get in the flat Sophie, and whoever it is knows where I live so if they actually wanted to harm me then surely they would wait under the cover of darkness and pounce on me when I leave the flat.'

Oh god! My brain just comprehends what I've just said. What if they do that? What if they actually wait for me and attack me when I'm alone and…

'Emma. Pack your bag and get over to my house right now.'

'No Sophie. I'm not being driven from my own home by some crazy person.'

'Well you're not staying there alone. I'll come to you.'

I think about this for a second. Some company would be good, even though I really do think that while I'm in the flat I'm safe it wouldn't hurt to have another person here with me just in case.

'That works for me.'

'See you in ten minutes.'

'Okay.'

'And Emma?'

'Yes.'

'Call those two police sergeants.'

'Right.'

I hang up the call to Sophie and find the sergeant's card in the kitchen cupboard and make them my second call. As I hang up the phone following the policemen assuring me they were on their way I contemplate having a glass of wine to calm myself but I think better of it. Although the criticisms of my drinking by those closest to me ring loudly in my head I realise under my own steam that I need to stay sober and alert this evening without alcohol numbing my senses.

Ten minutes later Sophie dutifully arrives lugging a huge overnight bag.

'Hey.' She gives me a huge hug as I let her into the flat.

'I'm okay Sophie.' And for some unexplainable reason I do feel alright. The initial fear has subsided and I'm just a bit numb now, as though it's not really real. Maybe it's just my mind's way of coping.

We head through to the lounge and sit down on the sofa. I switch on the television and put some R&B music on quietly as background noise. Sophie sees the letter on the coffee table and reaches for it.

'Don't.' I grab Sophie's hand and she jumps 'Sorry, the sergeant said not to touch it again. Whoever it is may have left a fingerprint on it.'

'Oh, I see.'

The intercom buzzes loudly causing us both to jump now.

'That must be the two policemen now.' I get up from the sofa and walk toward the intercom feeling nervous, although I suspect that a crazed psychopath wouldn't buzz his victim to ask politely to be let into their apartment so they could maim and kill them.

'Hello.' I say gruffly into the receiver.

'Miss Story? It's the police.'

I press the external door release 'Come up please.'

A few minutes later Sergeant Bulky and Sergeant Skinny are standing in my front room inspecting the letter and envelope with latex gloved hands.

'And it was just on the door mat?' Sergeant Bulky asks.

'Yes. The same as the last two.'

'We'll take this away for analysis Miss Story. Although the other two proved fruitless, this time whoever it is might have been careless and left some DNA.'

'Thank you.' I nod.

'Have you had any more thoughts on who could be behind this?' the other sergeant asks.

I shake my head 'I'm sorry. I simply have no idea why anyone would want to hurt me. I can't imagine anybody that I know doing this to me.'

'I realise that's not a nice thought, but it's more likely to be someone already in your life rather than a complete stranger trying to interject themselves into it.'

I bite my lip. The thought of this being someone I know scares me to death.

'Anyway, if you think of anything, however small, that might help then please get back in touch.' Sergeant Skinny places the letter and envelope in an evidence bag which shocks me a little as it's like something from a crime scene on the television, then I realise that's exactly what this is. A crime scene with evidence. I just hope that a further crime, such as my torturous death isn't about to conclude this whole matter. I force that disturbing thought from my head.

'We'll bid you goodnight then.' Both policemen make their way to the front door.

'Make sure you keep the windows and doors locked at all times.' Sergeant Bulky adds as they leave the flat.

'Great. That's not a scary parting note at all.' I say to Sophie 'I thought the police were supposed to make you feel safer.'

'Come on. Let's put the kettle on.' Sophie takes my arm and guides me to the kitchen but before the kettle boils the intercom buzzes again.

'Who the hell could that be?' I swing around and stare at the open hallway.

'Oh.' Sophie looks sheepish 'It's probably Simon.'

'Why would it be Simon? I didn't call him.'

'Um...I did.'

'Why?'

'I thought we might need reinforcements?'

'Reinforcements?'

'Well, we're only two small women. We might need protecting?'

'Against a nutcase intent on hurting us?'

'Um...yes.'

'So you called Simon?'

'Give him a break. He's worried about you, and honestly, Simon can catfight better that most when the mood takes him.'

I giggle at that image as the intercom buzzer screams loudly again, this time for longer.

'Okay, okay.' I call as I walk towards the front door even though I'm aware they can't hear me.

'Hello.' I say into the receiver.

'It's only me Ems. Are you going to let me in or not?'

'Keep your hair on Simon, I was just in the kitchen that's all.' I press the door release and a few moments later both Simon and James pile into my flat also armed with a large rucksack.

'Erm, what's happening here?' I gesture to the rucksack as Simon discards it next to the front door before kissing me on the cheek.

'James and I are spending the night here – no arguments.' Simon holds up his hand as I open my mouth to speak 'You're my best friend and you're in danger so we're staying put, and that's that.' He looks at me with an expressions that defies challenge.

'What about you're honeymoon. Don't you fly out to Ibiza tomorrow?'

'Not until tomorrow evening, and we're all packed and ready to go so we're fine to stay here tonight. Alright?'

'Alright.' I concede 'but all four of us can't fit in my double bed.

It appears that I was wrong as later that evening I glance around my bedroom as we all sit cross legged on my bed, pyjama-clad and drinking hot chocolate. I find myself feeling a wave of emotion wash over me as I'm torn between the contemplation that someone in my life, whom I may trust, is threatening me, and yet here I am in my moment of need, surrounded by friends who care for me deeply and who've dropped whatever they were doing this evening to come and comfort me and to make sure I'm safe. And I didn't need to even ask, they just came voluntarily without giving it a second thought. That's what friends do, and I realise how lucky I am to have the three friends I have sitting here with me in my bedroom.

Chapter Thirty-Three

As I turn into the college car park, late as usual, I almost run over a familiar figure. What is it with me and pedestrians? I nearly maimed Joe the night we met. I still to this day can't believe he asked me out after my car collided with his bicycle, causing him to bounce across the bonnet.

'Sorry, sorry, I wasn't paying attention,' I call to Tom as he walks over to my car and I clamber out, trying to balance my handbag and textbooks.

'Hi, Emma. How are you?'

'I'm good, thanks, just arriving at the last minute as usual.'

'Me too.' Tom takes hold of one of the books as it slips out of my grasp. 'Let me get that for you.'

'Thanks.'

We walk towards the college building at a quick pace.

'I've been meaning to ask you...' Tom says without looking directly at me.

'Ask me what?' I stop walking and face him.

'Whether, um, you have any plans this weekend?'

'Er, I'm working on Saturday until about five o'clock. Why?'

'You probably won't be interested, but a friend of mine is in a band.'

'Really? How cool.'

'Yeah, and he's playing at Corelli's Bar in town on Saturday night. I'm going along to give him some moral support and I wondered whether you might want to come with me.'

'Oh.' I hesitate slightly. Is Tom asking me out on a date? I don't feel that way about him. He's a great guy but –

'Just as friends,' he says, seeming to sense my quandary.

'That sounds great. Thank you.'

'They start playing around eight o'clock.'

'I'll see you there.'

I wave goodbye as Tom heads into his classroom, and I make my way down to my own. The last of the students are filing in, so I slip in behind them and take my seat next to Carly.

'Hi.' She leans across her desk towards me.

'Hi, Carly. How are things? How did you find the assignment?'

'Not too bad.'

She smiles and we enter into a short conversation about last week's essay question. I ponder for a moment whether I should mention Tom's friend's band and invite Carly to join us, but I decide not to say anythingt. If Tom wants to invite Carly then that's fine, but it should be up to him. I'm still not sure what's going on between those two – if anything.

Saturday has arrived and I'm feeling a little apprehensive as I drive to work. What if Tom does treat this as a date tonight? I know I've been out for drinks with him before, but never on my own – Carly has always been there too. And then there's the fact that Carly likes him. I feel like I'm doing the dirty on her by going to see his friend's band without her knowledge – but Tom asked me, not the other way around.

Maybe I'm overthinking things. Men and women can just be friends. I remember making this point very adamantly to Jenny and Lola not so long ago, specifically about me and Tom.

I'm right. We're friends, and I'm sure that's his intention too. He wants to get some support for his friend's band. It's that simple. I need to stop overcomplicating everything.

I turn the radio up and Alanis Morissette's "Ironic" blasts out from the speakers.

Ironic...hmm.

I arrive at the shop before Jenny, switch on the kettle and make my way through the shop, turning on the lights. I love this quiet time first thing in the morning when everything's calm. By the time I make it back into the staff area the kettle's boiled and I busy myself making two coffees.

Jenny walks through the door only seconds later. 'Morning.'

'Hi. I made coffee.'

I hand her a mug as she takes off her winter coat. The weather has taken a serious turn for the worst. I can't keep up with it. It's hard knowing what to put on in the morning. It wasn't so long ago that we were enjoying that lovely day of warm sunshine when I made the terrible error of walking to the coffee shop to meet Sophie and nearly sweated to death in the process.

'I'm so glad it's only the two of us today.' Jenny leans lazily on the worktop and takes a drink of coffee.

'I know.'

Julia Bamford has taken to reappearing on a Saturday recently, completely destroying the fun Jenny and I have together when the weekend's approaching.

'It's your turn to change the clothes on the manikins today.'

'No way. I did them on Tuesday when that new stock came in,' I protest.

Those damned manikins are defiant and refuse to move in any way, shape or form that might be helpful. They remain rock-solid statues, with their limbs barely moving, despite the use of brute force, as though they're rebelling against me with every ounce of their being.

'I did them twice last week!' Jenny argues.

'Oh.' I cringe. That's right, she did. 'That's not the point.' I don't sound remotely convincing.

'Oh, you're so childish.' Jenny shakes her head at me and then smiles. 'Rock, Paper, Scissors?'

Seriously? We must have this argument every week, and Rock, Paper, Scissors is our only solution. You'd think by now we'd have grown tired of the routine, but hey, you've got to bring a little amusement to your working day.

'Rock, Paper, Scissors.' I nod in agreement. 'One, two, three.'

Half an hour later I'm swearing at the poker-faced manikins, which are now naked, and wiping a film of sweat from my brow.

'It's no good,' I call out to Jenny from the depths of the window display. 'I need a cup of tea before I continue.'

'Sounds like a good idea to me.' Jenny lifts her head up from the desk she's been leaning over, buried in invoices.

I abandon the manikins and head to the staff area to prepare the drinks.

Jenny appears in the doorway as I switch on the kettle and rummage in the cupboard for teabags. 'What are your plans tonight?'

'I'm actually going –'

My sentence is cut short by the jingle of the bell as the shop door opens and swiftly closes. The atmosphere changes in an instant, and Jenny and I look at each other with a mixture of fear and annoyance.

'Where is everyone? You can't leave the shop unmanned to gossip in the back room.' The shrieking tone gets louder. 'And why are there naked manikins in the window? We're not going to sell many clothes on that basis.'

At that moment Julia Bamford's face appears behind Jenny, her lips pursed, scowling, as though she's been stung by a wasp.

'I was just coming back out,' Jenny whimpers. 'I needed to check… um…something with Emma.'

'Well.' Julia holds the door open with her bony hand baring perfectly manicured nails.

Jenny turns to me and rolls her eyes before scooting back to the shop floor.

'Cup of tea?' I ask brightly, sticking to my plan to kill Julia with kindness.

It doesn't work, and Julia is on both of our cases all day, following us around the shop sniping at this, criticising that. By the time five o'clock comes around I feel exhausted from the sheer volume of questions that have been fired at me for the last six hours, and the pressure to remain calm and not grab Julia by her hair and swing her around the shop until she shuts up once and for all.

I know that's wrong; I do. I don't really wish her any harm (well, not much). But I want to be left alone to do my job in peace.

As Jenny and I finally make good our escape and close the door behind us, leaving Julia still stalking around the shop like a predator, Jenny sighs heavily.

'Well, that wasn't the day I was expecting.'

'Me neither.' I pull my coat tighter around me, feeling the chill of the November night drawing in. 'Do you remember when Saturdays used to be quite fun, just the two of us?'

'I know. Julia does kind of kill the atmosphere.'

'And any potential enjoyment we could take out of a day's work.'

'Fancy a glass of wine?' Jenny asks. 'I think I need one after that.'

'I'd love to but I've got plans tonight, so I really need to get home.'

'Oh, anything nice?'

'I'm meeting Tom from college at eight pm to –'

'You're going out on a date with Tom?' Jenny interrupts me, her eyes wide.

'No, not a date.'

'I knew there was something going on between you two.' She looks smug.

'Something going on? No, Jenny, you've got it wrong. I'm –'

'All that rubbish you spouted that men and women can be friends. Huh.'

'It's not rubbish. Men and women can be friends, and will you shut up for a moment and listen to me, please?'

Jenny looks at me sceptically but remains silent.

'Thank you.' I pause for a moment before continuing in a calm monotone: 'Tom's friend plays in a band. They have a gig in town tonight. Tom simply asked me to go along to support his friend. That's all. No romance. No date. Just friends.'

'Okay.' Jenny bites her lip. 'I'll believe you.'

'It's funny how you don't sound that convinced, though.' I raise my eyebrows at her but Jenny smiles, saying nothing. 'Look, if you don't have any plans tonight then why don't you come along?'

'Really?'

'Yes, then you can see for yourself how that whole "man, woman, friendship" thing works.'

'Okay. I can watch a live band tonight. That sounds like fun. And I'd like to meet Tom anyway.'

'There you go then. We're meeting at Corelli's. They start playing at eight. Now I'm going to love you and leave you because I'm starting to lose the feeling in my feet. It's freezing.'

'Alright. See you later then.'

'See you tonight.' I wave before heading off towards my car, rubbing my hands together for warmth.

Chapter Thirty-Four

Okay. I'm standing in front of my open wardrobe with my towel wrapped around me, fresh from the shower, scanning my clothes. What do I wear that says "I've made an effort because it's Saturday night" but "I've not made too much effort as this isn't a date"?

Can men and women really be friends?

I think back to all the romantic comedy films I've seen over the years where the "just friends" couple turn into love's young dream and live happily ever after. But that's the movies, right? It's not real. They're compelled to have a happy ending. No one wants to leave the cinema after watching a film in which the hopeless singleton ends up living a lonely life with a thousand cats, where the local children run past her house with fear throwing eggs at the windows.

I don't know why I'm so fixated on this. I blame Jenny. In my own mind I know Tom is only being friendly. He doesn't have a girlfriend, to the best of my knowledge, but that doesn't mean he sees me as a potential one.

Jeans and a blouse? I reach into the rack of clothes and pull dark-blue skinny jeans from their hanger along with a cerise silky blouse. The colour looks great on me, but it's not revealing in any way – no cleavage on show (not that I have much to look at in the way of cleavage, but still…). I throw on some nude heels and touch up my makeup, applying a coat of mascara and swiping shimmery peach eyeshadow across both eyelids with my little finger.

There – a natural look. Perfect.

A car horn beeps outside and I look down from my bedroom window and see a taxi waiting at the roadside next to the block of flats. I grab my winter coat and hurry to the car. The temperature feels like it's dropped another few degrees and I hope this isn't the full onset of winter weather. Dark, cold mornings are so depressing without adding snow or ice to the equation.

The journey into town is only short and I arrive at the bar before I know it. It's hot and noisy with lively chatter and music. Tom catches my eye from across the room and waves me over. I make my way to him, weaving through groups of people.

'Emma. You made it.' Tom gives me a hug. 'What can I get you to drink?'

'Oh, um, a bottle of beer would be great, thanks.'

'Okay.'

Tom places his hands firmly on my shoulders and turns me to the three people standing around the tall table nearby. 'This is Emma, my friend from college,' he announces. I feel a bit a dog at Crufts being paraded in front of the judges. 'Emma, this is Phil, Dan and Zoe.' He points individually to the three faces staring back at me. 'Be nice to Emma while I get her a drink,' Tom says before releasing me from his grasp and heading over to the bar.

'Hi, Emma. Nice to meet you.' Zoe smiles warmly. 'Are you doing business management with Tom?'

'Me, erm, no, I'm taking a fashion design course,' I say, feeling nervous, and thinking how lame that must sound to two guys, but Zoe's eye brighten.

'Really? I'd love to do something like that.'

'Yeah, you've probably done enough research over the years, given how many clothes you own,' Dan chips in and then takes a swig of his beer.

'Not funny, Dan.' Zoe elbows him. 'Please ignore my fashion-challenged boyfriend who only knows two colours – blue and dark-blue.' She rolls her eyes at him.

'Hey!' Dan protests, but as we all stare at his shirt there's no denying that it's dark-blue, and instantaneously we start laughing.

Tom appears at my side and hands me a beer. 'Looks like you've made Emma welcome.'

'Thanks.' I take a drink gratefully. It's already far too warm in here. The place is rocking. 'I hope you don't mind but I invited my friend Jenny to join us?'

'Not at all.'

'Great.' I feel relieved. Perhaps it isn't good etiquette to invite a friend to someone else's evening, but there's a group of us now and Tom seems fine with it.

At that moment Jenny appears in the doorway of the bar and waves across at me. When she reaches us she says, 'Hi.'

'Hi, Jenny. This is Tom.' I turn to face Tom.

'It's good to meet you, Jenny.'

'Thanks for letting me tag along.'

'Any friend of Emma's is a friend of mine.' Tom smiles. 'Can I get you a drink?'

'Let me get that drink for you. I'm Phil, by the way.' Phil appears at

Jenny's side and she glances at him. There's a spark in her eye as she takes off her coat.

'That would be lovely, thanks.'

Jenny follows Phil to the bar and I can't help but smile inwardly. I'm always amazed at Jenny's ability to attract men within seconds of being in their presence. But why wouldn't she? She's warm and funny and confident, as well as pretty smart and attractive.

'I think Phil's smitten already,' Tom says as we both stand watching Phil and Jenny deep in conversation at the bar. She leans in close to listen to what Phil's saying. Then she tucks her hair behind her ear, her "tell" that she likes a guy.

I turn back around to face Zoe and Dan. 'I think the feeling is mutual.'

A few moments later Phil and Jenny return, chatting in their own little world. Tom's friend and his band appear on the raised stage. People are whistling and cheering; it looks like they've already got a group of fans.

Fifteen minutes into their set I understand why – they're fantastic, playing a mix of their own songs plus covers of classic tunes from indie bands such as Oasis but with their own take.

I tug Tom's sleeve to get his attention. 'They're really good. How long have they been playing?'

'A couple of years.'

Tom leans in close so I can hear him. With my three-inch heels on I'm nearly as tall as him, which makes a change; usually I wear flat pumps to college after being on my feet all day in the shop and I feel incredibly small next to him.

'Apparently a music scout comes in here on a regular basis,' says Tom, 'so fingers crossed they're in tonight, looking on.'

'Wow. That'd be great for the band.'

'They play a number of venues on a regular basis. If you like their music, you should come along again.'

'Thanks. I might do that.'

Tom takes a sip of his beer and carries on tapping his feet to the rhythm. I glance sideways and catch Jenny's eye. She raises her eyebrows and flashes a smile, before going back to listening intently to whatever Phil is whispering in her ear. Finishing the last mouthful of my beer, I start to relax and find myself moving to the music too.

'Another beer?' Tom waves his empty bottle at me.

'Yes, please.'

I smile as I watch Tom head off to the bar, saying hello to a few people on his way. This is turning out to be a really good night. I'm glad Tom asked me to come.

I'm impressed that the band play for a good hour and a half, before retiring to loud applause and shouts for more.

Zoe appears next to me with Dan by her side. 'We're going to head down to the club on Division Street. Are you coming with us?'

'You're welcome, of course,' Tom chips in.

I'm tempted. Tom and his friends are good company, but I'm exhausted. 'Thanks so much for asking, but it's been a long day so maybe next time.'

'What's this?' Jenny joins us.

'We're going to a club next if you want to come too,' Tom offers.

Jenny looks at me. 'Are you going?'

'No, I'm done for the night.' I glance at Phil. 'But don't let that stop you.' I don't want to ruin Jenny's potential romance.

'No, don't be silly. I'm not going to let you get a taxi home on your own. I'll come with you.'

'Are you sure?'

'Absolutely. I need two seconds, though.' She turns and takes Phil by the hand and they move away.

'Are you two going to be okay getting a taxi? I don't mind coming with you,' Tom says.

'We'll be fine, but thanks for offering, and thanks for inviting me tonight. I had a really good time.'

'You're welcome…anytime.'

Jenny appears again at my side. 'Okay. I'm ready to go.'

'Goodnight, Tom,' I say and he kisses me briefly on the cheek. 'Enjoy the rest of your night and I'll probably see you next week at college.'

'Have a safe journey home.' Tom smiles warmly at me. 'Nice to meet you, Jenny.' He kisses Jenny on the cheek too.

'Lovely to meet you all,' I say, waving goodbye to Zoe, Dan and Phil.

'Hope to see you again.' Zoe waves back.

As soon as Jenny and I get outside, a strong gust of freezing-cold wind blows around us and we link arms and huddle together.

'So, he's cute.' Jenny nudges me.

'Who? Phil? You two seemed to be getting on quite well.'

'No, you idiot. Tom.'

'Oh.'

'He definitely likes you.'

'Don't be silly. We're just friends and he's nice company.'

'So you can't see yourself being more than that?'

I pause as we reach the back of the taxi queue, which thankfully only consists of four people tonight or we might freeze to death waiting for a lift home after all.

'It's not…I'm…I don't…' I exhale loudly. 'I'm not in that place yet.'

'What place?' Jenny looks at me quizzically.

'That place where I close the chapter with Joe and start a new one.'

'I understand.' Jenny pulls me in a little tighter. 'I do, honestly.'

'I want to be.' I shake my head in frustration. 'And I know that enough time has passed for me to be there, but I'm not.'

'There's no rush. You need to take things at your own pace, and if you're not ready then you're not ready. It's as simple as that.'

'Thanks.'

We stand huddled together in silence for a moment as the queue reduces from four to two.

'So what about you and Phil?'

'I don't know.' Jenny shrugs nonchalantly.

'I think you do.' I giggle.

'And what does that mean, Emma?'

'It means that I saw your "tell". You like him.'

'What "tell"?' Jenny stares at me, aghast.

'You tuck your hair behind your ear when you like a guy,' I state as though it's the most obvious thing in the world.

'I do not!' Jenny protests.

'Alright then,' I humour her, but without conviction. 'So when are you seeing him again?'

Jenny purses her lips, clearly realising she's been caught out. 'Next Friday.' She huffs, teenage-like, and I laugh.

'See. You like him.'

'Okay, so I like him,' Jenny says defiantly, and we both giggle until two taxis pull up and we climb into the second car.

The taxi drops Jenny off at her house, before taking me to my flat. I'm so weary from the full day at work, being yelled at and interrogated by Julia Bamford. Having several beers and a distinct lack of food this evening has done nothing to improve my energy levels. Once I make it up the two flights of stairs to my apartment and let myself in, I barely take off my clothes (and don't even contemplate removing my makeup) before flopping face down onto the bed and pulling the covers over me.

Chapter Thirty-Five

The ringing of my mobile phone pierces the depths of my sleep, and I flap my hand around, trying to find the offending object. Once I locate it, I press the "answer" button without even opening my eyes.

'Hello?' My voice is gruff from lack of moisture.

'Have you decided what you're doing for Christmas this year yet, darling?'

Not this again! 'Mum? What time is it?'

'It's nine thirty, Emma. Are you still in bed?'

'No,' I lie. It's Sunday morning; surely it's illegal to make a phone call before eleven a.m.

'So, Christmas?'

'It's only the second week of November, Mum. I haven't given it much thought.'

'Well, do you want to fly out here again? I'll need to book your flight soon if you do.'

I think back to last year. It was great spending Christmas in New York. The decorations around the city are amazing, they go all out with Christmas trees on practically every street corner, and there's something magical about strolling through Central Park while it's under a blanket of snow. But I should really spend this year with Dad and Margaret. I think it's only fair that I take it in turns.

'That would be lovely, Mum, but...'

'But?'

Okay, I know Mum and Dad have a very amicable relationship, but I still feel like I'm choosing one over the other at times like this.

'I think I should spend Christmas with Dad this year, given that I came to New York last year, that's all.'

I hold my breath, waiting for the guilt trip I know is coming.

'I think you're right, darling. It's only fair.'

Oh...that was unexpected.

'We'll come to you instead.'

'What? Come to me?'

'Yes. It'll be wonderful, darling. We can all have Christmas together at your flat. There are two bedrooms, aren't there?'

Two bedrooms? Christmas at mine? Is she serious? My idea of

making a meal is calling for takeout food to be delivered – and I'm pretty sure nowhere will be open for delivery on Christmas Day.

'I'll call your father and invite him, and Margaret too.'

'Hang on there, Mum. Let me get this straight. You want me to host Christmas dinner for you, Dad and Margaret?'

'And Parker.'

'And Parker?'

'Of course, Emma. Parker will be joining us too.'

Oh my God. This is starting to sound ridiculous. Clearly things have become quite serious between Mum and Parker if she not only wants to share Christmas with him but also fly him halfway around the world to spend it with me. But having Christmas with my mum, her boyfriend, my dad and his new wife – surely that's not normal?

'Don't you think that might be a bit…weird, Mum?'

'What do you mean?'

'I mean, you and Dad with your respective new partners. Won't that be a bit uncomfortable?'

'Don't be silly, Emma. Your father and I get on absolutely fine, and we both moved on a long time ago. And Margaret and I are…civil. The most important thing to us all is spending Christmas with you, Emma. I'm sure your dad will agree. I'll call him this afternoon.'

'Okay, if Dad's alright with this then I guess I am too.'

And I'm pretty sure that Dad won't have much choice in the matter once Mum starts bending his ear over the phone. I'm yet to find the person who can say no to Rosalind Story and get away with it.

Wait a minute, this still means that I'm expected to cook Christmas dinner. I can't possibly do that unless they all want lunch to consist of wine and cheese.

'Right, that's sorted then. Christmas at yours it is. I'm so looking forward to seeing you, Emma. It'll be wonderful to spend Christmas in England.'

'Mum, one last thing.'

'Yes?'

'Um, cooking?'

'Don't panic, darling. I'll order all the food to be delivered to your flat and I'll prepare it on the day. All you need to do is be in for the delivery and put everything in the fridge. I'll do everything else.'

Thank God for that. Be in for the delivery. Put food in the fridge. I think I can manage that.

'Great, Mum. Thanks.'

'I'll text you later once I've spoken to your father.'

'Okay.'

'Bye, darling.'

'Bye, Mum.'

I end the call and pull the covers back over my head. I still have an hour's worth of lolling in bed before I need to be in the shower to get ready to meet Sophie for coffee.

'Can you believe it? My mum, my dad, Margaret and Parker all sitting around the Christmas dinner table? I mean, it sounds like the punchline to a joke, right?'

'It's a bit unusual, I admit.' Sophie nods in agreement as she takes a bite of her blueberry muffin. 'But it's nice that they all get along.'

'I know that, but it feels like it might be a bit odd, like I'm going to be sitting in the middle of them all having to watch what I say to who.'

'Maybe.'

'And speaking of sitting, where on earth are we all going to sit? I don't have a dining room table, or a very large kitchen table for that matter. It's small and seats four at a push. Damn Mum and her crazy ideas.' I scoop up a piece of Victoria sponge cake and scowl.

'So, what happened last night with Tom?' Sophie looks at me optimistically.

'It was a good night. His friend's band is really good.'

'That's not what I meant.'

'I know.' I take a drink of coffee. 'But I'm sick of telling everyone that Tom and I are just friends. I sound like a broken record.'

'Alright, alright, I'll take the hint. I'll never mention Tom in any way other than in relation to friendship.'

'Thank you…So what are you doing for Christmas?' I've been dreading asking this question. I'm not sure how I'm going to feel if Sophie tells me she's spending Christmas with Matt and his family, which includes Joe.

'I'm not sure.' She ponders. 'I'd like to see Mum and Dad but I'd also really like to spend Christmas Day with Matt.'

I gulp. With Matt probably means with Joe too.

'Would you feel weird about that?'

'Me? No. Why?' I can hear my voice rising an octave.

Sophie looks at me. 'Come on, Emma. I do realise it's not the most comfortable situation, me dating your ex-fiancé's brother.'

'Right.'

'And I'm pretty sure that me sitting around the Stark Christmas dinner table pulling crackers and drinking wine isn't exactly something
you want to envision.'

It hurts, it physically hurts, to even think about that.

'Don't be silly, Sophie. I'm fine with you and Matt. You know that.' I
hope the expression on my face is neutral and not displaying my true
thoughts.

'Yes…but…'

'No buts. I love you and I want you to be happy, and Matt makes you
happy.'

'Thank you, Emma. I love you too.'

'Stop it or I'll get all emotional.'

I take a drink of coffee and swallow down the tears that I can feel
creeping up on me. I don't know why, but thinking of Christmas makes
me feel over-emotional. I'll be spending Christmas alone (romantically
speaking; I realise I won't be alone – I've got all my crazy family mem-
bers descending on me). There'll be no snuggling up on the sofa with
a loved one, no sipping mulled wine together while listening to classic
Christmas songs, no exchanging thoughtfully bought gifts on Christmas morning. It feels so…sad.

I change the subject, keen to get on to something less emotive. 'Do
you think Simon and James will be home from their honeymoon now?'

'I think their flight landed early this morning, so they should be.'

'Perhaps we should call in on them on our way home, if only to make
sure Simon's still alive.'

'Good point. Two weeks in Ibiza – anything could have happened.'

'I know we joke about Simon and his crazy life, but I think he's really
settled down with James.'

'So you don't think he'll be in an alcohol-induced coma from spending the last two weeks clubbing twenty-four hours a day?' Sophie looks
sceptical.

'A few years ago I'd have said definitely yes, but now? He says he's a
changed man and honestly, I believe him.'

'And who says miracles can't happen?' Sophie chuckles. 'Come on
then. Let's finish these coffee and pay them a visit.'

Chapter Thirty-Six

I drive us the short journey to Simon's flat, and when we arrive I pause before pressing tentatively on the buzzer for his apartment. Maybe they'll be tired from their flight, or not in the mood for visitors, still wanting to enjoy each other's company in the immediate aftermath of their honeymoon. Or even worse, we might be interrupting them doing something intimate. Oh no – I don't need that experience twice in a lifetime!

'Hello?' Simon's voice interrupts my musings.

'Hi, Si. It's only me and Sophie. We were passing and wanted to see whether you and James had a good time in Ibiza. Are we okay to come up?'

'Hi, Em. Of course, babe.'

I hear the external door beep and Sophie pushes it open. By the time we make it up the flight of stairs to Simon's first-floor flat, he's already standing in the doorway, looking tanned and relaxed and nowhere near falling into an alcohol-induced coma.

'Hey, honey.' He sweeps me into a huge hug. 'I've missed you.'

'I've missed you too, Simon.'

'Hi, Soph.' Simon releases me and gives Sophie a kiss on the cheek. 'Come in both of you.' He ushers us into the flat. 'Do you want a cuppa?'

'We don't want to intrude,' Sophie says.

'Yeah, we wanted to say hi, that's all. You must be tired from your flight.'

'Tired? We've spent the last two weeks lying on sun loungers, only getting up to eat or drink.'

'So...no clubbing?' I ask.

'Maybe a couple of nights.' Simon grins. 'James and I are happy sitting in a bar with a cocktail, simply watching the world go by.'

'What happened to you, Simon?' Sophie admonishes jokingly.

'Cheeky!' Simon frowns playfully.

'See, I told you.' I smile at Sophie. 'We have a changed man here now that he's in love. Speaking of that...' I look around. 'Where's your husband?'

'James has just popped to the shop to pick up some essentials.'

'Such as milk and teabags?' I ask as Simon fills the kettle and switches it on.

'That's a good point.' He laughs. 'He won't be long, I'm sure. Let me show you some honeymoon photos while we're waiting.' Simon pulls his phone out of his pocket excitedly. 'We went in a hot-air balloon!' he exclaims.

Sophie and I stare at the mobile phone screen as photo after photo appears, showing Simon and James grinning, laughing and having the time of their lives.

'You look so happy, Si,' I croak, my voice heavy with emotion.

'I am, babe.' Simon puts his arm around me and squeezes me tightly. I hear the door to the flat open.

James strides into the kitchen, laden down with shopping bags. 'I hope he's not boring you to death already with the thousands of photos he took. I think we have a picture of every waking moment of the last two weeks,' he jokes.

'Ignore him. He's just grumpy because we're back in reality now,' Simon says gently as James starts to unload the shopping bags.

'Tea, coffee, milk.' He places the items on the worktop next to the kettle. 'I presume you'll be needing these.'

'Ta.' Simon busies himself making the drinks.

'How are you, James?' I ask, smiling warmly at him. He's also golden brown and looks very relaxed.

'I'm brilliant thanks, Emma. Couldn't be better.' He winks at Simon and the love for him is there to see, written all over James's face.

'So, how are you?'

'Ooh, that's my phone.'

As I pull my mobile from my handbag, my heart clenches and my stomach flips: Joe's name is flashing on the screen. I stare at the phone, holding it at arm's length. My hands are shaking so much that I struggle to press the "answer" key.

'Hello?' I whisper.

I'm met with silence, and for a second my heart drops all the way to my feet as I wonder whether he dialled my number by mistake. But then I hear his voice.

'Emma?'

My lips start to tremble and Simon looks across at me with a worried expression.

'Hi, Joe,' I manage. 'How are you?'

I see Sophie raise her eyebrows and then silently protesting as Simon ushers her and James from the room closing the door quietly behind them.

'Matt rang me,' Joe says, not answering my question.

'I see.' Matt obviously told him about me receiving stalking letters. Damn him and Sophie. I knew their relationship would cause some crossover into my life at some point. But Joe's on the phone. He called me, and that's something.

'I'm calling to...' There's a heavy pause. '... to make sure that you're okay.'

But his voice is cool and bears no resemblance to the soft, comforting tone that I used to love. That I still love.

'I'm alright, thanks.' I wipe away a stray tear that's formed out of no-where at the shock of hearing Joe's voice. 'I was a bit shocked at first but I'm not going to let it worry me too much.' I say sounding stronger than I feel.

'So you're okay.'

No. No, I'm not okay, I want to scream down the phone. I love you and I miss you and I wish I could go back in time and do everything differently – everything. I long to feel your warm, strong body next to mine in bed as I go to sleep at night, and I know I'll regret every day for the rest of my life ever suggesting that we postpone the wedding. Hearing your voice has made my heart break all over again and the pain is excruciating.

'Yes, I'm fine, Joe. I have my friends to support me. Thanks for calling.' I realise that I'm dismissing him, which is at complete odds to how I really feel but I can't allow my heart to open up to him again, even for a second.

'Bye, Emma. Take care of yourself.'

'You too,' I manage to croak before I hear the phone click off and I lay my head in my hands.

Simon appears behind me. 'Emma? Emma, what's wrong? What did he say?' He pulls me into a hug.

'How did I make such a mess of things, Si?' I sob into his jumper. 'He's the one. Joe's the one I'm supposed to spend the rest of my life with, and I broke our relationship.'

'Hey, hey. There are two people in every relationship, Emma. It's not all your fault.'

'Yes, it is.' I pull back from him, anger mixing in with my sadness. 'I was the one who suggested postponing the wedding. I didn't really want to postpone the wedding. I wanted to marry him. It all got a bit too much. Too many things going on at the same time. But I never stopped loving him.'

'I know, honey.'

'And now I can't fix it. It's gone too far.'

'You don't know that. He rang you, didn't he?'

'Only because Matt told him about the letters.' I glance at Sophie who's appeared in the kitchen doorway looking contrite.

'So he was obviously concerned. He wanted to make sure for himself that you're alright.' Simon continues.

'That's Joe. He's a gentleman, always doing the decent thing. I could tell in his voice that he feels differently about me. He wasn't warm or loving, just…clinical.'

'It must have taken a lot for him to call you. He was bound to feel weird about it. When was the last time you spoke?'

'I don't know.' I shrug. 'Months, I guess.'

'There you go then.'

'Hearing his voice though, it's brought it all back. The pain of losing him. I never meant for things to get this far. I thought he'd say something before it came to me moving out. That he'd tell me he loved me no matter what and that was enough.'

'For God's sake, Emma, why didn't you say something to Joe?' Sophie interjects.

'I figured that he must have wanted things to end. It was him who said that if I didn't want to marry him at that point then we didn't want the same things, and he couldn't be with someone who didn't want the same as him out of life.'

'It sounds to me like you did, and still do. You probably hurt him by saying you wanted to delay the wedding, and he was too proud to beg you to stay once you'd decided to split up.' Simon shakes his head. 'What a mess, Emma.'

'You don't need to tell me, Simon. I know what I've done and I'll have to live with it.'

'Joe's definitely the one, huh?'

'He owns my heart.' I sniff.

'Oh, honey.'

'Can you stay with me for a bit longer, Si?'

'Of course I can, Em.'

'I don't want to be alone right now.'

'You're never alone, honey.'

He squeezes my hand and I gulp to swallow down the huge wave of emotion that's coursing through my body.

Sophie and I spend the next hour listening to stories of James and Simon's experiences on their honeymoon, looking at numerous photographs and generally being part of their happy bubble. It's nice and heart-warming, and by the time we're ready to leave I find myself in a better mood, filled with optimism. If Simon and James can find true love then someday so will I again.

Sophie is quiet on our journey home until we're nearly at her house.

'Are you angry with Matt for telling Joe about the letters?' she asks.

'I suppose not.' I shrug dismissively. Honestly, I don't know how I feel about that, or Joe calling earlier.

'Are you angry at me?' She asks tentatively.

'Sophie – you and Matt are in a relationship so Matt is bound to know things about me. I just hope he doesn't share everything with Joe.'

'Like what?'

'Like how unhinged I've become over the recent months.'

'Don't worry. I don't think Matt has noticed.' She smiles widely 'he's always thought you were a little unhinged.'

'Oi, cheeky!'

'I'm just kidding Emma. Matt probably only told Joe because he's concerned about you and he must have thought that Joe would be too. Just because you're not engaged any more doesn't mean that you can't care about each other.'

I do still care about Joe. That's the whole point. That's why I'm unhinged....

I drop Sophie off at her house and make my way back to the flat, planning an evening consisting of taking a hot bubble bath, drinking a glass of wine, watching repeats of soaps on the television, flicking through celebrity magazines and stuffing whatever food may be left in my cupboards into my mouth.

Chapter Thirty-Seven

Two weeks to Christmas.

'It feels good to get the first term out of the way.' Carly shuts her textbook with emphasis. 'Now let's celebrate an end to our hard work for a few weeks and the start of Christmas.'

Tonight is our last college class before the Christmas break, and I can't quite believe that we've got here so quickly.

'You appear to be forgetting the essay we have to write and hand in the first week back in January.'

I slide my textbook and notepad into my bag as we stand up to leave. Although Carly's right, it does feel like we've achieved something in the last few months. Even if all other aspects of my life have been turned on their head, my studies are going well, and I'm grateful that Joe pushed me to do this course back in August.

As we make our way out into the corridor, Tom is walking towards us.

'Hey, I was just coming looking for you and Carly.'

He smiles and Carly blushes furiously. She never did pluck up the courage to ask Tom out on a second date, always making up some excuse about it not being the right moment.

'Are you still going for a few beers to celebrate the end of term?' asks Tom.

'Definitely. We're ready to go now. Are you coming with us?'

'If that's still okay? Plus some of my business management friends were going to come too.'

Carly finds her voice. 'That's fine – the more the merrier.'

'Absolutely,' I agree. 'Shall we go to The Crown at the top of the street first?'

'I'll go and get the rest of the guys.'

Tom turns around and jogs down the corridor to a group of people near the exit door.

We all head in a gang out of the building and up the hill to The Crown pub. It's a true December evening – crispy pavements and a chill in the air.

Tom's friends are really good fun – although they all seem very young, but maybe that's because I'm in my thirties and not my twenties. Jack, David and Lewis are doing business management too and they too seem relieved to have reached the end of their first term. They mess about, dancing ridiculously to the eighties tunes that are blaring out in the bar, and then trying to convince Carly and I to do some Christmas themed vodka shots with them. Usually I would decline (I've been much better behaved on the drinking front recently) but a few cranberry and orange vodka shots sound yummy and will certainly warm me up.

'Okay, I'm in. I'll get the first round, but I'm only drinking the nice flavours – nothing that tastes like death in a shot glass.'

'Come on then.' Tom tugs at my arm. 'We'll go and get them in, then you can choose the ones you want.'

'Deal.' I nod at Tom.

'Are you alright?' I ask Carly as she whizzes past me being flung around the dancefloor by David.

'I'm great.' She grins, and to be fair David is very cute, blond and blue eyed, so I'm sure she's more than okay. Her fixation on Tom seems to have momentarily waned in the presence of David anyway, and by the way he's dancing with her, not taking his eye off her, I think she might be in with a very good chance with him.

It's a little quieter at the bar, where Tom and I study the menu of flavoured shots.

'Dave seems pretty taken with Carly.' He glances back at the two of them.

'Yeah, I'd definitely say there's some chemistry between them.'

'It's nice when that happens unexpectedly.'

'What?' I glance up from the menu.

'When you meet someone out of the blue and there's a connection.' Tom's looking at me intensely and it feels like the atmosphere between us has become charged.

I gulp nervously, wondering where this is leading. Tom idly picks up a menu and begins scanning the list of drinks, as if purposely not meeting me gaze. I look down at my own menu.

'I'll have the cranberry and orange, and the mulled wine shots. I'll get the same for Carly. How about you?' I still stare forward, unsure whether I'm misreading the signs. Is Tom telling me that he likes me?

'They sound good to me.'

He waves the barmaid over and orders the vodka shots, and I fiddle with a strand of hair, not really knowing what to say now.

'It's been good to get to know you over the last few months, Emma,'

Tom states, handing me one of the two shots that the barmaid has put in front of us. 'Merry Christmas.' He clinks his glass against mine and we both hesitate for a second before downing our shots.

It's quite nice, fruity and refreshing, and in all honesty I'm glad of the shot of liquor to stem my nerves, which appear to have gone into overdrive and set a thousand butterflies flapping around my stomach.

As the barmaid prepares the rest of the shots, the proximity between Tom and I intensifies, and he's standing so close to me now that I can smell his crisp aftershave. My heart's racing as he turns to me and his hand grazes mine – whether intentionally or not, I have no idea. Neither of us speaks; we just stand together with what feels like electric static creating friction between us. I can't decide whether the alcohol is fuelling my desire or my feelings for Tom are real and he's been right there in front of me the whole time.

He leans a little closer....

'Hey, you two,' Lewis calls loudly, appearing right at the side of us, interrupting the silent spell that had fallen over me and Tom. 'I thought you'd gone all the way to Russia to get the vodka,' he jokes. 'Come on, Tom.' He reaches over us and picks up the tray of vodka shots. 'We need you to settle an argument. You know Jack, always thinks he's right, and Dave's having none of it.'

And with that he sweeps Tom away and the moment between us has gone.

The rest of the night is a bit of a blur. We all end up on the dance-floor and the eighties tunes continue long into the night. For whatever reason, maybe cosmic law, Tom and I don't find ourselves alone again for the whole night, and I wonder whether I imagined the entire thing earlier. Perhaps he was making observations about Dave and Carly, who seem completely smitten with one another, and not referring to his feelings for me.

We all find ourselves outside the bar a little before eleven o'clock, a little merry after further rounds of vodka shots, and definitely in the Christmas spirit.

Tom flags down two taxis and we exchange hugs and wish each other a great Christmas.

'Happy Christmas,' Tom whispers into my hair and he embraces me. 'Hope you get everything you want.' He squeezes me tightly and I inhale the scent of his aftershave again. Mmm, he smells nice.

'You too,' I say back as he releases me. 'I'll see you in the New Year.' I find myself grinning at him.

'I'm already looking forward to it.' He cocks his head to one side and studies me for a moment.

'Come on, Emma – it's freezing.' Carly takes hold of my arm and guides me to our taxi.

The guys all pile into their own car and I strain my neck to look through the windscreen behind me at Tom as he climbs into the back. Our eyes meet for a second and he holds my gaze and smiles before our taxi pulls away from the curb and he becomes a blur in my vision.

'You spoiled things, though. You called the police.'

Chapter Thirty-Eight

One week to Christmas.

Christmas shopping.

A day of hell.

My feet are throbbing, my arms feel like they've stretched three feet and my hands are dangling somewhere near my ankles. Even being on a sugar high from gingerbread lattes isn't enough to numb the pain.

We began what feels like three days ago with the best of intentions. Sophie had this great idea of "getting it all done in one go". It was an easy sell for me, as usually Christmas shopping takes me at least four trips of battling the crowds (including the high numbers of overly aggressive people who seem to turn out at this time of year). I'm often distracted by the yummy food and mulled wine on offer at the Christmas markets, which results in me getting slightly (okay, sometimes very) tipsy, and then I wander around aimlessly with no idea what to buy until I trudge home present-less, only to repeat the process again.

So a "one day and all presents sorted" plan seemed like a good one. Now? I can't remember what day it is, what I've bought or what I've got left to buy, and annoyingly my head is filled with the same dozen Christmas songs playing endlessly, intermingled with the whines of children.

'Are you alright, Emma? You don't look yourself.' Sophie glances at me with concern.

'I don't feel quite myself.' I blow a loose strand of hair from my face. 'Aren't you tired?'

'Tired? After all those lattes? Nope, I love Christmas shopping.'

'I know. In fact, I don't understand why I haven't yet utilised your obsession with Christmas and sent you out to purchase gifts for my family and friends on my behalf.'

'You'd still have to get mine yourself.' Sophie gives me a nudge.

'Haven't you heard of internet shopping?'

'You're such a Bah Humbug,' Sophie chastises.

'Mulled wine,' I suggest. 'See, I'm not. I'm suggesting we partake in Christmas-spirited drinks.'

'What?'

'I need mulled wine and that cart over there is selling some.' I drag my weary legs towards a wooden cart manned by a giant elf and order two drinks. 'Here.' I hand one to Sophie before paying the Christmas elf, and we stand to the side against the window of a department store, out of the flow of people charging by while attempting to balance the weight of shopping bags between their two hands.

'Mmm, that tastes good.' I sip the hot, fruity, potent liquid and exhale as the alcohol immediately permeates my brain and soothes the Christmas songs to a quiet hum.

'What have you got left to buy?' Sophie examines her own bags, counting off names one by one.

'I need something for my mum. Do you think I should get something for Parker too?'

'Who? Oh, yeah, your mum's boyfriend.'

'Male companion,' I correct her – Mum is very precise about that.

'He is coming to Christmas dinner, so…'

'So what do you buy for a man you hardly know who's dating your mother…and who dyes his hair?'

Sophie laughs at me. 'I don't know. Some aftershave maybe?'

'Come on.' I down the dregs of the mulled wine. 'Let's go in here and find something for them both.' I push open the door to the department store. 'And then I'm officially done.'

Twenty-five minutes later we exit the store, after queuing for approximately eighteen minutes to purchase aftershave for Parker and a bottle of Chanel perfume which I know is Mum's favourite.

'Shall we head back to mine and get a takeaway?' I suggest as we walk wearily to my car.

'Sounds great.' Sophie swings her shopping bags jubilantly. 'We can decorate your tree.'

'You're presuming that I have a tree.'

'No, I know for a fact that you won't have, which is why we're stopping to buy one on the way home.'

'I don't think that's necessary.' I shake my head. 'There's not enough room in my flat anyway.'

'There's plenty of room,' Sophie says dismissively, 'and I wasn't giving you a choice in the matter. We're stopping on the way home to buy you a Christmas tree and you're going to get into the Christmas mood this year, even if I'm forced to drag you kicking and screaming.'

'Since when did you become so bossy?'

Sophie looks at me with an expression of "really?".

'Okay. You've always been bossy.' I can't help but smile.

'And you love me for it.' Sophie grins.

When we reach the car we squeeze the vast number of shopping bags behind the front seats and fold down the back ones to make room for the Christmas tree that's been forced upon me. We climb in and I switch the engine on and turn the heating up to the maximum. It feels as though snow may be a possibility. They keep predicting it on the weather forecast, but so far it's just bloody freezing.

As we drive to the farm that sells Christmas trees, Sophie turns on the radio and yet another Christmas song blares out. She sings along to "Step into Christmas" by Elton John while dancing in her seat. I shake my head at her, not saying a word.

'What?' She notices my expression.

'Nothing at all. You enjoy yourself.'

But when we pull into the farm courtyard a few minutes later it's hard not to feel slightly festive at their vast arrangement of twinkling fairy lights welcoming us to the large barn that houses the display of trees.

As we approach the entrance, a biting wind whips around us and I clasp my hands together and rub them vigorously to try to improve the blood circulation.

'It's too cold for this,' I complain as we wander inside where it's marginally warmer. I begin to inspect the trees one by one with no idea of what I'm looking for.

'Don't be so grumpy. It's tradition.'

'What is?'

'To choose a real tree at Christmas. I always went with my dad each year to choose the tree, and it was special. Kind of the start of Christmas for us as kids. And of course it's cold – it's December.'

Before I can respond we're approached by a young guy who's far too hot to be hiding in a barn on a farm.

'Can I help you ladies?' he purrs and I feel slightly weak at the knees.

'Um,' is all I manage to say. His alarmingly good looks seem to have even stunned Sophie into silence.

'What are you looking for today?'

Oh my God, his voice is so sexy. I want to say "a tree" but that seems obvious given our location.

'There are several different types of tree,' he continues, clearly sensing our inability to answer his question.

'Of course.' Sophie comes to life at the side of me. 'She needs a small tree, about four foot high.' She nods at me and I nod along.

'What colour?' Hot guy asks.

Again, "green" seems too simple an answer.

'There are lighter-green pines or dark-green ones.' I swear he's trying to hide a smile.

'Dark green, please,' I say.

'This way.'

He marches off to his left, and Sophie and I scurry behind him. She glances at me with raised eyebrows and I wave my hands in the air in a dismissive fashion.

How has this happened? How have Sophie and I turned into bumbling idiots? We're buying a Christmas tree, that's all. It should be straightforward. Walk in, choose a tree, pay for the tree, get it in the car (oh yes, it seems to have escaped Sophie's mind that we have to fit a four-foot tree in the back of my small hatchback). Hmm.

We arrive at a row of dark-green trees with labels stating that they're "non-drop pines". I can't help but wonder why all Christmas trees wouldn't be of this nature. Surely it's their duty to remain looking like a tree for the duration of Christmas? Mind you, if I'd been plucked from the sanctuary of a forest only to be stuffed into a bucket in someone's lounge and dressed up with tinsel and baubles, I might not feel like fulfilling my Christmas destiny either.

'Emma?'

'Yep.' I snap back to reality.

'This one?' Sophie points to small tree.

'It's petite and well rounded.' Hot Guy states, ruffling the lower branches, and I have to bite my lip to contain a giggle as I immediately think, So am I.

'That one will be fine,' I manage without laughing. 'Thank you for your help.' I blush.

'Not a problem.' He scoops the tree under his arm and heads back to the entrance of the barn, where a machine trusses the tree up in white netting which at least makes it narrower for transportation, if not shorter.

'I'd better take some of these.' I grab a box of white fairy lights conveniently stacked next to the till and hand over the money for both.

'Would you like some help getting this into your vehicle?' Hot Guy asks, holding the tree at arm's length.

Sophie opens her mouth but I quickly interject, 'No need, thanks. We can manage.'

Sophie looks at me with utter confusion.

'Come on, Sophie. You grab that end.'

I take hold of the top of the tree and point to the bottom of the trunk. Sophie glances at the hot guy and smiles nervously before crouching down and taking hold of the trunk.

'Ready?' I ask confidently.

'Sure,' Sophie answers doubtfully.

'Thanks again.' I smile at Hot Guy, who watches with some amusement as we hoist the tree up to underarm level and shuffle towards the exit.

'Are you crazy?' Sophie asks once we're out of earshot, seemingly bewildered.

'Shut up, Sophie, and just carry the damn tree.'

We walk disjointedly across the darkened car park (I don't remember it being so dimly lit when we arrived. How long were we in there?). I step in something which I pray is only mud, because I'm wearing my favourite knee-high boots, but I fear may be something less acceptable given that we're on a farm. We finally make it to my car, at which point the real fun begins.

'A little more to the left.'

Sophie tries to negotiate the front of the tree as I hoist the trunk up and shove it forward, pushing the tip of the tree further between the two front seats. We've been jiggling this tree around for at least five minutes in what can only be described as a comedy sketch.

'Nearly there.' I hear her voice but Sophie is completely out of view now, buried somewhere under the tree.

I give it one last lurch forward and the base of the trunk finally slides into the boot, and I close the boot quickly before it attempts to spring free and make good its escape.

Climbing into the driver's seat, I brush some stray netting from my view. I'm wedged in between the car door and green spruce. Sophie gets into the passenger side and the tree is nudged further in my direction.

I start the car and set off gingerly down the farm track, struggling to operate the gear stick buried beneath the tree. Shaking my head, I'm drawn back to the reoccurring thought that someone is secretly filming my life for their own amusement and one day it will be broadcast live for all to see and laugh at.

'This is why...' I state, brushing pine tree from my view to no avail. Sophie remains hidden behind the giant green cone. 'This is exactly why I didn't want that very attractive man assisting us. We're ridiculous, and I think it better all round if we contain that fact between ourselves without a very handsome spectator.'

Sophie says nothing to either confirm or deny my accusation. She must be well aware that I can turn most scenarios into comedic events. Then I hear a giggle. It's soft at first but it's not long until it turns into shoulder-heaving laughter, and then I'm laughing too.

I'm laughing at the fact that I can't see Sophie over green spruce and netting.

I'm laughing at the fact that I could predict before we pulled up at the farm that the simple task of buying a Christmas tree would descend into a pantomime. (Seriously, why did the person serving us have to be that cute? There must have been a dozen or so guys working there but no, we had to get the hot guy "What are you looking for today?" indeed.)

And I'm laughing simply because it feels good to laugh so hard that my stomach hurts, so hard that I'm struggling to focus on driving; because it feels like a lifetime ago since I laughed uncontrollably. As Sophie stated earlier, I need to get into the festive spirit, and I think this has just about done it.

It's nearly Christmas, after all.

Chapter Thirty-Nine

We repeat the same hoist and shuffle action to force the tree up the two flights of stairs to my flat. Why didn't I pick a building with a lift? No – the question is: why did I let myself get talked into buying a four-foot tree?

We make it into the flat, and Sophie heads back down to the car to collect our shopping bags while I, severely lacking grace, drag the tree into the lounge and over to the corner next to the television stand. Leaning it against the wall, I gasp for breath. I feel incredibly unfit, although given the amount of Christmas shopping we've done today, I've probably walked the distance of a marathon whilst being hindered by carrying heavy bags bearing gifts.

Sophie bustles in, weighed down by bags which she discards in the kitchen. 'I'll nip to the off licence, shall I?'

'That would be great. I'll order the Chinese food to be delivered.' I wipe my brow.

'I won't be long.' Sophie grabs her purse and heads out of the door while I go in search of a vessel to stand the tree in.

By the time Sophie returns I'm slumped on the sofa admiring my handiwork. The Christmas tree has been released from its wrapping and is standing upright (somewhat slanting, but hey, it's a tree; they don't necessarily grow straight, do they?) and the Chinese food is ordered.

'Wine?' Sophie waves a bottle of Sauvignon Blanc around the door. 'What the hell is that?'

'What?'

'That thing that the Christmas tree's standing in?'

'Oh. I've no idea. I think it's what you use to make a vat of stew or something. My mother forced it on me when Joe and I moved in together. I used it to transport my toiletries when I moved out.'

Sophie scowls at it.

'It'll be fine with some tinsel wrapped around it.'

'Speaking of tinsel, do you actually have any Christmas decorations to hang on your tree?'

I ponder for a moment. 'I have fairy lights.' I hold up the box of lights that I purchased with the tree.

'You're hopeless,' Sophie chastises softly.

'May I remind you that it wasn't my idea to buy a tree, and didn't you say something about wine?'

'Yes. Of course. I'll grab some glasses.'

Sophie heads into the kitchen and returns two minutes later. She places the glasses on the coffee table before filling them with wine and handing me a glass, and then raises her drink in the air for a toast. 'To Christmas.'

'Yeah.' I clink my glass against hers. 'To Christmas.'

By the time the intercom buzzes, signalling the arrival of our food, we've demolished the majority of the bottle of wine, which on top of the mulled wine in empty stomachs has made us both a bit giddy. The fairy lights have been unravelled and are now placed haphazardly on the Christmas tree. It really is harder than it looks to get the lights evenly wrapped around the branches without garrotting yourself in the process.

We sit at the small kitchen table and I slosh the remaining wine into our glasses as Sophie shares out the Chinese food.

'Have you decided what you're doing at Christmas?' I ask tentatively and bite into a piece of prawn toast.

'I'm going to spend Christmas Day at Mum and Dad's.'

'Oh, right,' I say causally. I'm relieved that she isn't spending Christmas with Matt and his family, i.e. Joe. 'What about Matt?'

'We're going to spend Christmas Eve together at mine. I thought we could have some party food and champagne, and snuggle up on the sofa together watching Christmas movies.'

'That sounds…lovely.' I swallow. It sounds perfect actually.'I wonder how I'll be spending Christmas Eve. Oh yes, I remember: I have my mother and her boyfriend, no – male friend – staying with me, which will be, well, plain weird, I think.

'How about you?' Sophie asks, spooning chicken fried rice onto our plates.

'I'll probably be enjoying the calm before the inevitable storm.' I sigh and gulp the dregs of my wine.

'Christmas Day will be fine, Emma. You'll see.'

'What? With Mum, Dad, Margaret and Parker all pulling Christmas crackers and wearing paper hats?'

'They're all adults and they've all agreed to do this. Your mum and dad get along perfectly well, don't they?'

'Yes,' I mutter.

'And it'll be nice to spend some time with your mum.'

'It will,' I agree. 'So what have you bought Matt for Christmas?'

Sophie's eyes light up. 'I got us tickets to the Comedy Store. We went earlier this year and he loved it. There was a real mix of comedians on stage and they were all good.'

'Oh yeah, I remember you two going. That's nice.' I smile. Joe loved the Comedy Store too.

We quickly demolish the food. It would appear that Christmas shopping really builds up an appetite.

'We seem to be out of wine.' I wave the empty bottle. 'Fancy another?'

For the first time in a while Sophie and I make our way, a little tipsy, back to the off licence for a second bottle of wine. It didn't occur to me to tell her to buy two earlier, perhaps because I had good intentions of only having a glass or two. You'd have thought that after all these years I'd know it never works out that way.

The cashier in the off licence eyes us with suspicion as we present him with another bottle of Sauvignon Blanc.

'Ooh, mulled wine,' I say, grabbing a bottle from the display next to the tills.

'Is that everything?' the cashier asks.

'Yes. Thank you.' I smile over-politely and hand him a twenty-pound note.

Once safely back in my flat I proceed to search for a saucepan to heat the mulled wine in.

'Shall we have a glass of white while it's heating up?' Sophie suggests, having already opened the bottle and started pouring the wine into our glasses.

We leave the nulled wine to simmer on the hob and retreat to the lounge. The Christmas tree doesn't actually look that bad, and I concede that having it here makes me feel a bit more Christmassy. I won't tell Sophie that, though.

I switch on the television for some background noise and the film The Holiday with Cameron Diaz and Kate Winslet is playing. It's a romantic comedy set at Christmas, which seems perfectly apt, although I'm not sure I'm in the mood for romantic couples at Christmas tonight. My head's still not right about the whole thing with Tom.

I'm not exactly sure what, if anything, happened the other night. There was definitely a spark between us that I haven't felt before. Or maybe I have and I've been trying to supress it under some misguided notion that if I admit that I like Tom then I'm somehow cheating on Joe.

Which is stupid. Joe and I are over, and have been for a while now. Joe's probably got someone else by now anyway, and they're looking forward to sharing their first Christmas together.

I gulp my wine.

'Is everything okay, Emma?' I hadn't realised Sophie was watching me.

Feeling slightly braver due to the alcohol, I decide to be honest with Sophie about my potential feelings for Tom.

'I'm fine. Everything's fine.' I exhale deeply. 'I had a bit of a moment with Tom – or at least I think it was a moment. The other night. After our last college class before the Christmas break.'

'A moment? What kind of moment? How come you're only telling me about this now?' She takes a mouthful of wine and then places her glass on the coffee table and leans towards me, her eyes wide and intense.

'We…well, we almost kissed. I think.'

'What do you mean, you think? How do you "almost" kiss someone? Honestly Emma.' She sounds exasperated.

'I don't know. We were in a pub. There were a few of us having a good time, and towards the end of the night Tom and I found ourselves standing away from the others and we were close together. There was definitely some…electricity between the two of us, and he leaned in a little nearer, but then we were interrupted.'

'And you left it there?'

'The moment kind of came and went and there wasn't an opportunity to rekindle it.'

'So how do you feel about Tom?'

'I like him. He's cute, and there was something, or maybe nothing. Maybe I'm simply getting a little over-emotional at Christmas, you know.'

'Aren't you the one who's spent the last three months denying any feelings for this guy and protesting to all who'd listen that rubbish that men and women can just be friends?'

'Hmm. That would be correct.'

'So do you admit it?'

'Admit what?'

'That men and women can't simply be friends. That there'll always be some sexual chemistry on at least one person's behalf.'

'No,' I state defiantly. 'I don't concede that.'

'But you want to be more than friends with Tom?'

'Maybe. I don't know. I didn't ever...' I stop myself. 'That mulled wine smells amazing. I'll go and get us some.'

'Wait.' Sophie grabs my arm as I stand up. 'You didn't ever what?'

I bite my lip, feeling stupid. But Sophie's my best friend, and I'm sure she won't think any less of me, even though I feel pathetic thinking this let alone saying it out loud.

'I didn't ever...ever think of myself with anyone else but Joe.'

'Oh.' Sophie's voice is heavy.

'I couldn't imagine ever wanting anyone else to kiss me, to touch me, or being comfortable naked with anyone but him. I know it's silly.'

'It's not silly.' Sophie hugs me tightly. 'You thought you were going to spend the rest of your life with him. Why would you see yourself with anyone else?'

'But I'm not going to be spending the rest of my life with him, am I?'

'If you're not ready to start seeing someone else then that's your choice, Emma. There's no rush.'

'I know that. Tom's a nice guy, but I'm not sure it feels right. It's almost as though I want it to be okay in my head, but my heart isn't quite there yet.'

'I understand.' Sophie smiles gently. 'Come on, let's try this mulled wine.'

Chapter Forty

Four days to Christmas.

'I'd better get going.' I down the last of my bottle of beer and Jenny pulls on her coat. 'I promised Mum I'd be home to take delivery of the food she's ordered for Christmas.'

It's the end of our three last days at work before we close for Christmas and we're having a quick beer in the pub across the road from the shop.

'Are you cooking?' Jenny looks at me, aghast.

'No,' I answer 'I realise my limitations in the kitchen.'

'Such as opening wine and crisps?' Jenny grins.

Hmm.

I ignore her flippant comment. 'Anyway...'

'I'm only kidding. It's not like I'm some domestic goddess...although I do make a mean shepherd's pie.'

That's true. I've been to Jenny's house for dinner and eaten such pie and it was indeed very good.

'My mum's the kind of woman who enjoys the pressure of hosting dinners.' I shake my head. 'I, on the other hand, am not.'

'I agree. Christmas Day should be for getting tipsy and stuffing your face with chocolates and food that someone else has prepared, which is why I'm going to my family's house.'

We head out of the door and I pull on my hat, scarf and matching gloves as light snowflakes flutter tentatively down and settle like icing sugar on the pavement. A very obvious sign that Christmas is nearly upon us. I stare up at the swirling snowflakes.

'Only two more working days.' Jenny wraps a thick woollen scarf that must be two metres long around herself.

'I'm very happy about that. See you in the morning.'

I wave as I hurry in the biting cold towards my car. Christmas Eve falls on a Sunday this year, so our last day of opening at the shop will be Saturday. After the pre-Christmas rush at the end of November/beginning of December as people shopped for new evening dresses for festive parties, things have quietened down. Hopefully Jenny and I will be left to our own devices for the last two days and Julia Bamford can occupy herself elsewhere.

I reach the car with barely any feeling left in my toes and make the short journey home. It's six thirty and the delivery isn't due until seven. I arrive back at my flat at six forty and make myself a coffee to defrost my body. I contemplate throwing in a large shot of Irish cream liqueur for good measure but I think better of it. It occurs to me that so far I've spent December eating food that's laced with fat and/or alcohol, and drinking wine or beer on most evenings. But everyone does that at Christmas, don't they? I'll go on a diet in January and resolve to do more exercise – or at least some exercise. I realise that I'm a cliché, but so are millions of other people with good intentions for their New Year's resolutions.

Sipping the warm liquid, I start to regain feeling in my hands and feet. I hear my mobile phone ringing. Sophie's name is flashing on the screen.

'Hi, Soph. How are you?'

'Yeah, good thanks. I'd thought I'd ring you for a catch-up. It's nearly Christmas!' she squeals into the receiver and I have to hold the phone away from my ear.

'Okay, I need to tell you now that if you make any more noises like that during this conversation, I'll be forced to end the call.'

'Don't be such a scrooge.'

'I'm not a Scrooge,' I protest, 'and I fully accept your over-eagerness about Christmas. It's just that you reached an octave that only dogs can hear.'

The intercom buzzer interrupts before Sophie can respond.

'Sorry, Soph, I'm going to have to call you back. That's the delivery guy with the Christmas food.'

'No worries. Speak to you in a bit.'

I hang up the phone and press the intercom.

'Hello?'

'Hello, miss. I have a delivery for you.'

'Come on up.'

I press the door release and go to the front door, open it and stand in the doorway. I can hear the guy huffing and puffing as he makes it up the two flights of stars. And it's no wonder – when he appears I see he's carrying a large green crate that's brimming with food.

'Come in.' I hurry back inside and hold the door open for him. 'The kitchen is down the hallway.' I point.

'Thanks.' He brushes past me and I close the front door and follow him into the kitchen.

'I'll have this unpacked in no time.' I smile as he takes a moment to steady his breathing. 'Then you can get on your way.'

'Thank you.'

I stare down at the food, wondering how on earth it's all going to fit in my fridge.

'I'll pop down for the other two crates.'

'The what?' I look up at him, astounded.

'There are two more crates, miss.'

'Two more…but I don't have the room.'

'Not my problem, I'm afraid.' He looks at me a little uneasily.

'Of course not.' It isn't his problem. It's my mother's. What on earth was she thinking, and more to the point, what the hell has she ordered?

Ten minutes later, I'm still unpacking parsnips and red cabbage and I haven't come across a turkey yet. I fear that an incredibly large bird will be buried at the bottom of this last crate, and that really would be the final straw. Turkeys are huge, and my oven is neither wide enough nor tall enough to accommodate a full-sized turkey. Nor do I have room in the fridge to house it until Christmas Day, and there's no way I'm hacking at a chilled bird carcass to fit it in.

But as I pick up the last few items – stuffed dates? I hope they're for Mum and I'm not expected to eat them – I see a box labelled "turkey crown" nestled at the bottom and I breathe a sigh of relief.

'Is that everything?' the delivery guy asks, stacking the three empty crates.

I look around the kitchen and survey the vast amount of food piled high on the kitchen worktops, the small table and the floor. 'I hope so.'

'Then I'll wish you a Merry Christmas, miss.'

'And you too.'

I show the delivery guy out. Back in the kitchen, I don't know where to start. After a minute or two of deliberation, I pour myself a large glass of wine and dial Sophie's number.

'Hi, Emma. All sorted?' she asks.

'In a manner of speaking.'

'What does that mean?'

'It means that the food my mum ordered has arrived.'

'But?'

'But she appears to have mistakenly ordered food for the entire block of flats and hasn't taken into account my lack of storage space for food, especially the amount that needs refrigerating.'

'Oh.' I can hear Sophie giggling.

'Don't laugh,' I warn her. 'You're going to have to help me.'

'Help you how?'

'I don't know, but for starters you need to drive over here and fill your car with whatever food won't fit in my fridge.'

'And what am I supposed to do with it then?'

'Put it in your fridge, and your mum's fridge, and whoever else's fridges you can hijack.'

'I'm on my way.' Sophie chuckles before putting the phone down.

Ten minutes later she arrives at my flat and takes in the amount of food still strewn around my kitchen.

'Wow!' She puts a hand over her mouth. 'You weren't kidding.'

I look at her with an expression of despair.

'Don't panic.' She hold up her hands. 'We'll sort it.'

'It's like a cryptic game. To fit, the items need to be placed in a specific pattern,' I say, exasperated after spending the last ten minutes shoving food items into the fridge, moving them around and then taking them back out again.

'Calm down.' Sophie hands me my half-drunk wine. 'Go into the lounge and finish your drink. I can handle this.'

'Are you sure?'

'I'm sure.'

I walk through and slump on the sofa, exhausted. Christmas is far too demanding for people like me. As for Sophie, she has the mad organisational skills that you have to exhibit in the run-up to Christmas, and it's no surprise that a short time later she appears in the doorway with her own glass of wine and says smugly, 'All done.'

Chapter Forty-One

Two days to Christmas.

I cringe inwardly as the ringing of my alarm clock permeates my deep sleep. Stretching out a hand I silence it, then quickly pull my hand back under the covers where it's warm and snug. Maybe I can have another five minutes' sleep; that won't hurt, I'm sure.

My conscience wakes up just as I close my eyes and prods me sharply. Oh, crap.

I sit bolt upright in bed and acknowledge the fact that it's still pitch-black. That's because it's five a.m. The reason for my rude awakening at this unearthly hour is that my mother and her "male companion" are arriving from New York on the night flight and I promised to collect them from the airport at seven a.m. Damn it.

I slide my body gingerly out of the bed, grab my fluffy dressing gown and wrap it tightly around me, and shuffle, one eye still closed, through to the kitchen, turning the heating thermostat up as I pass it in the hallway. At this moment I'm extremely grateful for my coffee pod machine, which makes really good – and, more importantly, strong – coffee instantaneously.

I sip the hot liquid as I pace the kitchen in an effort to wake my body up, while also trying to calm the nervous feeling in the pit of my stomach. Having Mum and Parker staying here with me feels a bit odd. I don't really know him, and I have an awful fear that I'll bump into him in the middle of the night as we simultaneously head to the bathroom, and I'll be completely naked having forgotten, in my sleep-weary state, that I'm not alone in my apartment. Oh, the shame of it!

I'm also slightly concerned about my mother sharing a bed with a man in my flat. I know that's silly: they're both adults. Maybe that's what's worrying me. I try to push thoughts of my mum's sex life forcibly from my brain. I don't need to think about that over the next few days – or, in fact, ever.

When I've finished the last of my coffee, I head into the bathroom. After a hot shower, I feel like I'm functioning at about ninety per cent. I pile on layers of clothes, protection against the sub-zero temperatures we're currently experiencing. The snow seems to have bypassed us, apart from the rare light flurry which teases our hope, and instead the winter weather has gone straight to severe frost and ice, which should make the journey to the airport interesting, to say the least.

When I step out of the building and into the dark morning, I'm glad to be dressed like an Eskimo, as the freezing air instantly hits my cheeks like a slap around the face. Ice covers the windscreen of the car, but when I pull the can of de-icer from the boot and give it a shake, I realise it's practically empty and curse under my breath. I start the engine, turn the heaters up and climb out armed with the ice scraper, which I leave in the glove box as a last resort – it looks like it's my only option this morning.

After a few minutes of jabbing the ice, I've finally cleared enough of the screen to be able to drive and I jump in the car, rubbing my now numb hands vigorously together. It's six fifteen and the airport is only half an hour away, so I still have plenty of time. Maybe I can grab a takeaway latte in the arrivals hall before Mum and Parker appear.

Thankfully at this time of the morning the traffic is sparse, and I arrive at the airport twenty-five minutes later having carefully negotiated the slick iced roads. The arrivals hall is bustling with people, many of them holding handwritten signs displaying the names of their passengers.

I buy a latte from the coffee shop and perch on the end of one of the rows of cold metal seats. Christmas decorations line the walls, and taking pride of place in the centre of the area is a huge real Christmas tree with hundreds of colourful baubles. I think of my own tree, with fairy lights and nothing else. Never mind. At least I have a tree. Without Sophie's persistence after our Christmas shopping, I doubt I would even have that. Images of the hot young guy who served us at the Christmas tree farm spring into my mind and my cheeks flush. I gulp coffee as a distraction but it has little impact, so I allow myself a few moments to browse those images in my mind and simply enjoy them.

'Emma?'

My mum's cheerful tone interrupts a daydream of me and the guy from the Christmas tree farm in a passionate embrace under some mistletoe. I glance up and see Parker pushing a trolley laden with suitcases and my mother marching alongside him, dressed impeccably, as usual, in a caramel-coloured floor-length coat with a chocolate trilby and a matching scarf wrapped elegantly around her shoulders.

'Hello, darling.' Mum flings her arms around me as soon as she's in touching distance. 'It's so lovely to see you.'

'Hi, Mum,' I mumble into her scarf.

'You remember Parker, don't you?' Mum beams at Parker, who's also dressed impeccably, in a black woollen coat with what looks like a red cashmere scarf tucked neatly into the open neck.

He shakes my hand firmly.

'It's nice to see you again, Emma. And thank you for inviting us to stay with you over Christmas.' He smiles, showing even white teeth. Potentially as fake as his hair colour, I think, and I quickly supress a giggle.

Also, I don't remember inviting Mum and Parker to stay exactly; I was instructed by Mum that it was going to happen and I was too browbeaten at that point to argue.

I offer to assist with their luggage but Parker politely refuses. As we head to the car park, Mum links arm with mine.

'It really is good to see you, Emma, and you look really well, like you're back on top of things.'

Oh yes, the last time Mum saw me I was in a deep depression, hibernating under my duvet and detached from reality, with an appearance that would scare even the most hard-faced horror movie fan. That was also when Mum and Sophie had their "intervention" about my drinking habits.

'I'm feeling much more positive about things.' I smile genuinely at her.

'That's good, Emma.' She squeezes me tightly to her and we walk in silence until we reach the car.

Getting their vast amount of luggage in my hatchback provides a similar challenge to the Christmas tree, except that this time we have a third human being to fit in as well. After a brief struggle we get the two larger bags into the boot and Mum slides elegantly into the front passenger seat, leaving Parker to climb into the rear seat with Mum's pink vanity case perched on his lap. I have to stifle a giggle, but as I watch Parker making himself comfortable I realise that he doesn't seem to mind at all.

'Did all of the food that I ordered arrive?' Mum asks as we head out of the airport car park and onto the ring road.

'Yes, it's all here.' I think back to the other night when I was surrounded by unusual food parcels in my kitchen and required the organisational skills of an expert, i.e. Sophie, to fit them into the fridge, freezer and every spare centimetre of my cupboard space. 'At least I hope it is.'

'What do you mean?'

'Well, you do realise that there are only five of us, don't you, Mum? I think there's enough food to feed the whole street.'

'Don't be silly, Emma. And anyway, it's Christmas. It's better to have too much food when you're having guests over than not enough.'

'It's only Dad and Margaret.'

'They're still guests in your home, Emma.'

'You're right,' I concede. 'But you can keep the stuffed dates for yourself.'

Mum laughs. 'Alright.'

Once we arrive at my flat, Parker very kindly offers to lug the suitcases up the two flights of stairs while Mum and I make a cup of tea.

'I only have about half an hour before I need to go to work,' I say as I carefully extract a bottle of milk from the fridge.

'That's fine, Emma. Parker and I can amuse ourselves today.'

I don't even want to know what that means.

'I thought I might take him into town to show him a few sights. Is the Christmas market still here?' Mum asks, stirring the mugs of tea.

Ah, she means sightseeing. 'Yes, it's the last day today.'

'Wonderful. We can enjoy the festivities with some mulled wine.'

'Sounds like a lovely way to spend the day.'

'Just one more bag,' Parker calls from the hallway as Mum and I take the drinks through to the lounge.

'Emma! What is that?'

'What, Mum?' I look around, startled.

'Your Christmas tree.' She stands in the middle of the room assessing my tree with her mouth open.

'Um, it's a Christmas tree?' Why do people keep asking me questions in relation to trees that appear to have a literal answer but in fact, I fear, have some underlying meaning?

'Why is it bare?'

'It's not bare,' I protest. 'It has lights on it.' I walk over and flick the switch and the fairy lights come to life.

Mum furrows her eyebrows and shakes her head at me in a way that only mothers do when they want to convey disappointment without saying a word.

I sip my tea as Parker walks back into the apartment and joins us in the lounge. Mum hands him a mug of tea and he stands next to her. We all stare, transfixed, at the Christmas tree.

'What a lovely tree, Emma. Very classy and minimalist,' Parker states before taking a drink of his tea.

I fail to hide a smug grin. 'Thank you, Parker.'

Chapter Forty-Two

A short while later I kiss Mum on the cheek and wave goodbye as I head off to work. It's the last day in the shop before we close up for Christmas. I can't believe it's Christmas Eve tomorrow. Thankfully the thick ice which greeted me earlier has now started to thaw, which makes the journey to work a little easier.

'Morning!' Jenny calls jovially from the shop floor as I close the door behind me and step into the staff area at the back of the building.

'Coffee?' I call back, and I hang up my coat and switch on the kettle. Thankfully it's quite warm in here; Jenny must have got here early.

Jenny pops her head around the door. 'I'm doing a last stock check. I'm so excited that it's Christmas in two days!' She beams. 'I'll get the Christmas CD on, shall I?'

'Sounds good to me, Jenny.'

I busy myself making the coffees and a few moments later "Last Christmas" by Wham blares out of the speakers. My heart flinches. I love and hate this song with equal measure. It's one of my favourite songs to sing along to, but the words make me feel emotional.

'Come on.' Jenny grabs my hand and starts swaying to the music. 'It's Christmas!' she shouts, and we dance and giggle around the kitchen area until "Last Christmas" ends and "Rockin' around the Christmas Tree" reverberates through the shop.

The whole day is spent laughing, singing and dancing as customers are few and far between. We complete the stock check together, and it quickly reaches four p.m. Jenny's on a major high, counting down the minutes until we close at five.

At four thirty we get the shock of our lives as Julia Bamford appears, as if by magic, at the rear of the shop. Neither of us heard the back door open and close (perhaps due to the volume the Christmas CD is playing at) and we both freeze, eyes wide and mouths closed, awaiting the reprimand that's sure to come. However, Julia Bamford simply smiles at us, displaying her neat white teeth.

'I've got something for you both,' she says loudly over the music and I instinctively jump over to the CD player and press pause.

Julia walks over to us and hands each of us a white envelope. For a second I wonder whether all of her moaning and complaining at us for the last few months has culminated in this moment, and the envelopes contain our P45s.

'Merry Christmas,' she states, rather than says, and Jenny glances at me warily.

I take the initiative and rip open my envelope. It's much better to know the truth than to speculate. I pull out a Christmas card with a winter scene of a forest and deer covered in white glitter. As I open it two fifty-pound notes fall out, and I look at Julia Bamford with wonderment.

'Um…thank you.'

Jenny opens her card too. 'Yes, thanks very much,' she says quietly, clutching her own two fifty-pound notes.

'It's a little something to show our appreciation for your hard work,' Julia says. 'Hope you both have a lovely Christmas. Why don't you get ready to close up now and get off home? No more customers will be in today.'

And with that she turns on her heel and heads for the door.

'Merry Christmas to you too,' I call after her.

I hear the back door open and close as Julia disappears as quickly as she appeared only a moment ago, and I swing around to face Jenny. 'We're both going straight to hell, you know.' I wave the card in the air.

'Don't be overdramatic, Emma.' Jenny rolls her eyes at me.

'All the name calling we've done about Julia in the last few months and now this…this kind gesture.'

'Exactly. This is a peace offering because she knows she's been dreadful to us and she's probably worried we might not come back after the Christmas break and then she'd have to find two more lackeys.'

'Maybe.'

'You know I'm right. Now come on, she said we could lock up and go home and I don't need telling twice.'

I grin. 'Merry Christmas.'

'Merry Christmas.' Jenny hugs me. 'Hope you have a great one.'

'You go; I'll lock up.'

'Are you sure?'

'Of course. Have a lovely Christmas and I'll see you bright and early the day after Boxing Day.'

As the door closes behind Jenny the shop stills, and it's silent for the first time today. For some reason, nostalgia maybe, I make myself one last coffee and wander over to the CD player. I find track six, hit the play button and walk slowly over to the shop window as George Michael sings "Last Christmas" once again.

I won't get to experience Christmas with Joe, and today that bothers me more than ever. As I swallow down the surprise of tears welling in my eyes, I see a snowflake tumble down in the light cast by a streetlight right outside the window, then another, and another. By the time the track has finished playing, snowflakes are dancing down from the sky and covering the pavement in icing sugar.

I switch off the CD player and remove the plug, then for the second time I check all the other plug sockets are switched off too. The last thing I need is the shop burning down over the Christmas period due to an electrical fire when I was the last one to leave.

I wash my cup and leave it to drain next to the sink. Then I pull on my coat, turn out all the lights and step out into swirling snow and what now looks like the picture on the front of a Christmas card.

The car journey home is a little tricky as the snow has started to settle and there's not much traffic to dissolve it, but I make it back to the flat unscathed – if you don't count nearly slipping on my bum as I climb out of the car. I walk up the stairs to my flat, suddenly feeling weary and thoughts of a large glass of wine and a hot bath fill my mind. I wonder what Mum and Parker have planned for tonight?

As I reach my front door raucous laughter is coming from the other side and I frown as I hear Mum's voice; she's clearly in high spirits. I unlock the door and walk in tentatively.

'Mum?' I call as I head down the hallway towards the lounge.

'Emma, darling!' Mum exclaims as I stand in the doorway, taking in the scene before me. She and Parker are standing either side of the Christmas tree, which is now adorned with red and gold baubles and sparkling strings of beads that shimmer under the fairy lights.

'I hope you don't mind, Emma, but your tree looked, well, not like a Christmas tree should. It looked sad.'

'The tree looked sad?' I raise my eyebrows, feeling a slight edge of annoyance creeping in.

'We thought we'd cheer it up a little, that's all.' Mum winks at Parker, her co-conspirator.

I take in Mum's flushed cheeks and Parker's inability to meet my gaze.

'Mum, are you drunk?' I ask, my hands placed firmly on my hips.

'Absolutely not, Emma.' Mum looks back at me sternly.

'Okay, I'll rephrase that question: how much mulled wine did you drink at the Christmas market, and how much sherry has followed that?' I stare accusingly at the open bottle on the coffee table. After all that spouting she did last time she was here about my drinking and now Mum's not been here two minutes and she and Parker are clearly sloshed.

'Honestly, Emma' – Mum's expression softens – 'we've had a couple of drinks to start the festive celebrations, that's all.'

'Hmm,' is about all I can manage. Mum wobbles slightly to her left as she stands defiantly – a complete giveaway, if I ever saw one. I can't believe that Mum and Parker are at the very least tipsy.

'Why don't you join us for one?' Mum picks up the bottle of sherry. 'I'll go and get another glass.'

'No, Mum, really...'

She looks at me a little hurt and glances at Parker, whose face is solemn, and now I feel like a complete bitch who's ruined the party. I take in a deep breath and exhale.

'I don't really like sherry, Mum, but I'll go and get a bottle of wine from the fridge instead. You're right, tomorrow is Christmas Eve and I'm done with work for the next three days.'

I kick off my winter boots in the hallway and hang up my coat, and then fetch a bottle of white wine and three glasses and return to the lounge.

'So what have you two done today, apart from rearrange my Christmas tree?' I ask while pouring wine into the glasses.

'We walked around the Christmas market and sampled some of the wonderful food from the stalls,' Mum gushes.

'And the alcohol, clearly,' I chip in, but Mum ignores my comment and continues regardless.

'I took Parker to the cathedral and around the art gallery on Houseman Street.'

'Oh, that's nice actually.'

'You've been there?' Mum looks at me with surprise.

'Yes.'

'I'm sorry, Emma, I didn't mean to insult you. I didn't think art galleries were particularly your thing.'

'That's alright, they're not really. Simon dragged me along to look at a sculpture of, well, something that was unrecognisable to me, but he thought it was amazing.'

Parker joins in the conversation, having been quiet since my accusation about them being drunk; now he's relaxing a little and sipping his wine. 'They do have some unique pieces. I saw a few items I'd like to have purchased myself if I didn't have to get them back home to New York.'

'I know, the shipping costs are a nightmare,' Mum states. 'Do you remember that vase I bought a few years ago when we went to London, Emma?'

'Yes.' I smile at the image of a huge dark-blue vase with coloured glass twisted around the outside. Mum fell in love with it instantly and bought it on the spot without considering how she was going to get it halfway around the world to her home in New York.

Mum laughs. 'It cost almost half as much again to get the damned thing to my apartment.'

'I remember. But you love that vase, Mum.'

'I know. It was worth every penny.'

'Is that the one on your wall unit in the lounge? It's exquisite,' says Parker.

'That's the one.' Mum nods. 'Now, what are your plans for Christmas Eve, darling?'

'I'm meeting Sophie for a quick coffee in the morning to exchange gifts, and I need to call in at Simon's flat on my way home to drop off the present I bought for him and James. Then, nothing I guess.'

'I'll need to do some food preparation during the day,' Mum says.

I silently pray that she won't ask for my assistance with that. I know that's selfish, but this whole cooking thing was her idea and it's not my strength.

'And I think I'll take Parker to the Christmas carols at the cathedral at seven p.m. Why don't you join us?'

Actually that sounds like a really nice way to start Christmas.

'We could have some mince pies and mulled wine before we go – keep us warm in that big, old cathedral,' she suggests.

'That sounds lovely, Mum. Count me in.' I glance at my watch, feeling weary. It's ten p.m. After drinking the last of my wine, I decide to call it a night. 'I think I'm going to go to bed.'

'We should too.' Mum looks at Parker. 'We've had a very long day, and my body clock's all over the place with the time-zone difference.'

'The spare room is made up and there are towels in the airing cupboard.' I stifle a yawn.

'Thanks, Emma. We'll be fine. You get yourself off to bed; you look a bit tired and you need to be fully refreshed for Christmas Day.'

'Goodnight, Mum.' I kiss her on the cheek.

'Goodnight.' She tucks my hair behind my ears like she used to when I was a child. 'See you in the morning.'

'Goodnight, Emma.' Parker gives me a slightly stiff hug. He's trying, and he seems like a nice guy. He makes Mum happy, which is all that really counts.

I head through to my bedroom and close the door behind me. I need to remember to do that, and especially to lock the bathroom door. Living on your own makes you very lackadaisical about these things, as there's no need to worry about anyone walking in on you semi-naked.

I take off my work clothes and pull on a t-shirt and pyjama bottoms, then drag an all-in-one facial wipe across my face to remove the majority of my makeup. As I climb into bed and pull the covers up tightly around me, I feel that nice sense of anticipation that only Christmas Eve can bring. It's the one day of the year that feels truly magical, and in some ways I love Christmas Eve more than Christmas Day itself. Thoughts of snow and mulled wine fill my head as I snuggle deeper under the covers and drift into sleep.

What's that noise?

My ears prick up and I listen intently. Silence, then I hear it again. Giggling, followed by my mother saying, 'Shush.'

Oh no, it's Mum and Parker. What could that mean? More importantly, what time is it? I roll over and pick up the clock from the bedside table, squinting at the display screen. It's a few minutes after midnight, two hours since I left them in the living room together with my mum stating that they needed to go to bed too. And now that's where they're heading – to bed. Giggling.

Mum seems to behave differently with Parker, more relaxed and very comfortable. She obviously cares about him. Maybe she loves him. People in love do that though, don't they? Relax in each other's company. They don't hide behind any barriers; they're honest and have no reason not to show the other person exactly who they are, because they're loved for that, for being themselves.

I had that with Joe.

I hear footsteps shuffle past my bedroom door and then the door to the spare room opens and closes. Pulling the quilt up over my ears, I bury myself in the bed. I do not need to hear anything that goes on in that spare room between my mother and her "gentleman friend". Urgh! That's far too much for my imagination to take.

My mum and Parker do not have sex.

Mum and Parker do not have sex.

I repeat the mantra even though I'm one hundred per cent sure that there'll be no funny business under my roof. Okay, maybe ninety five per cent sure.

'I was scared; I am scared.'

Chapter Forty-Three

Christmas Eve

I open my eyes to find a bright streak of sunshine glaring through the crack in the curtains, signalling a cold but sunny day. I climb out of bed and pull on my fluffy dressing gown and fling the curtains open to see a thick frost covering everything and twinkling in the sunlight.

I pad through to the kitchen, taking note that the spare room door is firmly closed, and shake my head to dislodge the thought of Mum and Parker locked in an embrace. I'm sure they're simply having a lie-in following their long flight yesterday morning.

After turning on the coffee machine, I locate a cappuccino pod and a mug and take bacon from the fridge. I might as well start as I mean to go on over the Christmas period by eating food that's bad for me. To be honest, it's unlikely to make much of a difference given that I've eaten my body weight in mince pies since the beginning of December. I place the pod in the machine, press the start button.

I switch on the light above the hob, spray oil into the frying pan and then gaze out of the kitchen window. Despite the bright sunshine there are heavy grey clouds in the distance and I wonder whether snow might arrive later today.

Throwing a couple of bacon slices in the frying pan, I then butter two slices of bread. The meat starts to sizzle and the kitchen fills with that fantastic aroma that only bacon can produce.

'Morning, darling.' I hear Mum's voice behind me as I take my cappuccino from the machine and I spin around.

'Good morning.' I can't help but smile as I take in Mum's slightly bedraggled appearance. 'Although maybe you're not feeling that good yourself?' I sound smug and I know it, but I'm taken aback by Mum's less than glamourous exterior – it's so unusual for her not to look pristine and be full of energy the moment she hops out of bed.

'Is that bacon I smell?'

'Yes, would you like some?'

'If it's not too much trouble.'

Mum eases herself down onto a chair at the small kitchen table and I take pity on her, having woken slightly (or, in some cases, very) worse for wear myself over the last few months before I curbed my incessant alcohol consumption.

'You can have the first one.' I place the bacon onto the buttered bread and hand the plate to Mum.

'Thank you; that's very kind, Emma.'

'Coffee?' I ask, placing another couple of bacon slices into the frying pan and adding a further spray of oil.

'That would be lovely.'

I slip another cappuccino pod into the machine as the bacon cooks.

'Where's Parker?' I ask tentatively.

'He's having five more minutes in bed,' Mum answers between bites of bacon sandwich. 'I think we had a little too much to drink yesterday.'

'Really?'

'Don't be smug, Emma.'

'Sorry.'

Mum smiles and sips her cappuccino. 'I think it was the flight and time change. The alcohol appeared to affect us more than usual.'

'Of course.' I turn back to the frying pan to hide my smile.

'What time are you meeting Sophie?'

'At eleven thirty. It's only nine fifteen now, so I've got plenty of time.'

'That gives me a couple of hours to prepare the food for tomorrow. Your dad and Margaret will be here for about noon. We'll have plenty of time to exchange all of our gifts before we sit down to lunch.'

'That's fine.' I join Mum at the table with my bacon sandwich. 'What time did you get to bed last night?' I ask, although I already know the answer.

'We had a nightcap of brandy.' Mum rubs her temples. 'I don't know what came over us – well, me really. Maybe I'm feeling a little pressure because it's my first Christmas with Parker.'

Wow. That thought had never occurred to me. I guess no one is immune to insecurities about their relationships.

'I'm sure Parker will have a lovely time with us.'

Mum nods and we remain in our own quiet thoughts as we finish breakfast.

As I stand up and place the pots in the sink Parker appears in the doorway, looking a little sheepish but thankfully fully dressed in his day clothes – I'm not sure that I could cope with seeing Parker in his pyjamas, assuming he wears any. Oh no, don't go there again, Emma!

'Good morning, Emma,' he says in a polished voice.

'Good morning, Parker,' I manage, equally polished, as I walk past him towards the bathroom, hiding my smile until I'm safely out of sight.

I shower and dress at a leisurely pace, enjoying the feel of Christmas Eve. It's the nice calm, before the storm. The moment of anticipation of Christmas itself. The shopping, parties and generally running around like a headless chicken is done and now there's just the lull before the overexcitement of Christmas Day.

When I return to the kitchen, Mum's already elbow deep in pots and pans. I look around with some amusement at my small kitchen, which has been turned into an industrial production line, with Mum shouting instructions to Parker, who hands her implements or ingredients.

'I'm going to meet Sophie now,' I announce, interrupting their flow of chatter.

'Okay, darling. Do you want to join us for lunch?'

'Thanks for the offer but I'll grab some food with Sophie, and then I need to drop off Simon's present so it might be late afternoon when I get home.'

'That's fine. When I'm done here' – she waves her arms around – 'we're going to lunch and then maybe we'll stroll around St Paul's Park. It's a lovely, crisp winter's day.'

'That sounds lovely.' And quite romantic.

'Are you still coming to the cathedral carols tonight?'

'Yes, I'll definitely be back in time for that. I'm looking forward to it. It's a nice way to officially start Christmas. See you later.'

I walk over and kiss Mum on the cheek. Then I grab the wrapped presents for Sophie and Simon from the lounge and head out of the front door.

Mum's right, it is a perfect winter's day. The cold air tingles on my face as I make my way to the car. There's only a thin film of frost covering the windscreen, so I decide against scraping with freezing-cold hands and go for the lazy option of sitting in the car with the heaters on full blast, waiting for it to melt. I reach for my mobile phone and text Simon to make sure he hasn't forgotten that I'm calling in later. He quickly texts back: *Sure, Ems, I'll be in. See you later xx*

The windscreen's just about clear so I set off to town to meet Sophie.

Chapter Forty-Four

The coffee shop is warm and welcoming, with Christmas music playing and the baristas wearing red Santa hats. The whole atmosphere is jovial, and I find myself smiling as soon as I walk to the counter to order.

"Two skinny lattes, please, and two large mince pies." I think I'm now up to four thousand and two mince pies, but I figure if I have skimmed milk then at least I'm making a small effort to reduce my huge calorie intake.

As I'm waiting for the drinks to be prepared, Sophie comes up behind me.

'Hi. Have you ordered?'

'Yes. I got us mince pies too.'

'Good! I'll grab a table.'

A few moments later I teeter across the coffee shop, trying to balance a tray with two large mugs of coffee and the mince pies while carrying the bag containing Sophie's present. I place the tray down gingerly and Sophie unloads the mugs.

'Can you believe it's Christmas Eve already?' She bounces in her seat like a child.

'How are you going to contain yourself until tomorrow morning?'

'I know, I do get a bit giddy at Christmas.'

'A bit?' I laugh.

'Okay, a lot. But it's Christmas!'

'Eat your mince pie.' I take a huge bite of my own; I never tire of the taste. 'What time are you meeting Matt?'

'He's coming over to mine around five. We're having champagne and nibbles.'

'That sounds great.' And very romantic, I find myself thinking for the second time this morning. What is it with everyone: Mum and Parker, Sophie and Matt? They're all loved up and doing intimate things together today. Maybe because it's Christmas, the rational part of my brain reminds me; that's what people do.

'What are your plans?'

'I'm going to see Simon and James to drop in their Christmas presents. Speaking of which…'

I hand over the bag containing Sophie's present. It's a makeup set from a new brand to which she's addicted, so I'm pretty sure she'll love it. It's wrapped beautifully in silver paper with snowflakes, and a red ribbon is tied in a bow around it. I'd like to claim the credit for that, but in all honesty it was gift wrapped by the store. Every shop should offer this service; it would save hours of stress and masses of unused sticky tape being stuck randomly to things.

'Thank you!' she squeals. 'Yours is in my car.'

'I'm having a not so romantic Christmas Eve though - I'm going to the carol service at the cathedral with Mum and Parker.'

'Ah, that'll be really nice.'

Hmm. Not as nice as snuggling up with your boyfriend and sipping champagne.

'Yeah, it will be.'

'Are you going to be okay?' Sophie looks at me with her head cocked slightly to one side.

'Why wouldn't I be?'

'Because it's Christmas, and it's a time to spend with loved ones...'

'Yes, and?'

'And I think you still miss Joe.'

I remain quiet, a little taken aback by her comment. I thought I was hiding my feelings of despair at a boyfriend-less Christmas quite well, but maybe not.

'I know you had a bit of a "moment" with Tom from college, but I don't think he's who you really want to be with.'

'Sophie –'

'Look, Emma, I'm not saying this to hurt you. I'm saying it because I care.'

'But what exactly are you saying?'

'Don't you think there's any hope that if you saw Joe and spoke to him then you could work things out? It's Christmas, after all. If you can't freely tell someone that you love them at Christmas, then when can you?'

'That's a nice idea, Sophie.' I take a gulp of coffee to drown the emotion that's rising inside me, and I forcibly push back the tears that feel imminent. 'But that sounds like a love story to me, and life's not like that.'

'Who says it can't be? Why can't life be a fairy-tale romance?'

'Don't you remember me calling him and some woman answering his phone?'

'Yes, but...'

'He's moved on Sophie. He's found someone else.'

'She might just have been a friend.'

'I thought men and women couldn't just be friends.'

'Don't be facetious.'

'Look, I'm just saying that I think I've had my heart crushed enough this year without declaring my love to Joe only for him to tell me that he doesn't love me anymore and that he has a lovely new girlfriend to share his life with, and that I should never darken his door again.'

'But if you never tell him that you still love him then there's no chance that he's going to say it back, is there?'

I remain silent, chewing on my bottom lip.

'Maybe you two just need to be in the same room as each other again to get a dialogue going.'

'Don't even think about trying to make that happen Sophie.' I've experienced Sophie's well intentioned meddling before. 'Leave well alone. Joe has found someone else and that's the end of it, oaky?'

'Okay.' She grumbles.

I allow myself to think just for a moment. Dare I believe that if I turn up on Joe's doorstep and tell him that I still love him, he'll throw his arms around me and declare his love for me too? Do I still love him? Do I have feelings for Tom? It's all too confusing and I'm not sure I have any hope of figuring it all out in the near future.

Sophie looks at me for a moment, seemingly deciding whether to push this conversation further. She takes the hint and retreats, changing the subject completely.

'So my mum and dad have booked a cruise for the end of January. It's not my thing at all. I can't imagine anything worse than being stuck on a big boat with hundreds of strangers and confined to a bedroom the size of a coffin, but they seem really excited about it...'

She gabbles on and I ad lib every now and again, distracted by the last conversation. The Christmas music's still playing loudly and I glance around, people-watching, looking at happy faces and animated conversations. The whole atmosphere feels charged with excitement and anticipation.

We finish our coffees and make our way outside to the pavement.

'I'm only parked around the corner,' Sophie says. 'You need to get your present.'

We link arms and walk to the end of the street.

'It's a new start soon,' Sophie says quietly.

'What?' I stop walking and turn to face her.

'A new year. A time for change, for positivity.'

'Sophie, stop worrying about me. I'm no longer sad and depressed about things ending with Joe. Do I wish things had worked out differently? Yes, I do. But life carries on regardless, and you have no choice but to adapt.'

'So you're definitely okay?'

'Of course.' I hug her. 'I really appreciate you caring so much, but I'm looking forward to spending Christmas with my family, even if it's a bit of an unusual gathering of people.'

'Alright.' She studies me for a moment.

'Enjoy your evening with Matt, and Christmas Day with your family.'

'I'll call you in the morning anyway – to wish you a happy Christmas.'

'I'd be disappointed if you didn't.'

We carry on walking until we reach Sophie's car. She retrieves a perfectly wrapped box from the boot, which I know is all her and not store gift-wrapped at all, and she hands it to me.

'Merry Christmas, Emma.'

'Merry Christmas, Sophie.'

She takes hold of my hand and gives it a little squeeze before she climbs into her car and I watch her drive away.

Ten minutes later I pull up outside Simon's and James's flat and slip the two presents for him and James into my large handbag. I've bought Simon an autobiography of some artist whose name I can't pronounce. Simon loves him, and has three of his clay sculptures, which he shows off when people visit the flat, much to James's amusement; he has very little interest in art and just humours Simon.

I press the buzzer for their flat.

'Hello?'

'Hey, it's only me.'

'Come up, Ems.'

The door clicks open and I head up the stairs to the flat where I'm greeted by a huge wreath of holly and berries hanging on the door.

'Wow,' I say, admiring it, as Simon opens the door, looking causal in grey jogging bottoms and a navy t-shirt.

He grins. 'Wait until you see the rest of the flat.'

I walk into what looks like Santa's grotto. Festive decorations hang from every possible point and most of them are covered in glitter. Every surface is adorned with a Christmas character or tinsel.

'I know it's a bit much.'

'A bit much? No.' I giggle.

James appears behind us. 'It looks like a wonderland from a Disney film.'

'Ignore him.' Simon scowls playfully at James.

'So this isn't your creativity?' I ask.

'Hell no, it's all Si. But if he's happy then I'm happy.' James kisses Simon affectionately on the cheek.

'See, I definitely married the man for me.' Simon laughs. 'If he can put up with spending three weeks living in this then he can put up with anything from me.'

'Coffee?' James asks.

'Yes, please.'

We all head into the kitchen where the Christmas madness continues.

'Have you had any lunch?' Simon asks.

'Are you offering to make us something to eat?' My eyebrows raise instinctively. Simon is as crap at food preparation as I am, unless it involves bacon, eggs or something that requires simple heating in the oven. Chocolate biscuits and a packet of crisps is usually the best I can expect to receive.

'No, silly, but James makes a mean toasted cheese sandwich.'

James rolls his eyes at Simon.

'No, it's alright. I don't want to be any trouble. I only came by to drop off your presents.'

'I'm making them for me and Simon anyway, Emma, so you're welcome to join us.'

I ponder for a moment. Mum and Parker will be having lunch out, so all that awaits me is an empty flat.

'That sounds lovely. Thanks, James.'

And so I spend the rest of the afternoon snuggled on the sofa between Simon and James as we reminisce about old times. It's lovely, and I realise that I might not have a boyfriend but I have got some really good friends who make me feel loved and wanted on every occasion, and for that I'm extremely lucky.

I return home to find the flat still empty. Mum must have whizzed Parker off to a museum or something. I glance at my watch. It's only four thirty but it feels much later as it's dark outside. That's the worst part of winter. I hate dark afternoons and dragging myself out of a warm bed on dark mornings. I switch on the Christmas tree lights and a warm glow fills the room. I notice a large red candle has appeared in the centre of the coffee table, so I go in search of a box of matches in the kitchen and then light it. Immediately the aroma of cinnamon and berries fills the room.

The bottle of sherry Mum and Parker were drinking the other night is still on the bookshelf. I grab a small tumbler from the kitchen and pour a measure. When I take a sip, I realise it's actually quite nice. The liquid is sweeter than I thought and it warms my throat. I take another sip and it feels like Christmas has finally arrived.

Chapter Forty-Five

I hear the buzz of the intercom as I finish the glass of sherry.

Who on earth could that be? I've seen everybody I was expecting to see today. Who would be dropping by the night before Christmas? Isn't this the night where the whole world goes out and gets drunk and messy and there's chaos in every town throughout the UK?

I walk over to the intercom and pick up the receiver.

'Hello?'

'Hey.' I'm surprised to hear Tom's voice. I know I've mentioned where I live before to him but he's never been to my flat.

'Hi, Tom. What are you doing here?'

There's a pause.

'Sorry,' I say, realising that sounded a bit rude, but I was taken a bit by surprise. 'Please come up.' I press the door release button.

'Hi, Tom.' I smile at him as he reaches my door.

'I was in the area.'

'Where are my manners? It's freezing. Please come in.' I stand to one side and Tom walks in, bringing in a cloud of freezing air so that I shiver. 'Can I get you a drink of something?'

'Are you having one?'

'Well, it is nearly Christmas, so why not? Beer? Wine?'

'A beer would be great, thanks.'

'Okay, go in and sit down' – I point to the lounge door –'and I'll get the drinks.'

The sensible part of my brain nudges me and I force back the notion that this isn't a good idea. I like Tom, and he's very good looking and clearly charming, but I'm still not sure whether I'm interested in being anything other than his friend. I'm don't know whether there was something between us the night we all went out at the end of college – a moment. Even if there was, I'm unsure that I want to do anything about it right now. But my conversation with Jenny and Lola from months ago replays in my mind: 'Men and women can't just be friends.'

When I walk into the lounge Tom's seated on the edge of the sofa, looking decidedly nervous.

'Is everything alright?' I hand him the bottle of beer and sit down next to him.

'Um, yeah. Everything's fine.'

'Okay.' I nod. 'So what are your plans for Christmas?'

'I'm going back home to my mum's tomorrow morning for the holidays.' Tom takes a sip of his beer.

'Back to London?'

'Yes. My sister and her husband and their kids will be there.'

'Sounds nice.' I think of my own Christmas, which has the potential to be a minefield with Mum and Parker, and Dad and Margaret. Having everyone together at Christmas will either be lovely and cosy, or very weird.

'I lied, Emma,' Tom blurts out, puncturing my thoughts.

'Erm, about what?'

'I wasn't just in the neighbourhood tonight.'

'Oh.' I swallow, now sure where this is going.

'I wanted to see you.'

He takes another drink of his beer and I suddenly feel the need to do the same. I reach for my bottle and take a sip before placing it back down on the table. I note that my hands are shaking a little and I can feel my heartbeat quickening.

'I wanted to see you, to say something to you, before Christmas.' Tom fiddles with his hands in his lap. 'I like you, Emma. I've liked you since the moment I saw you hovering outside the revolving glass doors on that first evening at college.'

I press my lips together, unable to formulate a response at this point. I did kind of get the feeling that Tom liked me, but I chose to ignore it. I wasn't in the right frame of mind to jump into another relationship. But he obviously felt a connection the other night too, and the fact is that Joe and I broke up months ago. He's probably moved on and doesn't give me a second thought. I should be ready to start looking towards another relationship, and Tom is a good guy, so why not him?

'I thought, if you can't say what you really think at Christmas then when can you?' Tom edges slightly closer to me and I look into his deep brown eyes. He really is a good-looking guy, and he's a lot of fun. We've become friends over the last few months and I enjoy his company.

I'm aware of the proximity of our bodies. Tom's eyes meet mine and hold my gaze for a second, and before I can think any further he leans in and his lips gently brush mine. I only hesitate for a second before I kiss him back. It feels good as his body presses against mine and I enjoy the sensation of being caught up in his embrace. His lips are warm and comforting. It's been a while since I was kissed by anyone, and I kiss him back, feeling a kick of adrenaline as he pulls me closer.

But then my conscience prods me:

If you go through with this then you're admitting that things are definitely over for good between you and Joe.

So what? Things are over. There's no hope at all of getting back with Joe. He has someone else.

Don't you want to try one last time?

Why? So I can get shot down and have my heart broken all over again? Joe doesn't want me any more. It's too late, isn't it?

Don't you want to find out?

I pull away from Tom and he looks at me with a kind smile but his eyes are full of knowing.

'I'm sorry, Tom.' I lean forward, holding my head in my hands. This is hard, this is so hard.

'It's okay, Emma. I understand.' Tom picks up his bottle and downs the remainder of his beer. 'You don't feel the same way.'

'I'm sorry,' I repeat.

'Don't be.'

'You're a really nice guy, and I want to feel the same way.'

'But you don't.' He shrugs. 'You can't help how you feel.'

'I could go out with you and we could have a good time, but I wouldn't be being honest with you or with myself, and I like you far too much to do that to you.'

'But as a friend?'

'As a friend.'

'You're still in love with that other guy, aren't you?'

I nod.

'I'm really sorry, Tom. I like you, a lot, but Joe owns my heart. It's taken me a while to truly realise that, but he does, and he always will.'

I feel suddenly overwhelmed by this realisation. I have to tell Joe how I feel. I must try to get him back. If I still love him then there's a chance, however small, that he still loves me too.

'I appreciate your honesty, Emma. I wish the outcome was different, but I understand. He's a lucky guy; I hope he knows that.'

'Can we still be friends?' I say earnestly.

'I'd like that.' Tom smiles. 'But perhaps we can avoid mentioning this, or it might be a bit weird for a while.'

'I won't mention it, Tom, but I'm flattered. You're a great guy.'

'Have a lovely Christmas, Emma.' Tom stands up and pulls on his coat. 'And I hope next year is a good one for you. You deserve it.'

'Merry Christmas, Tom. Have a safe journey to your mum's.'

'Thanks.'

We stand a little awkwardly.

'Can we at least hug goodbye?' I ask.

Tom pulls me into an embrace.

'I shouldn't have said anything,' he whispers into my hair.

'No, I'm glad that you did.'

'Take care, Emma.' He pulls away and I follow him to the front door.

'Take care, Tom.'

As I close the door behind him I feel an unexpected sense of clarity. All this time I've been trying to get over Joe when I should have been trying to get him back. I need to tell him that I love him, and I need to do it now. I can't possibly wait until after the Christmas break. I need to see him. I have to see Joe right now.

Am I really going to go charging across the city on a romantic whim, hoping that my tragic love story might have a happy ending after all? But what if Joe says he doesn't love me anymore? What if he is seeing someone else and she's not "just a friend"? – oh God, what if they're with him? What if he's not even home? It is Christmas Eve, after all.

I exhale deeply. I haven't thought this through. This isn't some lame romantic comedy where the girl turns up unexpectedly and declares her love for the leading man, only for him to tell her how much he's missed her, and that he was stupid to break up with her in the first place, and that he has loved her from the moment they met.

Am I really expecting Joe to say any of those things to me? He might be really angry that I've turned up on his doorstep unannounced, spoiling his Christmas fun. I might be heading for seasonal suicide once he's slammed the door in my face after telling me to never darken his doorstep again.

But Joe's not like that.

He's not vindictive. Even when we were separating Joe was never shouting and nasty, he was more sullen and hurt. Maybe that was part of the problem. Perhaps if we'd had a screaming match to clear the air then we could both have said what we really thought. Maybe it wouldn't have made any difference. My suggestion to postpone the wedding was the last straw, and at the time I needed to say that, although now I wonder what on earth I was thinking.

Well, there's only one way to find out how this is going to go. I grab my bag and coat and pull on my boots with some difficulty as my hands have begun shaking violently.

I glance at my watch. I have plenty of time to get over to Joe's and to still make it back in time to go to the cathedral for the Christmas carols with Mum and Parker. I hurry out the front door and down the stairs taking them two at a time. My heart feels like it's climbed up into my throat and it's doing its best to suffocate me. My palms are starting to sweat, despite the freezing chill that's creeping in. I can't believe my own stupidity at not realising that I had it all, for the desolate months I've allowed to pass pretending that I was over Joe.

I practically run out of the door to the building, and nearly slip on some ice in my hurry to get to the car but then I hear a familiar voice call out my name and my stomach does a nervous flip.

'Chris?' I turn around and find him standing only a few feet away from me, just off the pavement on the grass surrounding the flats.

'Hi, Emma. What are you doing around here?' he asks.

'I live here.' I frown, wondering exactly the same about him.

'A friend I play football with lives a few streets away,' he explains as if reading my thoughts. 'So how are you, Emma?'

'Um, I'm okay, thanks.' I fidget awkwardly with a strand of hair. This is the last thing I was expecting today. Bumping into Chris twice in quick succession. It's a little…unnerving.

'It was nice to see into you the other week in that coffee shop.'

'Yeah.' I nod a little dismissively. I thought it was a bit weird, if I'm honest. Plus I looked completely hideous at that moment. Not exactly my idea of nice.

'It's a shame you didn't have time to have a coffee then.' He shrugs. 'It would have been good to catch up.'

'Yes.' I force a smile, wondering where this is going.

'Do you have the time now?' He looks at me intently.

'Oh…um…It's Christmas Eve.' I stutter. I really don't have the time for this now.

'Did you say you live here?' He points to my building. 'We could grab a quick coffee in your flat. It is Christmas, as you say.'

I take a deep breath and exhale. What's the worst that could happen? I can have a quick coffee with Chris and then still make it to Joe's house before it gets late.

'Sure.' I nod. 'Why don't we go up to my flat then and I'll make us a coffee. But I only hasve half an hour. You kind of caught me on my way somewhere.'

We walk, without speaking, over to the building and I swipe my card on the door keypad to let us in. As we head quietly up the two flights of stairs to my flat I can't help but feel odd about this whole situation. Chris is the last person I'd have expected to see here today, and seeing him twice after not seeing him for months and months seems unusual. I'm not sure what we could possibly have to say to one another at this point in our lives, or how to get him in and out of my flat as quickly as possible without appearing rude – although why I'm worried about that is beyond me. This is the man who dumped me over dinner when I thought he was going to propose, so who cares if I seem a bit rude?

As I turn the key in my front door my heart sinks as an unfortunate thought pops into my mind. When I last saw Chris, I told him I was happy with someone else. But I live here alone, and there are no signs of a man living here with me anywhere in the flat. So it's going to be obvious that I lied to him, which makes me look pathetic, and he'll probably rub my face in it by telling me how happy he and Lucy are. Damn it.

Chapter Forty-Six

'Do you remember when we went to London for the weekend for... what was it? Our first anniversary?'

'Yeah, I remember.'

I watch as Chris hovers next to my electric fire, picking up red scented candle from the coffee table and sniffing it like he cares what it smells like. He's acting a bit weird now, and I'm feeling a hint of panic as my quest to get him in and out of the flat quickly seems to be way off track. I'm starting to regret asking him to come up here for coffee. But he was just there in the street and it felt like the polite thing to do given it's Christmas Eve, the season of goodwill and all that. Come to think of it, did I actually ask him or did he invite himself?

'We were happy, though, weren't we?' He turns and looks at me, still holding the vanilla spiced candle tightly in his hand.

'I thought we were. But then you slept with someone else, remember?'

I don't want to pick a fight but I feel like I need to state the obvious as we reminisce. I was very happy until that night when Chris confessed he'd been cheating on me. But the confident swagger he had that evening seems to have evaporated into thin air, and he now seems...

'I suppose you're right. I met Lucy and things changed.'

'Do you want to sit down?' I say, as I do the opposite and stand up. 'I'll go and make that coffee, shall I?'

'Have you found happiness again, Emma?'

I'm thrown a little by this question and not really sure how to answer it, what with the fact that it's my ex-boyfriend asking and I did find happiness, I found true love, and then I lost it.

'Yes, I met someone else. I was happy,' I say in an even tone, although all I can think about now is that I need to get to Joe. I need to tell him that I do still love hime.

'Joe?'

'Yes.'

'But you're not now? I thought you two were getting married.'

'Um, I guess not.' I clear my throat noisily. 'We broke up.' It's irrelevant to me now whether Chris knows the truth about my life or not.

'It hurts, doesn't it?'

'I'm sorry?'

'When the person you love leaves you. It hurts.'

As I look at Chris I notice that his whole demeanour has changed. His body looks tense and he no longer has the jovial smile that was so evident earlier. In fact, he looks like a different person now and I'm starting to feel more than a little uncomfortable.

'I'll get that drink then,' I say, taking a step towards the door, suddenly feeling the need to get out of the room and put some space between me and Chris. But as I make my move to escape he slides in front of the door, blocking my exit.

'Chris, you're scaring me now.' I meet his gaze as I stand rooted to the spot. 'What's this about? I thought you were happily planning an imminent wedding?'

'Lucy dumped me.'

Shit. No wonder he's a bit unhinged.

'I'm sorry,' I say softly.

'Yeah, I'm sure you are.' His voice is heavy with sarcasm.

'What's that supposed to –'

'Do you remember that day when you saw us together in the coffee shop?'

I stare at him blankly. My brain has gone into overdrive and the hairs on every part of my body are standing to attention. I'm scared, and I probably have good reason to be.

'You were with your mother.'

I nod silently as my mind plays a vision of my mum wandering over to their table. She made some stupid comment to them about infidelity and they left in a hurry. Oh God.

'Do you know what she said?'

'Um, not really.' I'm hoping this is the least provocative answer.

'Yes, you do,' he sneers. 'She basically said, "Once a cheat, always a cheat." She put the seed of doubt in Lucy's mind that because I'd cheated on you with her, I'd do exactly the same to her at some point too.'

'Chris, you can't possibly think that –'

'Shut up!' he snaps. He turns back to the coffee table and puts the candle back carefully where he found it, then he turns to face me. 'It was the beginning of the end that day, if only I'd realised it then.'

I stand silently, realising that I'm a prisoner in my own living room and there's no way I'm getting out of here until Chris has said what he came here to say. This was no chance meeting outside my building; he came here looking for me. How he knew where to find me is a question whose answer I think I'd rather not know.

'Every time I was late home, she worried. Every time my phone rang or I got a text message, she strained to see who it was from. She began to doubt me, to doubt my commitment to her, and she called off the engagement. You destroyed us.'

I've no idea what to say to this revelation. Could a simple comment from my mum really cause this girl to lose faith in Chris or was the doubt already there? Was his own behaviour to blame? At the end of the day, he did cheat on me with this Lucy, and if I were her then that would always be at the back of my mind. Can people really change? I don't know, I really don't.

'You bumped into me on purpose earlier, didn't you?' I ask, already knowing the answer. 'You don't really have a friend you play football with who lives a few streets away.'

Chris chuckles to himself, an unnerving sound. 'I knew you'd try to be the bigger person and that you'd pretend you were interested in how I was and then I could get you to invite me up here into your flat.'

'You always knew how to manipulate me,' I state coldly, remembering now how much our relationship had deteriorated under my nose without me even realising it before Chris found his conscience and broke it off with me.

'When I came to see you at the shop that night to tell you Lucy and I were engaged, I could see it in you then. You wanted to tell me exactly what you thought of me, but you didn't. You tried to pretend that you were happy for us and you wished me well. I could see that it was killing you not to be able to scream and shout at me. But it's not your style, Emma. It never was.'

'Yeah? Well you might also be surprised to know that things have changed. I've changed!'

My voice is raised and Chris looks surprised, and so am I. But I'm sick of being taken for an idiot by horrible men. I had enough of Chris and his games the first time around, and what with Connor then making an appearance, only to cause hell for me and Sophie, I think I've about had enough of playing nicely.

'So you're blaming me for the fact that Lucy dumped you, is that it? Always looking for someone else to blame, aren't you? It couldn't possibly be your fault, could it, Chris? It couldn't possibly be that you don't know how to be a decent boyfriend, or a decent human being for that matter.'

A vision spins through my mind: me fleeing a busy restaurant after Chris told me, over such a lovely romantic meal, that our relationship was dead, when I'd been suspecting a marriage proposal. I can remember the humiliation like it was yesterday.

'You don't think you're the one to blame?' Chris sneers nastily. 'I mean, what happened with your last love? Did he fall out of love with you all by himself?'

This hurts like a sucker punch. I've crucified myself over and over for the fact that I ruined things with Joe.

'What do you want, Chris?' I snap. My patience is wearing dangerously thin.

'I want you to hurt too. I want you to feel the pain that I've felt.'

'And how exactly did you think that would go, Chris? What was your plan? Did you think that you'd get me to invite you back here and then you could go through all this shit and suddenly I'd feel horrible about myself and you'd magically feel better?'

'No.' Chris bites his lip. 'That isn't it.'

'Then what do you mean?'

'You spoiled things, though. You called the police.'

'The police...I don't...'

Holy fuck. The air is sucked violently from my lungs and I stand aghast, not wanting to believe what's been placed right in front of my face.

'The letters...you sent the letters. How did you...? Why would you do that to me?'

Chris stands there with his hands stuffed in his jeans pockets, a sullen expression on his face, and I'm shocked into silence. I could never have imagined that Chris could do something so callous, so hurtful. That he'd want to scare me in my own home. That he could sink to that level.

'Well, I hope you're satisfied.' My voice is choked and strange sounding even to my own ears. 'I was scared; I am scared. I check every room, every night, the minute I walk through the door. I feel terrorised. You made me a victim. Is that what you wanted? Did you get what you were looking for, Chris?'

The slap takes me by surprise, so much so that I wobble unsteadily backwards before righting myself. It takes only a second for the burning sensation to hit full force and the whole side of my face feels like it's doubled in size as it begins to throb.

I want to scream at Chris, shout in his face. Why would he do that? How dare he lay a hand on me? But I'm stunned into complete silence and instead find myself staring at him warily while gingerly rubbing my cheek with the palm of my hand.

He watches me with cold blue eyes. No hint of the Chris I once knew, and loved, evidenced anywhere in his expression.

It's surreal.

The front door to the flat opens and closes and I hear a familiar voice calling my name.

'Emma? It's only me. Now don't be mad, you know I only have you're best interests at heart.'

Chris's head snaps around to face the closed living room door as Sophie's footsteps approach. My breath comes in short sharp gasps but my voice is nowhere to be found. What's Sophie doing here? I only left her a few hours ago. I don't know if I'm relieved to find her here in my flat or if I'm concerned for her given Chris's outburst of violence and his deranged mood.

'Emma?' The door opens and Sophie appears displaying red cheeks and snow twinkling in her hair. She looks at me then immediately at Chris who's only a few feet away from her. Her face screws up tightly as she glares at him.

'What the hell is he doing here?'

I try to swallow down the fear that's filling my throat.

Sophie looks back at me 'Emma. What's happened to your face? Did he do that?' She points an accusing finger at Chris.

'Why don't you but out and leave us alone?' Chris turns to Sophie, his voice gruff.

'It's okay Sophie.' I find my vocal cords at last 'Chris just called in to wish me a Merry Christmas.' I say as calmly as I can hoping to defuse the tension that's building in the room as I have no idea what the fallout of this situation could be. Chris seems unhinged and unpredictable, and Sophie is in major "protector" mode.

'Like hell he did.' She snaps at Chris 'and don't think for one minute that I'm going to just leave when you've clearly come here to cause trouble as that's clearly a red handprint on Emma's cheek and right now you look like the obvious culprit.'

'Sophie - '

'No Emma.' Sophie takes a step towards Chris and he eyes her warily 'He needs to leave, and right now.' She faces him squarely 'I don't know what you think you're doing coming here, but you're not welcome.'

Chris's expression falters slightly before his lips form a thin line and he appears to inhale deeply. It feels like time is moving much slower and everything is exaggerated like I'm in a bubble. I agree with Sophie, Chris needs to leave but I don't know how I'm going to get him out of the flat.

The flat door opens and closes once more.

Who the hell can this be? And how many people have a spare key to my flat?

This seems to throw Chris into a panic as he whips around shoving Sophie roughly to one side he attempts to push the living room door closed in a futile attempt to prevent whoever it is from joining us in the living room.

Footsteps approach and the door is pushed open. I'm astounded to see Matt looking tentatively at me with Joe hovering nervously in the background.

Joe...my heart leaps.

Suddenly there's movement to my right as Chris appears at my side taking hold of my arm in a vice like grip.

'Why don't you all get out of here and leave me and Emma alone?' He snarls.

Joe looks right at me and I see a flicker of anger cross his face. For a second I fear it's because he thinks that I actually do want to be left alone with Chris. But then I see his hands clench into fists.

What happens next is a blur.

Joe takes a step forward pushing past Matt.

A scuffle ensues.

Sophie's shrieking.

My body's being pulled in several directions then strong arms wrap around me and I'm pulled out of the fray and am lowered down to the sofa.

Joe appears to be restraining Chris and I can see that Sophie's talking to someone on her mobile phone but only muffled sounds fill my ears.

My mind seems to go into shut down as the next thing I know the room is filled with even more people. I take in the uniforms and realise that it's the two police officers who came to see me before when I reported the threatening letters. I watch silently as they handcuff Chris and he's led from the room by one of the sergeants.

'Miss Story?' The larger of the two, Sergeant Bulky, appears in front of me 'Miss Story, we'll need you to make a statement?'

'A statement?'

'I understand that you've been assaulted.'

'Assaulted?'

'You're friend reported that you had been assaulted by the man that we've just arrested?'

I gulp for air 'Yes. Yes that's right.' I reach up and touch the side of my face that's no longer burning but feels numb.

'Emma?' Sophie touches my arms as she crouches down in front of me 'Are you alright?'

I nod, wondering what on earth just happened, and how I keep finding myself in these ridiculous situations with what can only be described as seriously emotionally disturbed men.

'Okay, everyone out.' Sophie announces to the room 'Not you, of course Sergeant.' She adds.

Everyone is ushered from the room and the Sergeant sits down in the arm chair opposite me and takes out his notepad.

'Can you tell me exactly what happened here today please?' he looks at me with kind eyes.

I rub at the side of my temples and think back to the start of the madness. Tom had just left and I was on my way to tell Joe that I still loved him. Joe…he's here in my flat. What is he doing here? Nobody's supposed to be here – Sophie, Matt, Joe.

The door opens and Joe walk in carrying a steaming mug.

'Here, drink this.' He places it in my hands. My heart tightens as his fingers brush mine. Then he sits down next to me on the sofa.

The Sergeant opens his mouth.

'I'm not leaving her.' Joe says with some authority.

'Is that alright with you Miss Story?'

I glance at Joe and he gently takes hold of my hand.

'Yes. It's okay.'

'If we can begin then?' Sergeant Bulky has his pen poised.

I realise that I need to start from the point where I was leaving my flat to go to Joe's house but somehow it doesn't feel right saying that here and now. Yes, Joe is sat right next to me but I don't know what brought him here, and yes, he's holding my hand but that could just be because I've just been assaulted in my own home. He may just still care about me as a friend and is simply comforting me in a time of need.

'Miss Story?' the detective prompts.

Okay. Here goes.

I tell the tale from the beginning recapping everything except my reason for leaving the flat. I say that I was nipping to the off licence for a last minute bottle of wine – I mean I don't think my reason for going out is in any way related to the events that followed with Chris so I'm sure it's okay to tell a white lie about that. Everything else is the whole truth.

Joe sits quietly beside me throughout. His hand tightens around mine as I describe the slap on my face from Chris and as I look at him his gaze it still forward but he appears to be gritting his teeth.

I end the statement by confirming that Chris admitted to me that he was behind the threatening letters.

'We'll put that to him during questioning Miss Story, but he didn't appear to be very cooperative as my colleague escorted him to the police car. However that's everything that I need from you at this point in time.' He gets to his feet 'I'll be back in touch.'

'Thank you Sergeant.' I slide my hand from Joe's grasp and stand up a little unsteadily.

'I'll see you out.' Joe addresses Sergeant Bulky and the both leave the room.

Sophie scurries in, saying nothing, she simply pulls me into a huge hug and I collapse against her. 'I can't believe that it was Chris all along.'

A tear trickles down my cheek and I wipe it gently away. The throbbing in the side of my face is back with a vengeance.

Sophie releases her grip on me 'I'll get you some ice.' She says brushing my cheek with her fingertips 'That bastard.'

'Wait, Sophie.' I grab her hand. 'What are you doing here? And Matt, and Joe?'

She bites her lip 'Matt and I were just talking over a glass of champagne and I said to him that I was sorry that you and Joe couldn't work things out as I knew you still loved him.'

Sophie!

'But then Matt said the exact same thing about Joe. He said that Joe still loves you and hasn't stopped pining for you since you left.'

'But what about the other girl? The one that answered his phone when I called the other week?'

'I told Matt about that. It was his cousin! The one who was backpacking in Europe. She's come to visit for Christmas. It was only his cousin Emma.'

His cousin? Oh...

'So you coming here, Matt appearing with Joe, this was all just an elaborate plan conjured up this afternoon by you and Matt to get me and Joe in the same room?'

Sophie looks at me sheepishly 'I know you hate it when people interfere but...are you mad at me?'

Joe appears in the doorway before I can answer. Sophie looks from me to Joe.

'I'll leave you two to it.' She says walking from the room and closing the door behind her.

Joe and I just stand there for a moment. I'm nervous; really nervous. I haven't seen him in months. I'd forgotten what effect he has on me but the instant I saw him behind Matt earlier I knew in my heart that he's the one. He's the only one I ever want.

Matt apparently says he still loves me too but I need to hear that from him. I really, really need to hear that.

Joe takes a step towards me, his hands still stuffed in his jeans pockets. Our eyes meet and I bite my lip wondering if this is all too good to be true and I might just be letting myself in for another huge fall if I say out loud how much he means to me. I suddenly feel incredibly vulnerable which is silly really given the closeness we have shared in the last year but now it feels like there's a huge divide between us.

But then Joe's right in front of me, taking my face in his hands. His lips are on mine, strong yet gentle, and my knees weaken I kiss him back with every ounce of my being, reaching my arms around him and holding on to his warm toned body as if my life and future happiness depends on it. And honestly, I think it actually might.

Epilogue

I wake groggily, opening one eye at a time as weak sunlight seeps through a small crack in the curtains. It takes me a moment to realise that we've finally made it to Christmas morning and I smile. Despite my protesting I do actually like Christmas and this one feels extra special. I roll over and snuggle next to the warmth of Joe's body tugging the quilt a little tighter around me.

I've woken to this dream on many occasions; having Joe by my side, laying in his arms feeling safe, protected, loved. But today this is no dream. This is real. The last few months can now simply form of the past. Joe and I have a future together again. Despite the fact that a happy ending with Joe seemed impossible to ever recapture I was never able to fully let go of the tiny piece of hope that it could happen. Even when it appeared hopeless, Joe was still firmly in my heart, and he always will be. He is the one, the one that owns my heart.

I think of the day ahead. The current calmness will be taken over by the arrival of Dad and Margaret. I can already smell the faint aroma of coffee. Mum must already be up, probably making the final preparations for the feast she has created for us all to enjoy today.

After my reservations about the mixture of people sitting down together for Christmas lunch I can't help but look forward to the day ahead. All the people that I love celebrating the festivities together. And now that will include Joe.

'Good morning.' Joe rolls over towards me and kisses me gently on the lips.

'Merry Christmas.' I grin, already feeling like I've got the best Christmas present ever.

Thank you for taking the time to read my book; I hope you enjoyed it. If you did I'd really appreciate it if you could take a moment to leave me a review at your favourite retailer?

Thanks!

Sasha Lane

About the author:

Hi, I'm Sasha,

I love anything books, along with cats, wine, yoga and jogging when I find the time. I write Chick lit novels with a twist! They're Chick lit style with a hint of darkness. I write in first person as I find it much easier to get into character and tell their story that way. I try to create characters that are just everyday young women so hopefully everyone can find something about their personality or life that they can relate to, and fall in love with them as much as I have while writing about them.

Other titles by Sasha Lane:
Girl, Conflicted